THE POISON FACTORY

OPERATION KAMERA

LUCY KIRK

International Spy Thriller/Intrigue

© Lucille L. Kirk 2020

Print ISBN: 978-1-09830-548-2

eBook ISBN: 978-1-09830-549-9

Dedicated to the valiant defectors who helped us.

"Come Not between the dragon and his wrath."
William Shakespeare, *King Lear*

"Assassination is the extreme form of censorship."
George Bernard Shaw

PROLOGUE

I am done with the CIA.

I've been away from Langley for over four months now and have become a virtual expert on Syria. Al Jazeera was my go-to media source. But despite more hours of searching the world via the internet than I could possibly log, I'd gotten nowhere closer to finding my beloved Alex. In a slightly more productive use of my mind and time, I began tutoring Russian at Georgetown.

And then, as it does, life took another detour.

I was lounging in bed on one of those perfect June days before the miserable summer heat had set in, reading a book that had nothing to do with spies. The harsh buzz of the doorbell jarred me. I flipped my book over and jumped up to look out the upstairs window of my Georgetown house.

I could just make out a uniformed presence at the front door. No one called me, or dropped by, early in the morning—not in my rule book—and my friends knew it. I threw on my silk robe and raced down the stairs.

Another buzz. I glanced through the peephole, saw the capped head of a deliveryman, and asked who he was.

"FedEx," he said. "An envelope for D. Raines. I'd have left it, but you need to sign."

He sounded real enough, so I cracked the door open. "I'm Decktora Raines."

Barely glancing at me, he flashed his FedEx ID and then shoved the signature form in front of me. I signed and took a slim cardboard envelope from him as he dashed off.

CHAPTER 1

LONDON, MAY 21, 2012

Ivan Federov had almost forgotten those early years, the Cold War now long over. As he jogged along the bank of the Thames on his morning run, his past seemed foreign to him, as if it belonged to someone else. In fact, Ivan Federov no longer existed, hadn't for over ten years. Now he was Robert Casca Johnston. He felt the cool breeze flow over him as he ran in solitude on what would shortly become a busy path, full of people heading off to work, just before sunrise, when the light of day slowly emerges from the dark sky. The crunch of the pebbles and the undergrowth of the rain-soaked path were almost soothing. The smell of the wet grass held the promise of warm summer days ahead.

Could he be happy after what he'd been through? Content, he thought. He would settle for that. The fog today was thicker than usual, but delicious compared to the bitter cold he'd endured in his past, during those days in Moscow. Sometimes he found himself reaching into his pocket for his gun, like an amputated appendage, no longer there. When that happened, he always smiled and felt grateful for its absence. The gun wouldn't be comfortable while jogging, he thought with a smile.

* * *

Not even a twig cracked as she made her move. It happened so fast he didn't have time to turn his head. And though she was sure she'd gotten the jugular, she gave an extra push of the claw to clinch it. A speck of the white powder dropped on the ground. Her target fell quickly, without making a sound. Ivan Federov was dead. She gave it the proper two minutes and then ran calmly from the site, like a normal jogger, her weapon held tightly in her hand.

CHAPTER 2

Detective Chief Inspector Cransford Garvin couldn't believe he'd gotten himself into such a mess. He didn't do crime call-ins anymore. He was too senior. Too close to retirement.

Most days he took it for granted that he'd slide right into that so-called golden age of life along with his wife, Wallie. They'd been married thirty-eight years and she'd been a loyal and supportive wife, especially with the demands of his career. It was her turn now.

But an emergency call to his cell phone proved too much of a temptation. A body had been found along the bank of the Thames.

Garvin drove onto the grass when he got to the identified location. He assumed that prerogative in view of his status, and this was an emergency. A junior colleague, Sergeant Benjamin Fawkes, and the murder squad were already on the scene. Garvin braked the car to a stop and, straining with the extra weight he'd put on in the last few years, twisted his bulky frame out the door of his convenient, but compact, car.

His left hip hurt more than usual today, slowing him as he walked over to the younger officer. Garvin extended his hand to Fawkes.

"Detective Chief Inspector Garvin," Fawkes said, obviously recognizing the senior officer. "I didn't expect to see you here, sir."

"I was in the area when the emergency call came," said Garvin, sensing Fawkes's uncertainty about his presence. "Old habits die hard, son—you'll learn that someday if you're lucky. Just thought I'd take a look," Garvin lied, fully aware that he simply hadn't the willpower to resist the call.

"Jogger over there called it in," Fawkes said, nodding toward the runner who was bouncing back and forth, from one foot to another, as if waiting to continue his run. "We were about to question him," Fawkes said as he pulled on rubber gloves.

"Let's take a look at the victim first," Garvin said.

They walked up to the mound, then leaned over the body—slender build, ashen face, graying dark hair and pale hazel eyes, wide open.

"What do you see?" asked the chief inspector. "Be careful what you touch."

"Of course, sir," said Fawkes, as he bent in close to the man's head to see if there was any breathing, but, of course, the neat red slice that opened his throat would prohibit that. "He's dead. No rigor yet. Hasn't been down long."

Garvin stood up. Something about fresh death, something frightening, even exciting, drew him. He recalled the many times he'd found himself in this position, and how much he'd loved every minute of it. He was, at heart, a street investigator, not an administrator. He stifled a sigh.

Garvin nodded at Fawkes, giving him the go-ahead to touch the clothing, but not the body. Fawkes cautiously reached into the pocket of the man's trousers to check for pocket litter and pulled out a wallet.

"Robert C. Johnston, says his ID, address in Putney. Business card shows an insurance company in his name."

"Get everything we have on this fellow," Garvin said, turning away from the body to go talk to the witness.

As he started to stand up, Fawkes gasped, "Oh, my God."

Garvin's head jerked back toward Fawkes. "What is it?"

"Besides the slice—there are scratches, something like a claw mark on his neck."

"Show me."

"And white powder or specks on the wound, like it's been cauterized, perhaps."

All the more reason to be present, Garvin told himself. Poison raised the case to a different level. He circled the body, leaned down near the neck, but touched nothing.

"This killer might have wanted to leave a message. Slitting his throat would have killed him. Haven't heard of any claw markings in recent murders—maybe never. The Scenes of Crime Officers, SOCO, should be on their way. Don't touch anything." They moved slowly, looking at the body from different angles.

Garvin felt an uneasiness in his gut. "I don't like this. Tell the SOCOs to get the white substance over to Forensics Sciences at Lambeth. They're the fastest moving. We need a chemical–biological analysis right away. Use my name, if needed. We'll check the records for killings with these markings when we get back to the station."

Fawkes nodded, then pointed at the ground. "Sir, look at the drag marks in the grass. Some blood, too."

The rush hour now beginning, a small group of onlookers had formed at the edge of the scene.

"Fawkes, get this damned area roped off. It won't be long before the media arrives," Garvin muttered quietly.

Garvin finally turned and walked over to the jogger, who was still pacing.

"Chief Inspector Cransford Garvin, Metropolitan Police," he announced, shaking the jogger's hand with the kind of self-confidence only time and success can build. "Thank you for contacting us. I'd appreciate any details you can recall. Nothing is too small."

"Jeremy Ashton," said the jogger, who'd taken the DCI's hand then provided the few details he had.

"Please contact me if you think of anything else," Garvin said and handed him a card. "And do not discuss this with anyone."

The jogger looked questioningly at Garvin, confusion evident on his young face.

"In other words, this didn't happen," the inspector said with a nod. Not until Garvin figured out how the victim was killed—and identified the white powder.

Fawkes had just finished roping off the area when Garvin spotted a heavyset man with a shock of white hair working his way toward the body and trying to step over the rope.

"Stop. This is a protected police area," said Fawkes firmly.

As Garvin walked toward the intruder, he immediately recognized one of his least favorite people, the tabloid journalist Alastair Sinclair-Jones, who would report anything, fact or fiction, and who had a nose for finding a murder the minute it happened. Directly behind him and nearly attached was a slight man holding a camera, taking pictures as rapidly as his fingers could move.

"Hello, inspector, good to see you." Sinclair-Jones grinned widely at Garvin and kept walking as if out for a stroll.

"Stop, I said. No photographs," Garvin growled. "You need to leave right now." He knew how aggressive Sinclair-Jones was and doubted he could prevent him from scooping a good story if he thought he had one. That knowledge made him furious.

"Surely you can give me a bit of a story here," said Sinclair-Jones, as his photographer continued to snap.

"No story, no cameras, nothing. Get lost. Now."

"Certainly, no problem," Sinclair-Jones said, nodding to his cameraman to stop.

"I don't expect to see anything in *The London Hour* tonight."

Sinclair-Jones smiled at him as he walked away. Garvin could only hope. But not much.

Garvin knew the press had to report something about the murder along the Thames. He worried the most about Sinclair-Jones. With good reason.

The day had been full of phone calls. Who was murdered? Why? How? Garvin deflected the calls, providing the most minimal details possible.

When he got home that evening, he immediately pulled an ale out of the refrigerator, then collapsed into his big, worn armchair, turned on the radio—his preferred media—and hoped Wallie wasn't home yet, which would allow him to converse loudly with the radio if need be.

But Sinclair-Jones, as Garvin suspected, was not one to miss an opportunity to be in the limelight. Soon Garvin heard the fake posh accent come over the airwaves.

"Thank you for having me on this evening, Sir Edgar," Sinclair-Jones said to the well-known radio host. "It's been a busy day for those of us in the media who cover murders, and it's been a long time since there's been a murder on the bank of the Thames so close to the Tower."

"Son of a…," Garvin muttered to the empty room. Sinclair-Jones was off and running. Next thing, he'd be talking about Anne Boleyn.

"I regret that the CI, Cransford Garvin, was reluctant to provide any details. He virtually ordered us away from the site. Luckily, my cameraman and I got close enough to the body to see that the throat had been cut and to take a few shots. When we enlarged the photographs, we saw that the jugular had been punctured. There was plenty of blood under the head and some sort of white powdery substance near the neck. I'm afraid that's all I could see, but at *The London Hour* we are looking into recent murders that mirror this killing in any way."

Garvin jumped up from his chair, cursed at the walls, and finished his ale in one long gulp. Perhaps he should speak with Sinclair-Jones, maybe offer him the first interview once he was ready to discuss the case?

The thought, unfortunately, made him shudder.

CHAPTER 3

Sergei Devlin was sitting at his desk in the small but elegant office he rented in Knightsbridge. Perfect for his fledgling business, Russian Antiquarian, whose market was old Russians seeking lost family wealth. It gave him a chance to speak Russian, to meet some like-minded souls, and to make a small but unneeded return on his investment.

He'd been on holiday with his family for more than a week and had a massive amount of mail to plow through, including his daily copies of *The London Hour*, which he always read from cover to cover. Reading the media was a habit he'd developed when he'd been sent to London after his escape to the West. But that was over now, and whatever dreams he may have had of returning to his homeland, there would be no going back, not with the latest managers of the Kremlin, who had begun to track down old defectors. Why now? Sergei didn't know for sure, but he was convinced the crackdown was due to the emergence to power of a former KGB chief who held these "traitors" in high contempt.

He didn't enjoy reading the obits, but he did as part of his discipline. One day far in the future, he hoped, he would see the names of people his own age, maybe some he would even know. He did not expect that to happen today. But it did—as his eyes fell upon the name Robert Johnston. Robert Casca Johnston. He knew that name. And he knew the man.

Sergei felt his throat constrict as he read through the column. He hadn't seen Federov in several months and hadn't bothered to consider why until this moment. The brief obit said the man was murdered while jogging along the river Thames. The police had no suspect.

Ivan Federov had been a defector who, like Sergei, lived in a new identity somewhere on the outskirts of London. They had met at an art exhibit in Kensington several years earlier, an exhibit by a Russian artist living openly in the UK in those still warm post–Cold War days. Sergei attended such events not to meet anyone from his past, but to gain potential clients for his new business in a genteel environment. The minute he met Johnston he knew—the ordinary English name, the strong Russian accent. This man, like him, had a dark past. Their eyes met, and call it a sixth sense, or clandestine training, they understood that they shared something. They also understood that they should not get together. MI5 had strict—and sensible—rules once they had given a defector a new life and a new identity. Maintaining their security, and thus their separation, was essential to their safety. Still, the temptation was there and they agreed to meet. Once alone together, they shared the basic secret of their past—Russian intelligence officers who had spied against their own, then escaped to the West. Over time, Federov introduced Sergei to those other few souls who lived secret lives like them.

As he reread the obit, a chill crept over him.

It had been over fifteen years since Sergei Dumanovskiy had become the Englishman Sergei Devlin. MI5 had given him the odd middle name of Ligurius, for reasons he didn't understand but never questioned. He rarely used it anyway.

In his soul, he still carried the pain of those early days in the United States, after the Soviets swapped him for a spy of their own. The death in Moscow of his beloved Katya from cancer the Russians wouldn't treat, the "reassignment" of his two young daughters to other Russian families, his imprisonment, had put him into a deep depression, and even though he was now a free man, his melancholy continued.

It was an insightful young CIA defector handler, Decktora Raines, who took over his case and ultimately arranged Sergei's transfer to London. For that, he would always be grateful to Raines. She'd agreed with him that it would help him psychologically, by removing him from the memories of his early years in Washington, those heady days back in the early 1990s when he was a Soviet diplomat assigned to DC with Katya and the girls. All before he began spying for the Americans in order to get medical treatment for Katya, and before he was rightly accused of treason by his own masters, sent back to Moscow and arrested.

They were both right. Everything changed for the better in London. There he met Johanna, and with the birth of their son, found his way into a new life. Johanna had no objections when several years after they were married, Sergei told her he wanted to start a small business. She knew it would be a distraction for him more than a moneymaker. He didn't really need the money. He'd received a large sum from the American government once his relationship with them had run its course. The intelligence he'd provided had been priceless, they'd said. The medal they'd awarded him for his contribution sat in a small office in Langley, where all the Soviet defector materials were held, and which, of course, Sergei would never see again. The US government had rewarded him well, but he was more than ready for London, and yet another new life after the Agency had finished their exhaustive debriefs.

With "Russian Antiquarian," Sergei had intentionally selected a name that would draw little attention; he'd also chosen a neighborhood where a smattering of other Russian antiquities experts and iconastas had their shops. There he could speak Russian and be among some of his own, whether old Soviets or descendants of the czarist world. In those early post–Cold War days, a few daring, perhaps unwise, souls became less secretive about their Soviet pasts. Information was not held as tightly as it had once been, but by the turn of the century, things had cooled once again between East and West, and the handful of old defectors would go silent.

Sergei worked alone in his office in Knightsbridge, with the occasional help of a techie and a legal consultant. He had no intention of handling any issues related to the actual recouping of lost money or art objects. Those he sent on to the lawyer. But because he worked alone and away from home, Johanna had insisted he install a security system in his office, which he reluctantly agreed to do. He bought a simple, inexpensive setup that was tied to a discreet service, one he had researched thoroughly. Once installed, he needed only to pay his monthly fee, and if there was ever a security problem, one tap on a small button within the kneehole of his desk would alert the service of an emergency. He told Johanna he thought it was a waste of money, but there was no arguing.

A call he received on Wednesday afternoon, on the third anniversary of his business, would prove Johanna right.

"Mr. Devlin," said the soft Russian-accented voice Sergei heard when he picked up the receiver. "I would like to make an appointment with you, kind sir, if you can so arrange."

"And to whom am I speaking?" said Sergei, detecting the formality of the language but not able to place the exact origin of her accent.

"My name is Yulia Semenyova. I understand through friends in London and Paris that you might be able to help me find some lost art objects that once belonged to my family. I'm the only one left now, and it would bring me great joy to learn more about my elders and to find anything left of them."

Ah, that was the accent—northern Russia.

"I have few records, but my people were originally from St. Petersburg. After 1917, they lost everything. My mother told me so many stories about them, especially about my great-grandfather, who was an adviser to Czar Nicholas. I believe he was what they call a White Russian. I was a fool not to make a journal of my mother's stories, but youth never appreciates such things."

"Miss Semenyova, would you be able to come to my office?"

"Yes, I would like that. I do hope that you can help me. Oh, those awful people. How lucky we are that they are gone. Ah, well, not to bother you with my thoughts."

"You are not alone in those thoughts, and I look forward to meeting you," Sergei said, feeling the small sense of pleasure he got from helping other Russians find their way back to a happier past. "Will you be able to meet me Friday at two in the afternoon? I will even serve you tea from a beautiful old samovar that recently came to me."

"Yes, of course, I shall take a late lunch from work. Thank you, dear sir, thank you. I am so grateful."

"I have a small office in Trevor Place in Knightsbridge." He gave her the address and told her to buzz apartment number 3B. "You need to bring nothing but your memory."

A sad soul, Sergei thought. She sounded as if she was on the verge of tears.

Yes, he would help her.

But Sergei was unable to find anything on Yulia's great-grandfather, a few names with similar spelling and derivation, but no one who appeared to have been connected to the Czar or any other of the old royals. It was not unusual, he reminded himself, as records were sparse at best. He collected the few bits he had and put them in a folder for her. Perhaps when they met she could add some additional details, related names on the matronymic side that could help him find something more.

The rain pelted down on the day of the appointment, and Sergei half expected Miss Semenyova to cancel the meeting. When she telephoned him in the morning to reconfirm, he offered her another date, but she turned it down. She was excited to meet him, she said, and had long ago learned to navigate London's downpours.

Sergei had just prepared the samovar and had hot tea ready, along with the Marks and Spencer sultana cookies he kept on hand for such occasions, when the buzzer sounded.

"Miss Semenyova," he said, opening the door and looking at the face of a woman he would recognize anywhere. His stomach wrenched. This woman's name was not Yulia. Sergei knew who his new client was, though he had not seen her in years.

Their paths had crossed in Moscow when she worked outside the office of Vladimir Ivanchukov, the KGB officer who had had Sergei arrested for treason. He didn't even recall if they'd ever spoken a word to each other. But hers was a face he could never forget. The eyes, those large, slightly bulging eyes. *Snake Eyes*, they'd called her. Sergei froze as he stared into that face. He remembered her as "Olga," but had no recall of her surname. He assumed that had changed anyway.

Her short hair was now a pale platinum blond, not the dull brown he recalled. And her huge eyes were pale blue, no doubt because she was wearing contact lenses that didn't fully conceal the deep brown that lay beneath.

Sergei hoped she hadn't noted the sudden flicker of his eyes when he first saw her. Why was she here? His mind flew to the alarm system. He walked toward his desk, close enough to push the button if he needed to.

"Come in. Let me offer you some tea," he said. *Show nothing,* he told himself.

"Thank you, Mr. Devlin. I am grateful to have found you and look forward to hearing what you have learned about my family line. I do so hope you will be able to find something as beautiful as this samovar from my own people."

Sergei responded in Russian, listening even more closely to her accent, her attempts at elegant speech, and her cover story.

"Your Russian is excellent. You must have spent some time in my country?"

"Little, really," Sergei said, in his own lie. "My parents emigrated when I was five. My father was not at all political and could not do well professionally in the Soviet system. Still, he missed Russia in many ways and insisted that we speak his native tongue at home, which has proven useful to me, since being bilingual is of great value in my business." He spoke as casually as possible.

She mustn't know I have figured her out. He knew instinctively it would be a matter of life and death.

"I'm sorry to report that I've only been able to find a few fragments that might relate to your grandfather, so I will be grateful for anything else you can give me."

Olga didn't show any disappointment in his poor report, he noticed. He listened to her spin out more family fiction, jotting notes once in a while, but he didn't interrupt her.

Sergei hadn't played this game in a long time. But it was in his DNA. *Once a spy, always...*, he thought to himself, almost amused.

"There is a fee, I assume?"

"Yes, but first let me see if I can find anything more." Sergei rose, acknowledged the end of the meeting, and walked her to the door.

"Oh, I'm sure you will. I'll be happy to pay, and I know you'll find something for me. I have a dear friend who is also searching his family history. Now that you and I have had a chance to meet and start working together, I shall definitely refer him to you."

Yes, she wanted to see him again. Of that he was certain. She'd confirmed his location and probably had done a quick assessment of his office, size, telephone placement, absence of colleagues, and more.

After Olga closed the door, a cold anxiety crept over Sergei, unlike any he'd felt in all the years since he'd left Moscow.

If Olga was in London and had gone to the trouble of tracking him down, could Ivanchukov be far behind? He never knew what happened to Ivanchukov after he himself got shipped off to the West in the spy swap. What Sergei did know was that he had made a vengeful, last-minute effort to destroy Ivanchukov. The chances it would work were slim, of course, but in the last debrief before he was taken to Sheremetyevo airport, Sergei whispered to the senior intelligence officer accompanying him that he had one last, dark secret. When he saw the officer's eyes light up, he delivered it.

"This man you admire so much, Vladimir Ivanchukov. He is as traitorous as I was. We worked together. How could you have missed him all these years?"

The officer stared sharply back at Sergei, mouth suddenly opening, but said nothing. And then Sergei was gone. He didn't even know if his tormentor was still alive. But whoever was behind Olga's discovery was calling him by his new name, Devlin.

After all these years, his enemies had found Sergei Dumanovskiy. Sergei Devlin was no longer safe.

It was only three-thirty when she left, and, though eager to get out of his office, Sergei didn't want to rush out earlier than his normal five o'clock closing time. He now had to consider the possibility that someone could be watching him. He looked out his window to a quiet, fairly empty street below. Yulia Semenyova was not there.

Sergei pulled the office curtains tight, then took the Russian print off the wall behind his desk. He spun the lock on the small safe implanted in the wall, rifled through the few files inside, and pulled out a slim folder tucked underneath the others. He hoped the details were current. It had been at least three years since he'd recorded them. Sergei memorized the address and tucked the file back into the safe, secured it, and headed for his office door.

He hadn't seen or heard of Decktora Raines since she left London. He knew the rules, but he would not go to his MI5 emergency point of contact. There was not enough history there. He would turn to the one person in the intelligence world he trusted.

Sergei had had an intense and often conflicted relationship with his CIA debriefers until she came along. She was smart, but more importantly, she was the only one who seemed to feel what he'd lost, what he'd been through. Sergei had long ago told her she would be his last case officer, and he meant it.

Was he under surveillance now? Of course, he was. This meant a long, meandering trip home. He called Johanna and told her he would be later than expected, then decided on a route that would include a stop at a FedEx office. There he would compose his document and send it across the pond, urgent delivery. Sergei double-locked his office door and walked down the lighted stairs to Trevor Place.

He hadn't been this unnerved in a long, long time.

CHAPTER 4

LONDON, MAY 25

Senior British intelligence officer Jason Drake always started his work-day early. It had been his habit since the height of his career at MI6, and more recently at MI5, since his transfer to the senior counterter-rorism liaison position there. Now it was the morning read board that called him in. There was always a pile of messages on it, seeming to grow by the day—a terrorism incident in Indonesia, more of the same in Algeria, Yemen, Iraq, and on and on. This new business was not his game.

It was Friday and Drake was ready for a long weekend. He poured a cup of hot tea and stirred it, thinking about how he'd got-ten to a place where his days started out with a mountain of hideous events. It hadn't always been so.

Nothing had been the same since the end of the Cold War. Of late, Drake got his greatest pleasure sharing war stories with old anti-Soviet colleagues who had fought that long, mostly bloodless bat-tle with him. He'd joined MI6 after studying International Politics at Oxford. It was the only job he'd wanted. After years in the service, mostly overseas, his devoted wife had gotten him to agree that he and the family would stay in London. Drake became one of the service's top Soviet Russia hands and rose in position accordingly.

The 9/11 terrorism attacks in the United States changed everything, and the subsequent call from MI5 Vice Chief Kilbourne was not a surprise. Drake knew what it was about before he headed up to Kilbourne's office.

"Not for me, Clive. I don't have the expertise, and I'm too old," Drake said to his longtime friend, now his superior and the one man whose orders he had to follow. "There are better people for the job. Let me do the post–Cold War assessments and put someone younger into counterterrorism." Drake was not one to beg, but he was very close to doing it now.

"You're one of my best people, and I need your help there now," said the VC. "You have the contacts at MI6 and over at Security and Counterterrorism, and you don't ruffle feathers the way some of our colleagues do. I need a top officer here to handle the liaison with both offices. Not to mention, counterterrorism is the future, and you'll still be in a senior position. The Cold War's done. Get over it. I've had to."

Kilbourne paused and looked at Drake with a smile on his face. "I promise I'll reassign you if the Cold War starts over again." That was a long time ago. Drake sighed.

Today's read board was especially thick. Drake reached for a cigarette, then quickly remembered he no longer smoked. He still retained that urge, but with the constant pressure from his wife and the fact that smoking was not allowed in MI5 headquarters, Drake had to make do with the empty satisfaction he could draw from his tobacco-less pipe, barely enough to soothe his nerves through increasingly unrewarding days at the office.

He finished the classified reading, then turned to a week's load of open-source material, which he usually tried to flip through as quickly as possible. As he reached the bottom of the pile, an article from one of the London papers leaped off the page at him,

The small item mentioned a murder along the Thames near Tower Bridge—the victim, one Robert Casca Johnston.

Drake straightened up in his chair and reread the article. That name was damned familiar. Especially the middle name—Casca.

"Evelyn," he called out to his secretary of over twenty years. "I need you. Right away."

If he was correct, the victim was of one of MI5's old Soviet defector cases. One of Drake's former colleagues, a Shakespeare aficionado, had come up with the idea of adding to the intentionally bland first and last names assigned to their Soviet defectors, a unique middle one. This, he said, would make it all but impossible for the KGB to track down any of them, but would allow British intelligence to spot the name if one should ever appear in the public domain. What could be better and more appropriate, he proposed, than to use the names of the conspirators who had killed Julius Caesar?

Casca had just been murdered.

Evelyn appeared at Drake's door. Slim and of medium height, she wore the kind of prim, navy blue outfit her salary could afford and that suited her position. With her hair pulled up tightly at the back of her head and her rigid stance, she looked every bit the assistant to a man of high position in MI5.

"I need you to follow up on something for me. Put everything else aside," Drake said, showing her the article and pointing to the name.

"The files on Casca are likely to be hidden away in the archives. I suspect it will take a while to retrieve them," she said evenly, though she didn't need to remind him that the records were retired to secure storage.

"I know, I know. Go down there and see how long it will take to get them. God knows, I hope they're not in that offsite storage abyss."

As she headed out the door, Drake went back into his office and started thinking about those special assets, some of whom he had handled himself: the Caesars, a handful of defectors who had provided invaluable intelligence to the West at great risk to their own lives. They'd been uniquely coded because each had worked in a highly classified laboratory involved in dark research, about which little was known in Western intelligence circles. It seemed so long ago.

Suddenly the ashen face of Alexander Litvinenko, dying in a London hospital, popped into his mind. A former KGB officer, who left Russia after falling out with the Kremlin, made the unforgivable mistake of publicly criticizing his old government and its leader. He'd been wrong to do so. Dead wrong.

After several failed attempts, two former KGB colleagues managed to deliver a deadly dose of polonium-210 to Litvinenko in the tea room of a posh London hotel. Drake knew who killed him. Everyone did. The assassins had been so unprofessional as to leave dregs of the toxin in their hotel rooms, not to mention on the murder site's teacup. Then they fled back to Moscow.

Drake felt a degree of guilt even though he hadn't been directly involved. He was, after all, a senior Russia hand, and hadn't his people owed it to Litvinenko to protect him? Some of his colleagues thought not. They would not toy with the Kremlin, not during this period of so-called good relations between the two countries. But this story became a staple of British media, resurfacing every few months. Each time it did, Drake sensed the dead man's ghost breathing down his neck.

Today was about another defector. He slowly sucked in on his empty pipe. Life was about to get interesting again.

Drake was still at his desk when Evelyn got back upstairs. She tapped on his door, which he'd left slightly ajar, so she knew he was available. He looked up, eyes widening as he saw the two stuffed files in Evelyn's arms.

"Casca is indeed a defector. One Ivan Federov."

Drake took the files, beaming at Evelyn. "What would I do without you?"

She smiled. "We both know you'd get nothing accomplished. Are there any appointments I should cancel?"

"All of them. Close the door, and no calls."

Drake remained closeted throughout the day, not bothering with lunch. He emerged later, full of energy.

"Evelyn, get me Chief Inspector Cransford Garvin on the phone," he said, looking again at the obituary that had started this whole exercise. It had few details. He hoped Garvin had more and would share them with him. "If he has a secure line, use it."

Drake wanted to find out what the police knew about Johnston aka Federov, most important, whether their background on him showed a Russian connection of any kind. Until he knew the story behind this murder, he would consider that the Russians were involved. And that, of course, he could not tell the chief inspector.

"After that, I want to talk to John Perlman, the Chief of Station over at Grosvenor Square."

As the door closed behind her, he ran his right hand through his hair. This could be a bloody mess indeed. His thoughts turned to another Russia expert—an American with the CIA who had worked with him on some of their shared defectors. She had been very good at getting their Russian expats settled in England. What would Decktora Raines think of all this?

Evelyn had to deliver the news to her now impatient boss that neither Garvin nor the COS was still in the office late on this Friday afternoon.

"Dammit, am I the only one who works late in this business?"

"Well, sir, the COS is out of...."

"Never mind," Drake snapped back. "I'll wait till Monday."

"Have a nice weekend, sir," Evelyn said, closing the door and working her way out of the office.

CHAPTER 5

It had taken Evelyn several tries to get through to Detective Chief Inspector Garvin on the secure line. When she did, she motioned to Drake, who was still going through old Caesar files in his office, to get on the line. Though Drake didn't know Garvin well, at their last encounter at a joint conference two years earlier, he'd felt a comfortable camaraderie with him.

"Long time, Drake. Can you hear me all right?" Garvin sounded as if he were in a cave. His equipment was definitely not state of the art.

"Yes, dandy," Drake said, chuckling quietly to himself on his highly engineered phone. "I'm sorry to take you away from your work, but something's come up that I hope you can shed some light on. Can you talk now?"

"Happy to take a break. Been too wrapped up in a recent murder that, except for the fact that it's a one-off so far, has the look of a signature killing. Fellow's neck slashed by some sort of claw. Damned puzzle, this one." Garvin knew he was being chatty, but a little letting off of steam with a colleague who dealt only in secrets couldn't hurt.

Drake cleared his throat. "Well, maybe that relates to the case I'm calling about," he said, looking for a good opening for his thin excuse for calling the inspector. "I saw an article in one of the newspapers on the murder of one Robert Johnston and was mulling it over in my mind, thinking it might have been an old associate of mine. Couldn't find anything here. The name's too common. Thought you might be able to help, as I'd like to contact his family if he's the man I knew."

Drake didn't like misleading Garvin, but he wasn't prepared to provide any details about the likelihood that Johnston was one of his defectors. The case was highly classified, and Garvin didn't have "need to know." He just hoped he could elicit enough from the DCI to see if the case was more than a straight-out murder.

"We're still very early in the investigation, and trying to get information on his background, family, the usual," Garvin said. "A common name, as you said. I can tell you that the death appears to have come from some sort of cutting into his jugular vein. We haven't identified the weapon yet, but it is not a marking we've seen in any recent cases. We also found some white powder on and near the wound, mixed in with the flush of blood that poured out of the jugular. Our forensic people are looking into this. All very strange at the moment."

"Strange indeed," Drake said. "I'd be most grateful if you would update me on anything you can share."

"Will do, but sorry I can't help you with the family or any relatives."

"Most appreciated, chief inspector."

Drake hung up the phone and the hair on the back of his neck stood up.

Someone had murdered one of his defectors.

CHAPTER 6

LONDON MAY 28, 2012

The chief inspector had been waiting several days for the toxicology report, pressing his underlings for quicker results. There had been no major news stories beyond the initial reporting by Sinclair-Jones. Thank God, the bastard hadn't written any more articles, though he'd tried to contact Garvin, who refused his calls. Garvin needed more time to sort things out without the media breathing down his neck.

Unfortunately, by the time the Scenes of Crime Officer had arrived at the murder site, only the tiniest clean remnants of the powder remained, the rest mixed with blood, soil, and dirt from where they found Johnston's body. How far it had been dragged, they had no idea, but they were analyzing the soil just in case they could determine exactly where he had been killed. It took too damned long to get things done, Garvin thought, quietly pounding his fist on his desk.

With the autopsy report now completed, Garvin knew for certain that the weapon had successfully pierced the jugular vein, and the victim would have died from blood loss. The role of the white substance remained a mystery for the time being. Even though the case was the only one of its kind, Garvin felt sure that the killer or killers wanted the murder to have a signature, as he had suggested to Drake, one unique enough that he suspected someone was sending a message. But what and to whom?

He'd had his people put out an all-points detailed bulletin to other constabularies in the United Kingdom to determine if there had been similar murders in the past few years. Thanks to the high technology information system the British had created after a grisly serial killing years earlier, police units across the country could coordinate with each other on any case that might need input from another jurisdiction. Nothing on other claw killings so far.

Despite all his years on the force, Garvin was not a patient man.

The phone in Garvin's office rang loudly, Jane nowhere in sight to answer it. He finally gave in and picked up the receiver.

"It's Fawkes, sir, I need to see you right away."

"Come on up."

Must be something good, Garvin thought, as Jane resurfaced at her desk. He buzzed her and told her to delay his next appointment.

Fawkes was at Garvin's door within minutes.

"What is it?" Garvin grumbled, nonetheless hoping he was about to get a break.

"Hawkesworth and I have found something."

"Go on."

"There was a killing earlier this year in southern Cornwall that appears to have had similar markings. On the wound, that is."

"What the hell!" Garvin felt his pulse race and didn't quite know whether he was pleased or not. He really didn't want a serial killer on the loose in England.

"Well, sir, as you know, we've been going over the murders in the records and just found the reference to the killing, with a notation that the weapon appeared to have been 'clawlike'. I found a short article in

The Cornwall Daily that referred to the murder as 'The Return of the Hound'."

Garvin's eyebrows rose as he waited for his overly polite but excited young officer to continue.

"The constabulary down there said they found absolutely no evidence of any other such killings in or around the area and concluded the victim was in fact killed by some sort of animal."

"The name of the victim?"

"Oliver Sempworth. Described as a loner who occasionally showed up in the local library but had no work history or anything that could be followed up on. Apparently, they didn't find any powder at the crime scene, but now they plan to review his case again and see if there are notes about any unusual detritus. The investigation died eventually; they couldn't find anything. No one even claimed the victim's body. It's now a cold case."

"I'll call the constable down there and see what he has to say," Garvin said. "Good work. Anything more on Johnston? Follow-up with his family, neighbors…?"

"Well, sir, we reviewed all the bits we had from Johnston's pocket debris. He worked in a small office out of his home, in Putney. We called there and got his wife, well, his widow, and set up a meeting with her. We tried to question her, but she was crying so hard we couldn't really understand her. I did notice she had a foreign accent. Couldn't tell what it was, maybe East European, Russian. We asked if there was anyone she could stay with, anyone who could help her, and she only carried on crying. I told her we'd get back to her."

Fawkes hated that part of the job, and Garvin was well aware of it.

"Do what you can and keep me posted."

As soon as Fawkes left, Garvin picked up the telephone. The Cornwall official provided nothing beyond what Fawkes had already reported.

Friendly and professional sounding, the constable said he was more than honored to hear from the esteemed chief inspector," then told Garvin he'd talk to the officer who'd handled the case and get back to the DCI forthwith.

Garvin hung up and decided to call Drake back.

CHAPTER 7

Drake finished speaking to Garvin, hung up the phone, and rubbed a hand over his face. A murder similar to Federov's, several months old, and now a cold case. Who was Oliver Sempworth? What the hell was going on?

"Evelyn," he called from his office. No reply.

He went out to her desk, pulled out her classified address book, and clicked through the "B" section. He found nothing but suspected she had probably scrambled her address book in some way to ensure the security of the contents. He was still searching unsuccessfully when she returned.

"Where were you?" he asked, the exasperation in his voice clear. She smiled. "At lunch. What's up?"

"I need you to find somebody for me. Do you remember Stanley Brewster, our Soviet ops intellectual-in-residence back in the day?"

"Of course. Haven't seen or heard of him in ages," she said.

"Do you know if he's still in the Russia department?"

"No, but I'll track him down."

Fifteen minutes later, Stanley Brewster stood quietly at the entrance to Drake's office, shoulders slightly slumped, as always. He hasn't changed a bit, Drake thought, looking up from his desk. The trademark shaft of white hair and huge eyeglasses were the same.

"Stanley, come in. It's been too long." Drake rose from his chair and went around his desk to shake hands with the diffident genius who had made him and his colleagues look smarter than they were back in the days of the Cold War.

"Delighted. You wanted to see me?"

"Yes, yes. Have a seat."

Stanley took the chair across from Drake.

"Something's come up, and I'm hoping you can help me figure it out," Drake began. "All preliminary at this point."

Drake briefed Stanley on the Thames murder, the identification of Ivan Federov, and Evelyn's review of the defector's files. Then he told him about the conversation he'd just had with DCI Garvin about this Cornwall case, which raised the obvious question, who was Oliver Sempworth and does this have anything to do with Federov?

"Stanley, I'd like you to find out if we have anything on Sempworth. I'm especially interested if he had a middle name, and if so, what it was. By the way, I haven't told the chief inspector handling all of this that I suspect a Soviet or Russian connection. It's way too early, and we have to keep that information compartmented."

"I understand, of course. I'll get on it."

"I'll take anything at this point. Evelyn and I already have some material on Federov, but you're the best at this and may find something more."

"I look forward to it," Stanley responded, in his familiar, quiet way, but Drake sensed his enthusiasm. He was a true gentleman of the old world; not many of those left, Drake thought.

Before the close of business, Brewster was back at Drake's office.

"Your suspicions were right, Jason. He was one of ours. The minute I got my hands on his full name, using some of the old Cornwall registries, I knew. Oliver Decius Sempworth. He is our unmarried defector of some twenty years ago, Oleg Karchenko. I've requested the rest of his files. Nothing yet, but I'll let you know as soon as I get them."

CHAPTER 8

GEORGETOWN, JUNE 3

FedEx package in my hand, I flopped down on the sofa and noted the strange address on the large envelope. It was from London, but an address I didn't recognize. Then I felt the envelope to see if there might be anything odd inside, but there were no bulges. It was clearly just documents of some sort, so I tore the flap and pulled out the letter inside.

Decktora, darling,

Must see you. Take the five p.m. British Airways flight to London Heathrow tomorrow, June 4. Meet me at our favorite place at St. James's at nine in the evening on the 5th. I know you'll be tired from the overnight flight, but I'm eager to see you. And though I don't want to give you an out, if your plane is truly delayed, we can meet the next day. You have a hotel reservation at the Savoyard, and I've already bought your ticket, so you have no excuses. I know you're not too busy to visit me. Soonest.

Love, Sergei.

There was only one Sergei in my life, a Russian defector I'd handled in Washington at a painful time for him. I managed to get him transferred to London, where we thought he'd have a happier situation. That turned out well, and during that time working together, we developed a close bond.

But 'Meet me at our favorite place in St. James's.' could only mean he was telling me to meet him at the Chequers Tavern on Duke Street, the last place I'd seen him, some three years ago, when I was working in London. The FedEx letter was sent Friday night, but got to me Sunday morning. My flight had to be Monday night. A simple phone call to the airline would confirm that.

If I couldn't make the meeting, the message translated in our language to one hour earlier the following night. "Soonest" was internal jargon for just what it sounds like, but the word assured me this letter was strictly business.

And urgent.

Sergei and I both understood that when our work together was finished he could never again contact me directly and vice versa. As always in my line of work, when the assignment came to an end, it was goodbye.

He'd been given an emergency contact number for a resettlement officer in MI5, so I knew immediately that if he broke structure and tried to locate me, something was very wrong.

Quick planning would be required for me to travel to London tomorrow. I'd have to move a few things around on my calendar. I reread Sergei's message, hoping I could sense something between the lines. But he hadn't given me enough clues, and there was no operationally secure way I could get in touch with him other than in person. The more I thought about it, the more concerned I got.

Decision made. I would go.

I had to find someone at CIA headquarters in Langley. Sergei had been a CIA asset, and I wasn't about to go off cowgirl-style and handle whatever it was without giving headquarters a heads-up.

Whatever was going on, his contact had to involve more than me, no matter how it seemed initially. Thank heavens I'd kept the telephone numbers of a few of my old friends still inside. Those were precious numbers. No one got them once out of the business, even on a leave of absence. I'd hoarded the few I had, rearranging the digits in a pattern I created for myself and that would keep me out of trouble if I ever had to go through another polygraph.

I was used to reporting my foreign travel, every detail: where I was going, where I was staying, who I was meeting, all part of the code of conduct of CIA ops officers. You didn't visit a foreign country without the approval of the local Chief of Station. The COS was next to God and had to sanction even personal travel. Reporting it now reminded me that somebody, well *something*, cared about my whereabouts. *Mother CIA.*

My clearances were still active, and I'd left the door open to go back if the CIA's psychic hold on me was too strong and I couldn't really let go. I'd seen former colleagues who were unable to move on, and I promised myself I could make the break when the time came. Most case officers were workaholics, often because their professional life was more interesting than their personal one, and the Directorate of Operations, the DO, was good about not terminating clearances for certain case officers. They wanted most of us back on contract because of our unique experience and language capabilities, and there had been a lot of turnover in recent years. Old blood was good.

Who to call? I needed someone who would react quickly and not get caught up in a mess of red tape. Sam Winslow. Perfect, if he was around.

We had a long history. He'd been my mentor during the early days of my career, and later a good friend. Sam was one of those type A's who'd retired on a Friday and gone back to work, on contract, the following Monday. I smiled as I thought back to a conversation I'd had with him just after he retired.

"What's the matter with you?" I'd asked impatiently. "You just retired. Why don't you do something else? Travel, take a vacation."

"I had a vacation. Saturday and Sunday. And I've already been all over the world. Time to get to the office."

"You're hopeless," I'd said, and that was when I told myself I'd never fall into the contractor trap. That was plain crazy. Still, as noted, I'd kept my clearances when I left.

I dug out his number and dialed.

Sam agreed to meet for a short lunch at Clyde's in Georgetown. He was busy but got the point that I wouldn't call him on a Sunday unless it was urgent. We couldn't discuss what I had to say over the phone. We both understood that.

CHAPTER 9

GEORGETOWN, JUNE 3

As the water massaged my body, I let my thoughts run, a luxury I couldn't afford to indulge in very often. *Will I stay out of the CIA?*

I'd had enough years in and enough heartbreak to last at least one lifetime. It had been a tough decision, but believe me when I tell you, it was time to take a break. My entire adult life—the professional part, that is—belonged to Mother CIA. Eighteen years in, but short of financially requisite retirement points. Not good.

The bureaucracy had been eating away at me. It was painful to come home from an overseas assignment—"the field"—to a desk job at headquarters, even for a seasoned officer. Everything was about terrorism, and I was a Russia expert, not an Arabist, and I had no desire to become one. Plus, there was the mess in my personal life. But do I miss the action? I haven't had the courage to look at all that honestly.

* * *

I'd joined the Agency in the 1990s after the Cold War ended. Living in Moscow as a child with my Foreign Service parents meant that I'd lived through the demise of the Soviet Union. My father had served two tours in Moscow, but the second was cut short when my mother was killed in an accident. The car that hit her on the wildly congested

Ulitsa Varvarka was never identified, but the entire tragedy was enough to cause my father to go home "short of tour," an expression I didn't know then but would eventually learn. All I felt at the time was heartbreak. By the time we left Moscow, I spoke and read Russian. Of course, I didn't have a political understanding of all the craziness of that transition period, but I'd decided I would become a Russia expert and follow in my father's footsteps, to Yale for both undergraduate and grad degrees in Russian Studies. And then I made the fateful decision to go into the CIA, instead of what the older and wiser told me was a more sensible choice, the Foreign Service. The CIA's offer to put me into the esteemed and male-dominated operational training program clinched it for me.

After a year of training, I was sent off to work on one of the Middle East task forces. Exciting as it sounds, it interested me not at all. Within my first few months, I was begging to get assigned to what I called Russia House.

"You're not using my skills. What about the Kremlin? Do you really think they've changed?" That was by now my routine line to my managers as I pushed hard to get reassigned.

"Decky, you're living in the past, your father's past," said my first boss, a longtime colleague of my elder. "Russia is not the hot target these days. You're smart as hell but starting to drive me crazy with your stubbornness."

It wasn't exactly stubbornness. I just never gave up until I was satisfied with the result I wanted. I'd inherited my mother's IQ and my father's drive, all good. In the end, my boldness was forgiven in part because I was legacy, but more likely because by being so dogged and aggressive with management, I was demonstrating just the character traits needed in a CIA case officer—I went after what I had to, and I didn't give up until I reached the end of the road. Not to mention that I didn't like losing.

So, I got my assignment to the Russia Desk, but once there quickly understood my mentor's warning. It was the early nineties and revelations of a spy in our midst had just been announced. To us, to the media, to the world. Our office had the pall of a funeral parlor. The identities of at least ten of our Soviet agents had been divulged to the Kremlin several years earlier, along with details of some of our most sensitive anti-Soviet operations. After nearly a decade of counterintelligence investigation, we learned why. We had a mole. A Russia Desk officer, sitting right among us. Aldrich Ames left a path of blood behind him. The agents he'd betrayed were recalled to Moscow, each under mysterious circumstances, executed, and buried in unmarked graves.

It was a strange time, but now I understood why management thought this was a bad assignment for me. The office seemed to be in its death throes. Still, I persisted, and I was not unhappy with my choice, especially after they gave me a few defector cases to handle, knowing this would educate me in the dangerous lives and challenges of those who dared to spy for us. The Russians would get back to their old tricks, Cold War over or not. I knew where my future lay.

* * *

I felt the warmth of the shower spill over me as my mind turned to Alex—my love of so many years—his arms massaging my body. I was floating in a soft but sad reverie. After I don't know how long, I flipped the water to cold. Get it together, I told myself sternly, quickly rinsed off the last of the suds, stepped out of the shower, and reached for my towel.

It was a year ago last June. Alex and I were just back from a joint assignment in London and living in what now seems like blissful happiness in our house in Georgetown. The house was full of light and cheer, already decorated for Christmas, when a call came from his office offering him a new assignment.

"Just one more job," he told me, watching my Christmas spirit vanish. "They said they need me on an urgent mission, that I'm the one most qualified to handle it."

What could I say to that? I'd had no trouble being supportive when we were younger, both building our careers, even though I was seldom allowed to know exactly where he was going on some of his assignments. But this time I was angry. After London, we'd agreed to and settled into this new life together.

I finished drying myself, then turned to the mirror. As I twisted my hair into a French knot, I noticed a tiny hint of gray creeping into the auburn. Well, truth was, I wasn't getting any younger. I dabbed on some eye shadow, applied mascara, all the while noticing that my eyes didn't seem as dark as they once had. Do eyes get lighter as we age? I let out a sigh, picked up my cooled coffee, and took a gulp. Whatever. Life is what it is.

I moved to the closet to get dressed and brushed past the few items hanging there that belong to Alex. In my determination, I leave them there for when he returns. I may be the only one in the world who believes he will, but I do.

He and I are opposites professionally. He's a paramilitary officer, a PM'er, who speaks Arabic, Farsi, and Hebrew. Every time a new crisis in the special ops area popped up, the chiefs went to him. Like me he wanted to be in the field, so he jumped when asked. It didn't matter that he was getting too senior for these assignments. It was in his blood and his training to take the hard jobs. He'd always served in the Agency's war zones—of late, Pakistan and Afghanistan.

One of those rare CIA couples, Alex and I often had to take "split assignments." I hated it and so did he, but there were not enough Agency positions overseas for us to get two in one spot. I came up with endless ideas, like letting me be a housewife undercover teaching at a local university where Alex was assigned. I would have found targets all over the place, but the Agency would have none of it. One assignment per couple. Fortunately, the man in my life honored my work and supported our less-than-perfect situation.

We'd met at the Farm when I was in ops training, a complete ingénue, while he was instructing some new PM'ers in search-and-rescue training. The romance started there, as many do in that closed, intense, and exciting atmosphere, and we've been together ever since.

Amidst our subsequent, crazy, all-over-the-world lives, we never took the trip down the aisle, though all our friends knew and treated us as a couple. Our goals and our characters were aligned, and we were connected at the heart. I was sure of that after all we'd been through. We didn't feel the need to marry. But now I had no legal connection to him. I'd never given that much thought, but after several months, I was reminded by his office that I did not meet the "need to know" requirements for continued briefings on his status. They were being "nice" to me in the beginning. All I got now was the promise that they'd brief me if he resurfaced. Their position was not intended to be cruel, but I viewed it as such nonetheless. It goes without saying that I could receive no spousal income from his *estate*—a word I could barely stomach.

Dressed and as put together as I needed to be, I closed the closet door, grabbed my coffee mug, and headed downstairs, but not fast enough to escape one particular memory that haunted me ceaselessly. We'd had a horrific fight when Alex accepted that offer last December.

In early January, Alex went down to the Farm for special training and then headed directly out to—wherever. I suspected he was going to a backwater somewhere in Pakistan, but the information was what the Agency calls "compartmentalized," in this case, even from me, a colleague.

A phone call the night before he left was the last I heard from him. My heart still hurts when I think of my last words to him: "You'd better not become one of those stars on the wall," I snapped, referring to the lobby of the CIA, where stars are emblazoned onto the marble wall, each signifying the death of a former colleague. I hung up without giving him a chance to say goodbye.

In mid-January, home alone, I got the dreaded call from headquarters.

"He's gone," they said, "missing" somewhere in the embattled morass of the Middle East. They didn't even state his name on the open phone call to my residence. Did they say missing or lost—or gone? I wasn't sure. I was stunned: the Middle East? I thought he was in South Asia.

The questions—where is he? How can we find him?—race through my brain relentlessly, and did so especially at Langley, where my memories of him, of us, floated through the hallways like ghosts only I can see. I've tried to move on, but my skills are in areas that don't involve the heart. I'm brilliant at compartmentalization in my career, but a failure at it in my private life. Now my thoughts flew back and forth between memories of my mother's tragic death in Moscow when I was a kid, and Alex. Another stab to the heart, not the same, but not unlike it, either.

Alex is still missing, along with two Agency colleagues and at least one Brit, perhaps more. He disappeared from a small reconnaissance team somewhere in or near Syria, I was told. No further information. NFI.

Syria? *Ouch.* ISIS and various Al-Qaeda offspring were alive and well in that part of the world. Some very ugly things happened in the region, and learning he was there, intensified my anxiety. To make matters worse, he was under nonofficial cover, a NOC, which meant that if he was captured, our government would disavow any connection with the officers or mission. In other words, he didn't officially exist.

Once I knew Syria was involved, I understood why there was so little information. We had to be especially careful because of the presence of the Russians. An accident of any kind in that air space would produce disastrous results for us all. And because of our limited access in the region, we had little intelligence on local insurgencies, which I assumed is why Alex was sent there.

Some six weeks in, the desk started using the phrase "*If* he is still alive." The first time I heard it, my lunch threatened to come back up. The words continue to echo in my head. The crisis in the region has shown no sign of lifting, and reporting from there is slim at best. Now only my closest friends say, "There's always hope."

So I've closed the Agency door for now, bored and angry and still expecting Alex to come home. Alive.

I will have to figure that out on my own. Right after I figure out what in the world Sergei needs.

CHAPTER 10

GEORGETOWN, JUNE 3

Sam was already at Clyde's when I arrived. He was early. I wasn't, but I was almost always exactly on time—that was my art form. I was so tuned in to time that I barely needed a watch.

"You're three minutes late," he barked as he got to his feet to greet me.

"Sorry, my dog ate the homework." I smiled at him. "Can you just give me a little break? I'm on leave now, and, hey, I'm being good enough to report my travel."

He gave me a quick hug. "I'm glad you called, Decky. I knew you couldn't take being on the outside. No action—and you miss your old friends," he winked.

"Wrong," I laughed.

Our jousting aside, we didn't have much time and needed to get down to business. Sam and Alex had been good friends, and I didn't want him to ask me how I was doing, nor did I want to press him for current information. Obviously, if Sam had learned something about Alex's whereabouts, he would have let me know. I was sure of that.

"One of my defectors contacted me. He sent me a letter by FedEx."

I still called them "my" defectors. That was too hard to let go of. Deep bonds formed between case officer and agent, and then suddenly you moved on to a new assignment, and could never see or communicate with any of them again: defectors, agents, assets. All were turned over to the next case officer. Your relationship was over if you were doing the turnover responsibly.

Sam's left eyebrow lifted but he didn't say anything.

"He wants me to fly to London tomorrow. No explanatory details." I showed Sam the letter, explaining that, in addition to the fact it was out of the blue, Sergei Dumanovskiy and I had never spoken to each other in any way that had a romantic tone.

Sam nodded that he understood. "When did you last see or hear from him?"

"It's been several years."

"Are you confident the message is really from him? I don't want anyone pulling you into a trap. The Russkies aren't so friendly these days, and you have a history."

I took his point. We both understood the risk, but that wasn't about to stop me.

"I'll send a priority out to the COS in London, give him a heads-up. I need your trip details. You know the drill."

Before giving Sam those details, I told him I'd decided to make one change to Sergei's plans. I had no intention of staying at the Savoyard and would make a reservation at the Langsford Club, where I still had a membership. I wanted to be in a place I knew and one that was not open to the public. Further, if the letter was not actually from Sergei, avoiding the Savoyard would be a wise move.

"Are you worried?" Sam said, noting my intensity and giving me a last chance to back out.

"Concerned. He was always a disciplined man. Knowing him as I do—as I did—I'm taking it seriously. Anyway, assume I'll be in London for at least a few days. Don't really know."

"Okay. Flights?"

"British Air, Flight 602. It leaves from Dulles tomorrow at five p.m., to Heathrow."

"British Air. Couldn't you at least fly on a US airline?"

We had to fly US airlines when we traveled, part of our regulations and service to the taxpayer. Fly American.

"Sergei bought the ticket, not me. You're not paying, and I'm not traveling for the Agency. Anyway, that's the situation."

"Okay, I'll pull the files and check them for any updates. Christ, I hope they're not in archives, or it will be next week before I can review them!" He paused. "And thank you, Decky. You're right to report this."

"I'll be home tonight if you need to reach me," I said, refolding the letter and tucking it into my purse. "As you know, there's no way I can contact Sergei, so I'll follow the yellow brick road as best I can. It's just so strange…. "

My voice trailed off with the incomplete thought. "And, Sam, my clearances are still in place for a few more months, just in case you were wondering."

"I wasn't, and I'll call you one way or the other before you leave. There's a possibility someone will want to meet with you before you go. If so, I won't go into details over the phone, but just assume any meeting will be in Langley. Go to the front entrance, and I'll arrange VIP parking."

The phone rang at six o'clock as I was going through my closet trying to decide what to take to London. I groaned at the disruption and grabbed the phone on the third ring.

"Hope I didn't interrupt your dinner," Sam said casually. "Meet me tomorrow morning at nine for breakfast?"

That meant Langley.

CHAPTER 11

LANGLEY AND DULLES, JUNE 4

The late-afternoon flight to Heathrow didn't leave me much time for discussions in Langley. I'd already packed, had passport in hand, and was just out the door when I had a flash. I turned around and dashed back into my small home office, pulled the framed Matisse print from the wall, and opened the safe hiding behind it where Alex kept his files. I found his old London folder and searched through it, looking for contact information on Bredon Aberforth, who was Alex's MI6 Middle East liaison when we served in London. It was there in his handwritten scribble. The phone number was scrambled, but I knew Alex's secrets and easily figured out the correct sequence.

My car knew its way to Langley. A twenty-minute drive brought me to the turnoff to the unmarked entrance to headquarters. The main building emerged from behind a forest of low trees, like a hidden village. As I drove over the spiked pass-throughs on the entry road, I quickly saw that the checks had gotten even more rigorous than when I'd left not so long ago. The first checkpoint was a metal box that requested my data.

"Decktora Raines for an appointment at 0900." A buzzer went off and I drove to the guard box, where I had to show my ID.

Eventually, a bodiless hand reached out and handed me a building pass and parking sticker. I reminded myself I was basically an outsider now, but the good part of that was that I got to park in the VIP lot, just steps from the main entrance. I parked and walked up the front stairs, nodding to the statue of Nathan Hale as I passed by. The large CIA insignia embedded in the entry hall lay beneath me as I gazed up at the wall of stars and counted them. No star had been added since I'd left, and I exhaled a breath I didn't realize I was holding.

The words I'd spoken to Alex in that last conversation popped into my head and choked me once again.

"Miss Raines. Nice to see you again," said the security guard, smiling at me.

I looked up from the sign-in sheet at a man I'd seen over the years in various posts throughout the main building

"Logan, good to see you as well. I'm here for a meeting."

"Yes, ma'am. Mr. Winslow is waiting for you. Room 106 to the right."

Sam was already in 106 when I arrived, a cup of coffee in his hand. The aroma swept over me as I entered the all too familiar sterile room, with its government-issued rectangular table, a couple of metal chairs, and the requisite framed black-and-white prints of Washington monuments.

"Thank God you still have your damned clearances. As soon as Harrison gets here, we can brief you. In the meantime, I got the file on Dumanovskiy. You can stay after we've finished and review it, though I doubt you'll find much that's new since you last saw it."

Harrison was chief of the British Desk. I'd known him forever.

Sam continued: "The Chief of Station wants to see you as soon as you get to London, *before* you do anything else. In other words, from

Heathrow you head directly to Grosvenor Square and meet with him. I'll give you the contact information, which you'll need to memorize."

At least he didn't say I shouldn't go. I would have anyway, but it was good to have Langley's okay.

"By the way, you know who the COS in London is, don't you?"

"No, I'm out of that loop."

"It's John Perlman. Mr. P. He finally got a European assignment. God knows he deserves it after all the hellholes he's been to."

Mr. P.? The Pear. Damn, he was one man I didn't want to see. My brain started racing. Calm down, I told myself. *He can't hold anything over me now.*

Sam caught my expression. "He's harmless. He's been defanged."

"Right. Whatever. So, did he say anything else? Like why he needs to see me right away?"

"He just shot a quick cable back, probably because I sent mine out *priority*, and he knew there needed to be a fast turnaround. Don't worry about him. Just meet him and tell him what's going on. London doesn't hold old ops files, so I'm sending him a summary of the Dumanovskiy case."

"Fine," I said, though I wondered what obstacles the Pear would present this time.

A tap on the door signaled Harrison's arrival. He entered, looking like central casting for a CIA European ops manager—double-breasted suit, minimally patterned gray tie, and a slash of silver hair combed elegantly back on one side.

"It's been too long, Decktora. I'm sorry about...." He stopped mid-sentence as I waved my hand at him, knowing he was about to mention Alex.

"Well, then, let's get right to it," he said, clearing his throat. "Sam briefed me, and I admit I have mixed feelings about this message from London and your response to it. I understand the temptation, but we can't confirm that it's really from Sergei, certainly not in the short time frame you've given us. The bottom line, we have nothing recent on Dumanovskiy, as you'll see from the file. The chief plans to contact MI5 for any updates on their side since they're now his official point of contact."

"That's what I wanted to avoid," I groaned. "I'd hoped we could contact MI5 after I've met with Sergei and found out why he reached out to me."

"Not going to happen. Too risky. Can't go around MI5."

"Our meeting will be in a public place," I argued back, "and I'll brief the COS immediately after my meeting," already a little miffed. Enter the bureaucracy: the layers of red tape were beginning to appear. Maybe I shouldn't have coordinated with headquarters.

"I don't consider your public meeting site secure, and we don't have enough advance time to coordinate with MI5 and arrange surveillance. Nonetheless, you're a quasi-private citizen at the moment and can proceed as you wish. You might want to do a full Surveillance Detection Route, however,"

"Harrison, you don't need to go there. I only left four months ago. SDRs are in my DNA."

The edge on the conversation irked me, though I, like my colleagues, was good at concealing my emotions.

"One more thing, Decky. MI5 recently reported something to the COS that might be relevant. It concerns a Russian who defected to the Brits some years ago and was given a new identity and resettled in the outskirts of London. They hadn't heard from him in a long time, no news being good news."

Uh-oh. Past tense. I braced myself.

"His body was found on the bank of the Thames quite recently. The murder squad of the British Metropolitan Police is handling the case. There were some bizarre details. Slashes on his neck, a claw mark of some sort that pierced his jugular, and a white powder around the wound, all being analyzed by the Met's forensics team."

I winced.

"A senior MI5 officer, who just happens to be our liaison contact, spotted a recent obit in a British newspaper. His colleagues had cleverly coded the names of a certain category of Russian defector, so when he saw the name of the victim in the media, he immediately recognized it as one of theirs, then briefed Perlman in case we had any history on him."

"What about the British police? Aren't they all over this?

"MI5 discussed the Thames murder with a senior at the Met, but did not brief him on the nationality of the victim, just told him diplomatic traffic showed the deceased to have been foreign-born. In short, MI5 is not, *repeat not*, telling MPS the true identity of the victim. They don't want the police digging into their defector cases. As far as they know, the victim was just a local citizen. So until we know more...."

"Until?" Decky interrupted.

"Until we know whether the Thames case is a one-off murder that has nothing to do with his Soviet background, or—"

"Whether it does," I finished.

"Decky, the Met gave our MI5 contact the impression they are going down the serial killer path. They think the Thames murder looks like a signature killing. And just so you know, the British press has few specifics—the name of the victim and the bare details of the killing. Let's hope it stays that way. The British tabloid culture is voracious and unrelenting, so, cross your fingers we figure this out before they do."

"So, the connection to Sergei..." I mused aloud.

"It crossed my mind last night when Sam called. We don't know, but we want you to keep us in the loop on what you learn."

With that, Harrison nodded politely and headed out, leaving me and Sam alone.

"Decky, see what the Chief of Station has to say when you get to London. I really don't think he'll hassle you, and maybe he'll have something more by the time you get there. We barely gave him time to review the case."

"Got it."

"I'm leaving you with Sergei's file. You might see something new, though I doubt it. Anyway, safe trip and keep out of trouble. Glad you're back on board. Ha ha."

"Right," I grimaced.

Okay, Sergei, talk to me. I dug into the files, reading quickly through old material that was pretty much already known to me.

I was close to the end of my reading when a cable from London caught my eye. It said there was a new London Rezident, the head of Russian intelligence at the Russian Embassy. The document requested traces, a routine matter, on one "Vladimir Ivanchukov, made known to our COS in London, by his liaison contact in British intelligence."

Ivanchukov? I felt a chill.

Harrison hadn't mentioned this. Maybe he didn't catch the significance. But then, he didn't know Russia like I did; he had other targets on his mind, especially these days. If Harrison didn't get it, I sure did. Most of the information we had on Ivanchukov came from the debriefings of Sergei when he first defected. He provided a full bio on the man, details on his ops projects, his staff, all of it.

Sergei's nemesis was in London.

* * *

At Dulles, I headed over to my favorite airline lounge for the two-hour wait, sat down in a comfortable leather chair in a vacant area of the room, and got a tomato juice with lime. I pretended it was a Bloody Mary and settled in, hoping not to be disturbed. I read through *The Washington Post* in fifteen minutes and looked around to see that I was no longer alone.

An elderly woman sat across from me. She nodded politely and smiled, then turned back to her book. But one chair group over, I could feel the presence of a man who had just sat down. I didn't want to make eye contact but gave a quick look, caught the glimmer of a gray suit and a newspaper in his hands. Had he glanced at me? I wasn't sure. But I was definitely getting back to my case officer self, aware of everyone around me and willing to be suspicious. Funny thing about my business: when a man looks at you, you don't take it as a compliment, you wonder if you should be worried. Paranoia was an acceptable neurosis. I opened the newspaper again, turned to the op-ed page, and eventually started to daydream.

Sometime later an announcement blared over the airport loudspeaker. I snapped to, in time to hear the faceless monitor state that my flight was delayed for three hours. Not good. Now I had a long wait.

Our recontact plan would be the same as we'd used in the past. If I didn't make it for tomorrow night's meeting, I would see Sergei the following day, same location, one hour later. No sense in worrying about it. But still, I didn't like meeting plans to change, especially in no-contact situations.

This much I knew. A Russian defector I'd once handled had just sent me an urgent cry for help; another was recently murdered along the Thames. On top of that, Sergei's nemesis was now the Rezident in London. These pieces had to connect. Of that I was sure.

As I settled back in my chair and accepted the delay, I noticed the man in gray speaking angrily to an agent. He sat back down, not even turning his head in my direction. He was as perturbed as I was, not at all interested in me. I felt a small sense of relief. I set my cell phone alarm, leaned back in the big leather chair, and closed my eyes once again. I would soon be on my way to London, the place where Alex and I had spent some of our happiest days. And I dared to imagine that being there would help me find him.

CHAPTER 12

LONDON, JUNE 4-5

Finally, I was on the plane. As I settled into my seat, my mind once again turned to Alex. The last time I was there, I was with him. I could almost feel his gray-blue eyes on me, eyes that changed shade with his mood. The excitement I felt when he gazed at me came back for a moment, but I shut off the thought. I refused to slip into that mood.

And I also refused to accept that there was nothing I could do about his situation. It wasn't in my nature. Alex had been the center of my life, and now he was lost somewhere in that war-torn mess in Syria. I reached into my bag to check my note on Bredon Aberforth. Langley would never approve what I planned to do, but nothing would stop me once my mind was set.

I came so close to marrying someone else. I tried. I really did. I dated other guys, but in time, they all seemed like brothers. They didn't get to me, at least not in that way. After one fateful encounter in Langley, when Alex had declared "my destiny was with him," while offering nothing, I tried to put him out of my mind, which was made easier when he was sent off on assignment shortly thereafter. The Middle East again, God knows doing what, but it was paramilitary, and no doubt dangerous. When we were separated, I could gradually get him out of my mind. And the fact that he never contacted me when he was overseas helped.

My father had come around to the idea of my career by now and even acknowledged that I was doing well for a woman in the DO. But he knew, and I knew, that the continuous moving and traveling didn't bode well for marriage. Like most parents, he wanted me to "be happy," which meant marry, have children, and do some sort of not-too-consuming work.

It wasn't an easy path my character had chosen for me. I was not destined for the suburbs and, over time, it became clear to me that I was not going to have what my parents had had. Maybe that stability had given me so much comfort as a child, that as an adult I didn't seem to be looking for it.

I threw myself into work and was saved, if that's the right word for it, by my first overseas assignment. It was when I returned two years later that my personal life took a dramatic turn. Alex tracked me down. He'd been back in the States for a while, and he knew exactly where I was and when my tour of duty ended.

Not more than a week after I'd settled into my new position at headquarters, he appeared in my office. I was stunned to see him standing in front of me, but there he was.

"Dinner tonight, Decktora?" he said, handsome and direct as ever.

"Hello, Alex, how are you?" I wasn't about to dive into what should be the middle of a conversation with a man I hadn't seen in two years. "Are you surveilling me?"

"Actually, I am. I'll tell you all about it—about everything— at dinner."

I wasn't happy with myself, but I agreed to the date. How easy this was for him. As I got dressed that night, I noticed that I was more finicky than usual about my hair, about what I wore. This is not going to happen, I told myself.

I wore a silk, sleeveless, teal dress with enough of a plunge to catch the eye of the waiter at the restaurant. When Alex picked me up, I saw the slight double-take as he saw me for the first time outside the work uniform—a black suit, jacket, and whatever on top. Romance was on my mind, but I had no intention of giving in to him. Tonight, I was going to tease, to make up for the way he had treated me, whether it was intentional on his part or not. It was my turn to get even.

He took me to a charming inn in Potomac, where we were shown into a cozy dining room with a fire already aflame. And yes, we sat in a dark corner. My god, this man is sexy, I thought. It was clear he was targeting me—that's what we say when we are trying to recruit someone. He chose the perfect place. Either he understood me better than I'd thought, or this was his routine. Whatever way, it was working.

I kept up my guard, flirting in a calculated way. I could almost count the seconds before I would let my eyelashes drop, look down, and then gaze back up at him. He gazed directly back. Over the wine and the dinner, I knew.

We didn't even get to dessert. He grabbed me as we walked to his car, pulling me close to him. I could feel his whole body against mine, and I knew he wanted me, badly and now. He kissed me deeply, and I heard his sigh as my head fell back, letting him kiss my neck and move downward.

"My God, we're in the parking lot," I gasped.

"Fine with me."

"No."

He smiled, cool once again. I wasn't doing so well in flirtation management now.

"Come on. Hop in," he said opening the door of his car. I folded into the seat and let him take charge. We didn't speak as we drove to his apartment. It was as orderly and masculine as he was. Not that I noticed

much as we pushed through the front door. We barely got inside before we were tearing at each other's clothes.

"Bedroom, over there," he said in a husky voice.

By the time we got to the bedroom, our clothes were off, and we fell onto the plush bed, now hungry for each other. His kiss went deep into mine and he moved down my body touching and kissing every part of it, as if he knew my every secret. But we couldn't wait long. Passion had overtaken both of us.

We made love most of the night, falling asleep in each other's arms sometime before sunrise, the slightest hint of light peeking between the curtains.

I smelled the aroma of freshly brewed coffee and knew that Alex was already up.

"Good morning, you beautiful creature," he smiled at me.

"Good morning."

"I told you."

"Told me what?"

"That I was the one."

I threw a weak fist into his arm, and he pulled me to him in a fresh embrace.

"You're so conceited."

"Not really. You'll see." That smile again.

I noticed how neat everything was. The colors in his apartment were shades of beige and white, the spots of color from beautiful oriental rugs, and much of the furniture seemingly hand-carved, probably from South Asia.

"I didn't expect you to have such good taste," I teased.

"Why not? You really thought I was a knuckle-dragger?" He actually seemed surprised.

"Yes. I think so."

"I collected all this in my travels. Rugs from the Middle East, furniture made for me in Burma. Everything here reminds me of someplace I've been."

"You're sentimental." I guess I sounded surprised.

"What did you think? A hard-core paramilitary type with no appreciation of art, beauty?"

"Yes, that would be an accurate description."

"You have a lot to learn about me."

As soon as I figured out what was going on with Sergei, I would track down Aberforth. I didn't know much about his and Alex's missions into the Middle East and had never asked Alex for details. We were past that, but I hoped that history might help. I didn't know him well, but we'd had a good connection when we were all in London, and I would find him now. This was my own mission.

Eight hours into the air, I looked down at the lush, green earth below as the plane descended into Heathrow. I didn't know whether I was happy or sad to be back; Sergei's irresistible invitation was mixed with bittersweet memories. After a typically bumpy landing, I worked my way through the endless passport and customs lines, no longer able to speed through as I had when I carried a diplomatic passport. Now I just wanted to get into central London, and the quickest way was the Underground. I caught the Piccadilly Line into town, then grabbed a cab for Grosvenor Square. The hassle of the travel was over, but I wasn't relaxed. Sergei was very much on my mind, as was the immediate meeting with the COS.

The security cordon faced me as we approached the embassy, a reminder of how much our world had changed in the short time since

I'd left. The new frontage did nothing to enhance the appearance of the embassy, which was not a thing of beauty to start with. Designed by the architect Eero Saarinen back in the sixties, it was the ugly younger sister to the elegant Mayfair competition that surrounded it.

"Nine pounds four," the cabbie said. I got out and handed him ten pounds, no twenty percent like at home.

Glancing at the American Eagle atop the building, I suddenly felt excited to be back. Inside the main entrance, I showed the security guard my driver's license as ID and said I had an appointment with Mr. Perlman.

"He'll meet you in the coffee shop downstairs," one of the guards said, handing me a pass.

I headed down to the American-style café. Perlman wasn't yet there, so I ordered a coffee and waited. My mind flashed back to our first encounter, when I was looking for my first overseas assignment, and I felt an urge to turn and run. I had been eagerly seeking a special assignment, and he was the boss-to-be. To get the job, I had to interview with him, and he chose the time and location: after work hours in a safe house in downtown DC.

He'd been known in hallway gossip as "the Pear," a title based on his girth and general shape. But that didn't keep him from being a prodigious ladies' man, a fact I hadn't known at the time, though I wondered why the meeting had to be held at six p.m. and outside the office. And, sure enough, he greeted me at the apartment door, with no secretary or office staff to assist him. His first words were, "Welcome, come in. What will you have to drink?"

"A drink, well...."

"Come on, you've had a busy day. We're not in the office."

I suppressed a smile. Short, stocky, with a bald pate, he had certainly earned his moniker. The piercing brown eyes instantly spoke to me of a quick mind. He was clearly a born extrovert, and cocky—the basic person-ality type of the DO case officer.

Sliding into a well-upholstered chair, he loosened his tie, opened his shirt collar, and took a sip, or maybe it was a gulp, of his drink.

"I've read your file. You've done some decent work. Tell me, what can you do for me in Paris?"

As I started to answer, he jumped up.

"Follow me," he said, leading me toward the bedroom. I walked hesitantly behind him as he patted the bed, motioning me to sit down, or worse. Now I knew. He hadn't read my file and probably didn't know a thing about my fieldwork. My hoped-for Paris assignment was about to come to an abrupt ending.

"Excuse me a moment," I said as I rushed into the bathroom to gather my thoughts. The job was important to me, but he had outmaneu-vered me. I'd have to risk bravado and hope for the best. When I stormed back into the bedroom, there he was, right where I'd left him.

"Sir, I'm leaving now. I won't tell you what I think of you and this situation. I'll leave it at that—and as a tale to tell my grandchildren some-day. They won't believe it."

"Oh, come on, sweetheart, you're no fun at all. Can't you take a joke?"

I shook myself out of the memory, but my jaw was tight. Talk about gall. "Can't you take a joke?" Every time I thought of the Pear, a cartoon bubble appeared over his head with that lame comment. I glanced around and saw him enter the room and pause briefly to speak with a colleague. I sipped my coffee, determined to be cool, calm, and composed.

"What the hell are you doing in London, Raines?" he barked, no words of introduction, as I splashed coffee out of the cup.

"I heard you'd taken a leave of absence. I got the cable from headquarters. Fill me in."

He was certainly not the flirtatious creep I remembered.

"Well, first of all, I'm on vacation."

"Not from what I hear. Tell me *exactly* why you're here."

I wasn't going to be bullied, so I drank some coffee and looked at him. That smirk I remembered so well was still in place. Perhaps it was a birth defect, not just a character flaw. But apparently, I'd delayed too long.

"Get to it," he sniped, sotto voce. "What's going on? I know we relocated a defector here, and headquarters cabled that he has requested an urgent meeting with you. You were his last case officer? He's the tragic one, right?"

"Aren't they all?" I said, though Sergei's story was among the most heartrending. "And, yes, I was his last handler. He had some serious problems, and the result was that I helped him resolve them and got him relocated over here, at his strong request." I wasn't about to let Perlman lead the conversation.

"Details."

I told him I hadn't had any contact with Sergei since I'd left London but that he had suddenly reached out to me, no explanation why. The British were to handle any problems that arose at this point. No further contact would be expected with the CIA unless he initiated it.

"And that's what he's done," I said.

He was quiet for a moment. "I don't like this. Unprofessional on his part, but I appreciate that you're coordinating. I wouldn't expect any less of you."

He must have noticed my eyebrows rise. Suddenly he sounded less gruff, and our meeting was going better than I'd expected.

Maybe—just maybe—it wouldn't be so bad dealing with him after all. I gave him a full brief on the FedEx from Sergei and my visit to Langley. But I had something more on my mind.

"I saw your cable reporting that Vladimir Ivanchukov is in London."

He nodded. "I'm still waiting for headquarters to get back to me. We all have our eyes on him, to the extent possible. I recognized his name, but Russia wasn't my theater and I don't have specifics. That's why I need the fill-in from Langley."

"I can give you the history," I said, then explained Sergei's relationship with Ivanchukov and their ugly past.

The Pear rubbed his forehead, irritation surfacing.

"Goddammit. It pisses me off that they didn't give me a heads-up that one of our old defectors, never mind that he's now in England, had a past relationship with the new Rezident."

"They may not have put the pieces together, but I know they're sending you a summary of his case. Sergei was no longer our concern, or wasn't till I heard from him on Sunday."

He dropped his hands to the table and sighed. "Never mind. I'll take care of it."

Yes, he will, I thought, not knowing what else to say, because I believed he was right. I was beginning to wonder if Harrison and his group were on top of things. Maybe not.

"Okay, Raines. I'll coordinate further with my British liaison, a decent fellow, Jason Drake, to see if they have anything to explain why Sergei contacted you and to let him know about your meeting. Don't want us tripping over each other. Not done, you know."

"I remember Drake. Met him when I was stationed here. We worked a few cases together. Impressive, very professional. Like me, he was still having a little trouble viewing Russia as a lesser threat."

"You Russia hands. Get over it. Anything else?" he asked, starting to get up from the table.

I mentioned that Harrison Anders had briefed me on the Thames murder and I could almost see the steam rising.

"But, Raines, what's that got to do with you? Are you looking for a link to Dumanovskiy?"

"I don't know. I'm trying to figure that out," I replied as he shook his head.

"Drake contacted me last week about Ivan Federov. Said he'd been their asset, a good reporting source on Russia and the SVR. Thought he'd once worked the American target for the Russians and wondered if we had anything new in our records on him. They did the relocation and hadn't heard from him in a long time."

The Pear told me the clever Shakespearean code they'd used to be able to identify any of a certain group of defectors if they surfaced somewhere in the public domain. Perlman didn't seem to know what that group had been involved in back in the Soviet Union or Russia, nor did I.

"The only problem—his, not ours—is that Drake is in touch with the senior Metropolitan Police officer handling the case. The Met doesn't know the guy's true identity or his past, and Drake doesn't plan to brief them. Dicey situation, I'd say."

"So, what we have is one Russian defector murdered, and another contacting me, us, on some sort of emergency. Coincidence. Do we believe in coincidence?"

"Let's not jump ahead just yet. See what Dumanovskiy has to say, and if need be, I'll arrange for you to see Drake. Okay, I have to go. Do you have a secure cell, anything that would allow us to talk?"

I shook my head and got to my feet. "No, let's keep this simple until I know what's going on. I really don't want the British service getting involved until I understand exactly why Sergei contacted me."

The Pear stared at me a little longer than he should have. I suspected he wanted to put surveillance on me—I just hoped it wouldn't be tonight.

"I want to hear back from you after your meeting. Every detail."

"Fine."

"My intelligence assistant, Grace, can find me if you need contact sooner." He slipped his hand into the inside jacket pocket and pulled out a card. "She'll answer that line, day or night. Hopefully, this is a false start of some sort, nothing of concern. If we need to do anything more in terms of phones or concealment devices, we can deal with it tomorrow."

I remembered his IA, Grace, and was happy for that contact. She was one of those COS support personnel who knew how to do everything well and let the COS take the credit.

"I hope it won't come to any of that. You know where I'm staying, and that should be enough for now. I'll let you know tomorrow why Sergei wanted to see me."

"By the way, you're still looking good, kiddo. A little long in the tooth, but still. Maybe Dumanovskiy is in love with you," Perlman closed, with his trademark wolf-grin.

Some things would never change, but this time I laughed at him. "That's ridiculous. Sergei's remarried, with a young child. He isn't that kind of man."

The half-grin turned into a throaty laugh. "Every man's that kind of man. Don't you know that, yet?"

CHAPTER 13

LONDON, JUNE 5

I taxied over to the Langsford Club in Berkeley Square. By now it was ten-thirty. That meeting wasn't how I'd wanted to start my trip, but I understood the necessity and was relieved that it was over, with no damage done. Now, the Pear had been fully briefed on the who and why of my visit, and I could get on with my "vacation."

Fortunately, I'd kept my membership at the club after my London assignment, knowing that I'd come back whenever possible, though I never expected to return on business. The Langsford had been renovated since my last visit. Shades of gray, beige, and white— all greige everywhere. None of the frilly flowery patterns I remembered so well, and though I didn't need all those flowers, the starkness of the new decor made me feel very much alone.

Then I saw Lionel, the head concierge and a fixture at the club. His appearance lifted my spirits, a familiar and heartwarming presence in the place. He always found me a good room, but this time, I'd messaged him that I needed as much privacy as possible, hoping he could come through, even with a last-minute request.

Clunky key in hand, I worked my way along several corridors, ending up in the older part of the building, where I found the back elevator. It was so small it could fit no more than three or four people. Its familiar creaking sounds were strangely comforting to me, as I realized the club hadn't updated everything. When the elevator door opened on the fourth floor, a tall man in a brown three-piece suit and I exchanged places. He nodded at me but didn't make eye contact, the mannerism so English. My room was at the end of a long, narrow hallway, well away from any melee. Lionel had understood completely.

I pushed the well-worn key into its slot and the door opened with a single turn to the right. I immediately saw that my room had not been part of the recent renovation. A not-quite-pretty bouquet of fake pink and white roses sat on the coffee table, matching the familiar British flowery drapes and pale green duvet. I wandered over to the bed and picked up the small piece of chocolate the maid had left on the pillow, the same kind as the last time I was here.

Which was with Alex.

The memories flooded back again. I'd joined the club when I'd been stationed in London, a plum job for me after a challenging but exciting posting in Kazakhstan, where I'd held the coveted position of Chief of Station. At last in overlapping assignments, Alex and I had two happy but busy years, together in the same city at the same time.

But now, I was here for Sergei, and my immediate priority was to cancel the reservations he'd made for me at the Savoyard. Under the strange circumstances, as I'd told Sam, I wanted to be in control of as much of my setting as possible and being at a private club allowed for that. I wasn't about to use the phone to cancel the reservation. I had no idea if anyone was tapping Sergei's phone, but I decided the wisest option was to go over to the Savoyard and cancel the reservation in person to avoid any phone records.

I was starting to feel the effects of jet lag, but had no intention of lying down even for a minute. I could reset my time clock tonight best by not taking a nap. The lobby of the Savoyard was crowded when I got there, which was fine with me. The more people, the less noticeable I would be, if, in fact, anyone was looking. The receptionist found my reservation right away and said there would be no problem canceling since the hotel was already overbooked.

"Madam, we will need a forwarding address and number for you in case there is need for follow-up regarding the change."

I paused—not what I wanted to hear. Still, I didn't want to draw any attention to myself, so I gave them the name of the Langsford, smiled, and quickly walked away as they asked me for the address. At least the club is private and anyone looking for me there would be checked.

I still had hours to pass before my meeting with Sergei, so I strolled back along the Strand to St. Martin-in-the-Fields, went into the old church and then down into the crypt café, a hidden jewel in my London. I was plenty hungry by now, ordered one of their homemade sandwiches, salad, and cappuccino. No tea for me today. I needed something stronger. I sat down and looked around at the brick-vaulted ceilings and historic tombstones lining the floor. I was starting to feel happy. I loved this place and couldn't leave without purchasing a tourist cup in the adjoining shop.

By the time I got back to the Langsford, it was midafternoon. I headed up to my room, desperate to lie down. Once there, I collapsed onto the bed, promising myself I wouldn't fall into a deep sleep.

But I did. When I awoke a few hours later, I turned my mind to the other, non-Sergei, mission I had on my agenda, my search for Bredon Aberforth. I dug out his number and dialed. I'd napped so long, I'd probably missed him. Still, I was more than disappointed when a recording answered.

"We are closed for the day."

Really, I thought. We always worked late. Whatever, I'd try again tomorrow.

My unopened suitcase sat quietly on its stand, tempting me to unpack, but I resisted. I didn't need to get distracted with that now. I could take a long time assembling and reassembling my clothes. Long ago I'd trained myself to travel in a dark pantsuit, one that didn't wrinkle, and one that allowed me to easily transition from day to night, work to pleasure. It only took a scarf to change the look, and I had plenty of those, all but the one I was already wearing, packed neatly into my suitcase in tiny scrolls.

Time for a shower. I pulled off my airplane clothes, laid them on the bed. After a long dousing, I got out of the shower and turned to the bathroom mirror which was now covered in fog. I wiped it clean only to see a tired face staring back, one with slightly bloodshot eyes. I needed color and some eyeliner. I pulled out my tools and started over. Charcoal eyeliner, a smudge of smoky eye shadow. Better.

"Sergei, why did you call me here?" I asked myself, redoing my hair and pulling it back behind my ears. I still had on the small gold serpent earrings my mother wore almost every day. My elegant, nurturing mother, whom I'd lost so many years ago in that horrible car accident in Moscow. The driver was never found, and my father refused to talk about the accident, then and now. I didn't know enough when I was fourteen to think about how or why she was killed, though I've since wondered. Wearing her earrings comforted me, like tiny protective angels.

At eight-thirty, back in the same clothes with fresh underwear and a different scarf—both of which I'd stashed at the top of my suitcase, which I allowed myself to open just for those items. I wrapped the scarf around my neck and part of my head and left my room. I had no idea if anyone might have an eye on me, but in my world, it was always wise to expect the worst. At the elevator, I passed the visitor I'd seen before. We seemed to be on the same elevator schedule, or rather the opposite, as he got off while I got on. We exchanged a quick social nod.

Downstairs, I smiled at Lionel. "I'll be back later. Don't wait up."

"I would always wait up for you, Miss Raines, but Nigel, the night porter, might be here when you return." My stomach was tightening in anticipation of my meeting. It was finally time to find out why he had brought me to London.

A big black London taxi sat parked in front of the Langsford as I exited, and I grabbed it, asking the driver to drop me a couple of blocks short of my real destination. I walked the rest of the way in a slightly circuitous route, resisting the urge to glance over my shoulder.

CHAPTER 14

LONDON, JUNE 5

It was just before nine when I got to Chequers Tavern in the old St. James neighborhood, a busy night on a beautiful London evening. There were no empty tables in front of the pub, and a cluster of people stood around, chatting noisily with friends. Fine with me. The more people, the better.

Before going in, I had a quick look around the entry area, using the peer-in-the-window-while-primping method to detect surveillance. It was my only option. I had no special equipment, nor did I have a surveillance team. My ops training had taught me not to turn and look directly behind myself. Never appear to be aware of surveillance, the rule book said, and more importantly, never make eye contact with the person who is surveilling you, no matter what. I pulled my scarf tight around my face and shoulders and walked into the pub, fairly certain that no one was watching me.

Sergei was standing at the bar, waiting for me. I felt a flash of relief that I'd read the signals right and he was there. It had been a long time, but he looked the same. Dashing as ever, though his hair was more silver than it had been several years earlier. He saw me, gave a quick smile, and walked over.

He pulled me to him in a hug, seeming none too edgy despite his messages. I was careful not to say his name, just in case we had any observers.

He whispered in my ear. "I go by Devlin now. But Sergei still holds."

Of course, I knew that, but he would always be Sergei Dumanovskiy to me, though it never hurt to remind me.

We went to a table in the back of the dimly lit pub. Fortunately, it was quiet inside; everyone else clearly enjoying the fresh air and activity in front of the pub. As soon as we were seated and had ordered a drink, I jumped in, cutting through the pleasantries. I didn't know how much time we had and didn't want to waste a minute. We could have a charming chat later, if time allowed.

"Why did you get in touch with me, Sergei? It's a no-no, and you have your British point of contact." I didn't use the word MI5. We were in a public place with a lot of ears. But warm and fuzzy I was not.

"All for a very good reason. I'll tell you everything, but this isn't the place to go into details. We can have our wine, and then walk over to the Forum." It was a well-known men's club on St. James's Street."

I smiled. Time for small talk.

"You're doing well. Looks as if your new life has proven very successful."

"Being a purveyor of Russian antiquaria has given me a little cachet with a few of the uppers, and the club tends to be quiet late at night, so we can talk more privately. My dear, my boy is five now, a bundle of energy and too much for an old man like me. Boys are a handful, and you know, girls are…."

He paused, and I saw the sudden sadness in his eyes as he remembered the two daughters he and Katya had loved and lost. He cleared his throat.

"But what of you, my friend?"

"I still have a bad case of wanderlust despite this leave I'm on."
His eyebrows rose when I said "leave," but I explained why I'd needed
a change.

"How is Alex? I hope you are both happily enjoying this
new phase?"

"Is anyone happy, Sergei?" I answered. "I'm restless. It's in my
nature. And Alex? That's a long story, and not for tonight." I'd hoped he
would not ask about Alex, whom he'd met briefly during our London
days. "Isn't it time to head over to the Forum?" I asked, brusquely
changing the conversation a mere half-hour after we'd arrived.

Outside, as we headed toward Piccadilly, there were more people
on the street. The lights shone brightly from antique lamps draped in
beautiful baskets of multicolored flowers.

Sergei and I paused to look into the shops along the way, speaking little. I saw no one directly behind us as I stared into the large,
beautifully decorated windows of Fortnum & Mason, grabbing every
chance to check if anyone interesting was near me, near us.

The doorman at the Forum nodded with recognition at Sergei and
ushered us in. We walked up the marble staircase to the upstairs living
room, which was all but empty, except for the uniformed butler, who
immediately asked what we would like to drink.

I'd been to the club before, but it still amused me to see extraneous white encased pillows lying on the sofas in this elegant, heavily
book-cased room. It had all the appearance of an enormous, private,
and slightly unkempt bedroom. It was, after all, a London men's club,
where some members took afternoon naps, while others stayed for the
night after a few too many whiskies. Fortunately, tonight we seemed
to be alone.

We sat down in two overstuffed, slightly tattered chairs in front of the remains of a fire smoldering in a huge marble fireplace, reminiscent of bygone days. The butler arrived with our Bailey's, just a taste of caffeine this far into the evening.

As soon as the butler was gone, Sergei's face turned somber.

"Ivanchukov is in London."

His words surprised me. I didn't tell him I already knew this. I wanted to hear his story before revealing mine, and I very much wondered about his interest. The diplomatic list wasn't classified, but it wasn't a popular public document either. Was he keeping track of new arrivals at the embassy? He was in a new life, a new business. How and why would Ivanchukov's latest assignment have come to his attention?

"That monster has managed to land a senior assignment at the Russian Embassy. I suspect he's head of the rezidentura. After what I told the KGB before I was sent to America, I thought I'd ruined his career. It seems I was wrong."

"And you know this how?"

"Contacts," he said after a slight pause.

I could feel my eyes roll.

"Go on."

"He knows I'm here, and I have every reason to believe I have a target on my back. Why do you think I called you here on such an urgent basis?" It wasn't a question.

The intensity in his tone took me aback, but I tried to mask my concern. Until a few days ago, I hadn't thought about Ivanchukov in a long time. Almost all of what I knew about him had come from the debriefs of Sergei all those years ago. If he was now in the Kremlin's favor, it was reasonable to assume he would be in a senior position. We had never known whether Russian intelligence had fallen for Sergei's last-ditch effort to destroy Ivanchukov. We simply didn't have intelligence on that. Now we knew. But London, now, for Ivanchukov? As I said before, I don't believe in coincidences.

"Okay, Sergei. Details," I demanded as evenly as possible.

"One of us has been murdered."

"Us?"

"Another defector. He came over before I did and has been in England for a long time. His actual identity has not surfaced in the media, but secrets can't be kept from people like us. You know that."

I started to say something. Surely Sergei knew that what he was intimating could undo all the security measures we had taken to protect him.

"Let me continue. A few of us with similar pasts occasionally encountered each other, quite accidentally, or should I say, spontaneously, at public Russian cultural events. I would say we almost self-identified. A simple conversation, coincidences in our past Moscow geographies. It was too tempting not to follow up. And over time, that's what we did—"

I flinched.

"—with utter discretion. We know tradecraft, Decktora, and our sole raison d'être is to contact one another if anyone of us seems under threat. There *have* been killings, you know."

Sergei's speech quickened as my face tightened in what I would have to admit was alarm.

"You surely can't be surprised to learn…."

"But, Sergei, one could have been an infiltration, a double agent. Did you consider that?" I interrupted.

"Yes, of course, but we knew that and we had ways of checking each other out. We all had the same concerns. My contact with the others is via pseudo clients who find me when anyone has something to report."

Now I understood why he wanted no MI5 contact. They would have been furious, and I wasn't exactly pleased now that I was the one he chose to tell.

"I hope Johanna is not expecting you home soon because this is turning into a long evening. Let's take things in order, starting with more on this murder."

"A Soviet defector was killed less than two weeks ago, his body found alongside the Thames. The story that hit the press was about an insurance broker from Putney who had been found murdered on a path near Tower Bridge. I recognized his name immediately when I read the obit, not a good habit, but a necessity for someone like me. I knew the fellow, liked him. The story basically died out, and I haven't seen any further reports of it anywhere else."

"Do you have anything else on him?" I asked, now assuming he'd been in contact with some of his cohorts.

Sergei's voice was soft, urgent. "The man's widow told a close émigré friend that the murder victim was her husband. I haven't even told Johanna—but it has, of course, been very upsetting. No one seems to know if it was a political killing—which some of us suspect—or a murder that has nothing to do with any of us. There were cuts on the man's neck, not knife wounds but something else, and a white substance was found at the site of the wound, according to the widow." Sergei offered no response to my admonition about talking to his old émigré friends. Now it was my turn to slip around the edges.

"I met with the London chief after I arrived. I was ordered to," I said, noticing his eyebrows lift as I told him I'd brought the COS into the picture. "He said nothing about a recent killing of a defector." I hated lying to him, but I couldn't divulge what I had, especially now that I knew of his network. "Why do you think Ivanchukov is after you? After all these years?"

Sergei described in detail the call from "Yulia" and his meeting with her. He recognized her as Olga immediately. Ivanchukov and his old sidekick were both in London. *Not good.*

"So, my dear, there it is. I can't tell you why Ivan Federov was murdered, and I don't know with certainty if Ivanchukov and Olga were behind that killing. But they have found me, and I would make an excellent target. The fact that she suggested she had 'a friend' she wanted to introduce to me gives credence to my concerns. She wants further contact with me. Based on the poor job I did for her, there's no reason other than to bring in someone else. And I believe that will be Ivanchukov."

I felt my body tighten. I didn't want to make him feel worse by agreeing with him, but had to say that his assessment made sense. A lot of sense.

"Can you give me a physical description of Olga? We know Ivanchukov, of course, but this girl, tell me all you can about her. I'll see if Langley can identify her."

"I would have recognized her anywhere because of the eyes, but otherwise, she looked different; older, of course, her hair now dull blond. She's still very petite and thin, could dress like a male or female, androgynous, I would say. The name she gave me was Yulia Semenyova. But she was called Olga years ago when I last saw her. Probably wasn't even in her twenties. I couldn't possibly tell you the surname she used then, and I hadn't given her a thought in all these years until she showed up on my doorstep."

I took a deep breath and paused to take in all he'd told me.

"You were right, Sergei. This information justifies my trip to London. So many questions, but for now, how do you think she found you?"

"I have no idea, but my question is, how and where does Ivanchukov fit in?" he said, his face tightening, his hands now clenched.

"Of course, you're worried, and rightly so. I'm going to see what I can do about getting some coverage for you and your family, but probably can't pull it off tonight."

I'd brief Perlman in the morning. He had to be in the picture now, not least because he was the link to headquarters and to getting whatever they might have on Yulia-Olga. The two of them together in London. I hoped Langley would have answers.

The fire was drawing down to a few hot embers. We were still alone except for the butler, who occasionally looked over at us. Our conversation had to end.

"Sergei, let's call it a night," I said in a low voice. "We've gone over too much sensitive information in one place, and I don't like it. I have to get you some equipment so we can communicate securely."

I had to assume that he was being monitored. Priority for me tomorrow would be to get him a burner phone, all the more reason I had to get to Perlman. Sergei and I agreed to meet at a coffee house in Chelsea at six.

In the meantime, the jet lag was taking firm hold, and I was feeling the beginnings of a headache and bone-deep fatigue.

CHAPTER 15

LONDON, JUNE 5

It always gave her a rush to be working on a new assignment, a sense of the unexpected, the unknown. But targeting Dumanovskiy was even more exciting; he was high up on the list because of her mentor's particular animus toward him. Not a forgiving man, Ivanchukov could not forget what Sergei had done to him—the torture, Lefortovo, Yakutsk, the collapse of his marriage, the temporary failure of his career—and Olga knew all of this. She had rarely experienced a thrill like the one she felt when he set her on his trail. Now her target was only steps away from her, and she would wait.

The street was full of greenery and customers were sitting at outdoor tables, making plenty of noise, making it easy for her to hover outside the pub without attracting attention. She could move about comfortably, her nondescript attire helping her fade into the crowd. Olga was adept at surveillance, had done so much of it she almost felt invisible at times, a sensation she liked. Being stealthy, easily able to hide in plain sight, were her special assets. Ivanchukov was well aware of her talents and had even praised her for them in a rare moment of generosity.

A woman entering the tavern had caught Olga's eye. Why was she pulling her wrap up to cover her head? It wasn't the least bit chilly, nor was there any breeze in the air on this warm evening. The woman stopped and primped in front of the pub's large glass window before going in. Why bother? She looked good enough from what little of her face could be seen. Oh well, maybe she was meeting a man. Women could be so silly about their looks.

Olga watched as customers wandered in and out, the place getting livelier. There was no way to see her target now. Nothing to do but watch and wait. She was sitting quietly on a metal stump across from the pub when Dumanovskiy emerged, a half-hour later. But now, he had a woman on his arm, the very one she'd noticed earlier. Who was she? Older than Sergei's wife, she thought, but attractive from what little Olga could see of her face.

Sergei was not known to be a womanizer, certainly not when he was in Moscow with that first wife, who had caused so much trouble. He was almost a joke among some of them, for being such a devoted husband, too easily cowed by his wife, not one of the club. But now it appeared that Olga's very married target had a lover.

Ivanchukov was going to be pleased to learn that, and Ivanchukov was the only man who really mattered to her. She was so tired of other women's chatter, those women who got emotionally involved with men and then were shocked at their infidelity. Sure, they were unfaithful. Why not? She was the same way. No need to form a bond just to get sex.

She unclipped the barrette holding back her hair, removed it, and touched the tiny button on top of the clasp. Always prepared, she had tested the camera before coming out tonight. Holding it now close to her face but positioned to look as if she were fixing her hair, she clicked three times, just to be sure. Maybe they would be able to identify the woman.

Olga followed them as they walked away from the pub and turned up Jermyn Street. She smoothly dipped in and out of the small human clusters, tucking herself behind a large man, a tree, whatever she needed, keeping just enough distance that they wouldn't notice her, even if they turned around. Then they paused, and he took her arm and leaned in to whisper something to her. *Ah, he was human after all.* What if his wife should learn of this love affair? An anonymous letter might add to Sergei's troubles. Yes, that was a good idea and she was certain Ivanchukov would agree.

Olga suddenly felt the urge herself. It had been at least two weeks since her last sexual encounter. The married security officer in the embassy was a suitable choice for her, available often enough, sexually needy, and emotionally distant. And he was great in bed.

She followed as they walked toward the Forum, then went up the stairs into the inner sanctum of the private club. Now all she could do was wait. She moved into the shadows, concealed in her dark hoodie. It would likely be some time before they'd resurface. But she had patience, a great deal of it. As often happened in those pockets of time, the memories that made her strong came back to remind her why she had become who she was.

MOSCOW, Matrosskaya Tishina Prison, 1998

"Fortenskaya, get out here. Someone wants to see you," the guard yelled, opening her cell door with a large clanking key. "He's back again. You're the lucky one. Don't know why."

Thinner than ever, Olga passed by the guard, her head held as high as possible. She knew who her visitor was. And she also understood that no one would dare to touch her now.

"Hello, little one. Have you been behaving?" said Vladimir Ivanchukov, towering over Olga. *Now a rising star in the KGB, Ivanchukov was on rotation to the federal prison service. He had his pets, and she, Olga Fortenskaya, was among them.*

"Try to outwit me today," he challenged her, *pulling out the portable chess set. A table was already set up and the tea poured. No one dared question Ivanchukov, including her, though by now she knew exactly why Ivanchukov liked her. She played chess as well as he did, but was smart enough not to win, just to make it a close game. Pawn to knight, knight to bishop, but never checkmate. Ivanchukov was her key out and she knew it.*

"Are you teasing me?" he asked, *watching her eye his queen.*

"Of course, not," she responded, *showing absolutely no emotion, not even a sardonic smile. The smile was inside her head. She had learned over the years not to reveal emotion.*

"Fortenskaya. Tell me what you did. No lies.…"

Olga looked directly at him. "I have no stories. Pawn to knight," she said.

"I think you're all brains and no emotion, my malen'kaya."

She never answered his question. And he wouldn't make her. He knew why she was in prison; there were no secrets from him. But he had other plans for Olga, and her stubborn secretiveness was another plus.

Olga had killed three men.

It had started with a school incident a few years earlier.

"Snake Eyes, come over and play with us," yelled one of her four tormentors from the schoolyard.

She sensed what was coming but had little recourse, no one to turn to. She glanced around the area but there was no one to help. She could run, but what about tomorrow? Next week?

"Don't make a sound, you freak. If you do, we will do this anytime we want to."

Like a prisoner aware of her sentence, she stood her ground, but they surrounded her and dragged her out of sight of the building. In terrified silence, she learned just how cruel the physically strong could be to the weak. They took turns holding her down in the dirt, viciously plunging themselves deep into her until she was sure she would die. Their laughter rang in her ears and even with her eyes tightly closed, she could see their sneers. Would she die? Would it even matter? Her mind closed down when the pain got too bad. Then they were gone and she was left bleeding and torn in the dirt behind the school.

Three years after the rapes, all but one of the boys was dead. The bodies had been clawed to death, in mysteries the local police were unable to solve. Unfortunately for Olga, her fourth intended victim survived and turned her in.

But that was long ago and Olga's life now was different. In a good way, a very good way.

She felt her evening coming to an end. It had been an hour and they had not yet emerged. They were probably in there for the night or at least for a quickie before he went home to his wife. She had stayed in place long enough for tonight.

CHAPTER 16

LONDON, JUNE 5

Johanna was asleep when Sergei got home from his meeting with Decky. Having a young son meant early to bed for her, and usually for Sergei too, but tonight was different. He decided to give her the bare-bones version of his evening, having long ago chosen not to upset her with some of the more troubling parts of his past and to protect her as he had not been able to do for Katya and his daughters. But he would tell her tonight what was going on and about the meeting with Decktora. No time for delay. If something happened to Johanna or their son, he would never forgive himself.

She knew he was a defector, had been imprisoned in the barbaric Lefortovo, and that the Americans had brought him to the West in a spy swap. Her nature was not to question, and for that he was grateful. To Johanna, Sergei was a hero, albeit a secret one, and she was content with that. They had their own lives to live.

He jostled her slightly, and she reacted with a start.

"Johanna…," Sergei whispered. "Wake up. We need to talk."

"What is it?" Johanna spoke in the same calm way that Katya had, even when she was alarmed, probably one of the reasons he had been drawn to her in the first place.

"I don't want you to worry, but I need to tell you something."

Johanna sat up but did not interrupt him.

"There was an incident recently, a fellow found dead near Tower Bridge, early in the morning."

"Was it someone you knew?"

"Only slightly. Another Soviet defector. He lived somewhere outside of London, with a false identity. I don't even know if the police know the full story, but one of my comrades figured it out."

Johanna flinched, tightening her arms around her chest. "I didn't think you were in touch with any of those people," she said, sounding like Decktora, but more alarmed than accusatory.

"We're careful, but when necessary we find each other. Please, I don't want to go into those details right now. All that is for another day. The important thing is that my friend's wife, also a Russian, was approached by the widow, who was distraught and turned to this woman in desperation. She told her the police had visited her and asked a lot of questions."

"But what does this have to do with you? With us?"

"If one of us was murdered, it could mean that someone is interested in the others."

Johanna's face paled as she put the pieces together.

"My friend investigated and was able to find some reporting in the media, which mentioned the man by name and described his death as a murder. It didn't get much news coverage, but enough to get his attention. When he told me all of this, I decided to contact Decktora Raines. You know her. She's the only one from the past I trust, and I wanted to find out if she had knowledge of other incidents involving Soviet defectors elsewhere." Sergei left out the fact that a nemesis named Ivanchukov was now stationed in London. And that he believed he was a target, the real reason he had contacted Raines.

"If you are worried, with your instincts, there must be reason to be. Sergei, this is awful."

"Hopefully the murder had nothing to do with his real background." As sincerely as possible, he lied to her. He couldn't let her know the full extent of his concern, not yet.

"Until I know for certain why he was killed, I want you to try to limit your outside activities with Georgie, less time at the playground, things like that."

What he wanted to say was, "be alert to any changes around you, anyone who seems unduly interested in you, any hint you are being followed." But he realized those words would terrify her, as they should.

"You're scaring me."

He wrapped his arms around her, rested his chin on the top of her silky hair. "I don't mean to. I really think it's nothing that concerns us, but with my background, I always have to think of the unusual."

"Are you overreacting?" she mumbled into his chest.

"Yes, my love, I think so, but indulge me by being cautious until I learn more."

He would never tell her how afraid he was—for all of them. He had lost one family. He could not lose another.

CHAPTER 17

Sergei had tried to get me a taxi, but I told him I wanted to walk. We left the Forum and headed off in different directions. Though a headache was creeping in, I thought a walk would be good for me. I needed to think.

It was well after eleven, and the restaurant and after-theater crowds were thinning. I'd forgotten how early in the evening Westminster shut down. The narrow, curving streets from Bond to Stafford and on toward the club normally felt deliciously charming to me, but the discussion with Sergei had put my old instincts on alert. I turned onto the tiny and short Hay Hill Road. The air was getting chilly, and a slight fog was setting in. As I paused to tighten my wrap, I sensed someone behind me and glanced cautiously back. No one. The evening's unsettling conversation and my jet lag were making me jumpy.

At the next corner, I saw the light of a small coffee shop down the street. Someone was awake and still serving? I walked faster, then turned into the shop.

"Coffee please, decaf."

"Miss, you can have coffee but no decaf. We're not American."

"Thank you. Fine, fine." I got the dig. The only other customer chuckled.

I really wanted a quick break and a chance to glance around, not the caffeine. There were only the three of us, though one or two people were walking past the shop. I got the coffee but didn't take a sip, finished my reconnaissance, and walked the remaining ten minutes back to the Langsford.

Nigel, the night concierge, was on duty. He smiled as I approached the desk.

"Good evening, ma'am, there's a message for you. It arrived earlier this evening, when Lionel was still here," he said, handing me an envelope. I nodded a thank-you, opened it, and pulled out the single page.

"*GO HOME,*" it said in solid bold letters, with a signature that was all but unreadable.

A chill ran down my spine and prickled the back of my neck. Maybe my imagination hadn't been overactive after all.

"Nigel, do you know who delivered this letter?"

"Yes, Miss Raines. Bobbie Grey, a fellow from Yellowfin Bikes dropped it off an hour or so ago. They're located near Burlington Arcade, if you want to contact them. I have their business card as well, he said, extracting it from a small pile that suggested ongoing business.

The card said they opened at nine-thirty. I had a lot on my plate tomorrow, starting with Perlman, but this would be my first stop. Letter and business card in hand, I said goodnight to Nigel and wended my way to the back of the club. Despite my jet lag, the threatening migraine, and a painfully long day, I was now wide awake. I stopped outside my door and listened for a moment, but heard nothing, then twisted the key in its slot and opened the door. I let out a long breath.

There was nothing I could discuss over the phone about my meeting with Sergei, even if I did make a late-night call to the Pear. I would just have to wait until tomorrow, when I could see him in person. I rummaged through my cosmetic bag and found the small medicine pouch. Regardless of the coffee, the head med would keep me up half the night, but the migraine would go away. Unpleasant as these headaches were, I sometimes did my deepest and most intuitive thinking when I had one. I popped the pill, washed my face, dropped my suit onto the overstuffed chair near the window, and got into bed just as the dreadful migraine medicine delivered its caffeine high.

CHAPTER 18

LONDON, JUNE 2–6

The simple interception of a phone call on the morning of June 2 from their target Sergei Dumanovskiy—encrypted Kamera/1, K/1—to the Savoyard Hotel would change the course of the Kamera Operation for the Russians.

The team was well into its coverage of K/1, cyber-hacking his easily identified cell with their latest technology, and surveilling him on and off, depending on other work priorities. The twosome handling most of the surveillance on Ivanchukov's team was known as "the Couple." Though not actually married, Ivanchukov called them that to avoid using their names unduly.

Tracking Dumanovskiy had been boring so far, endless hours of street surveillance and mundane phone calls, mostly to his wife. Until Saturday morning when their eavesdropper caught him making a phone call to the Savoyard to request reservations for one Decktora Raines. Her arrival date was stated as June 5, but no final date was included. K/1 even left a message for her, saying, "Look forward to seeing you."

Who was she? Did their righteous family man have a lover?

They had to get this little filet to Ivanchukov.

"Contact Yasenevo. Immediate. Request anything they have on this Decktora Raines and try different spellings of her name," Ivanchukov said in an unusually tense voice as soon as they briefed him on the Savoyard morsel. "Of course, you'll check records here first." It wasn't a question.

The Couple didn't like it when he got upset. Everything always had to run smoothly with this man, and it usually did, but they had suffered through some cringeworthy times in their history with him. He could get very nasty when he was angry—or anxious.

"Right away, sir," they said together.

"Get to it," Ivanchukov spouted, turning in his chair to look out the window onto the magnificent view from his new perch. As they closed his office door, they could hear him saying in almost a whisper, "And good work."

Two hours later, they were back in his office. Yasenevo had already responded.

"Sir, she's CIA, or at least she was a few years ago, when she worked at the American Embassy here in London."

"Show me the cable." He was clearly pleased.

"Any photographs?"

"No pictures in any of the records."

"Increase surveillance on the target and let me know anything that surfaces on this woman," Ivanchukov said, his voice animated.

On June 5, the female half of the Couple called the receptionist at the Savoyard and asked for Decktora Raines. The guest hadn't yet arrived, she was told. She would not draw attention to herself or her voice by flooding them with calls. On June 6, she called the hotel once again, this time in the late morning. It took several attempts before she got to the right person, someone malleable enough to fall for her questions.

"Sorry, Madam, we've canceled her reservation."

"Oh dear, I'm trying to find her."

"Again, I'm sorry, but we cannot provide any information about our guests."

Drawing on her covert training and her skill with accents, the woman said she was in from the States and "just had to find her cousin, who was going to the same surprise party."

It worked.

"Well, Madam, I believe she will be at the Langsford Club, but that is all I can tell you."

"Thank you so very much. You're such a gentleman."

People talk too freely, the Couple told each other after she hung up. It always amazed them how much untrained people gave away. The Savoyard should instruct its employees to be more careful.

Without a photograph they couldn't identify her, but they could start watching some of the comings and goings at the Langsford. They would have to spend less time surveilling K/1. Ivanchukov quickly gave his approval. He would have to enlarge his team to fill in for them, now that there was more activity. The Couple started covering the Langsford the afternoon of the sixth, looking for females with suitcases, anyone who looked like a new arrival. They hoped they hadn't missed her if she had in fact arrived on the fifth. They really had little to go on but they weren't about to tell that to their boss. Now they were surveilling the Langsford, acting as tourists and snapping photos of every female who entered.

As they reviewed the take of their first day of watch, they had an idea that might just help them identify her.

* * *

It was evening and Bobbie Grey was the only one on duty at Yellowfin Bikes, a message delivery service near Burlington Arcade. He looked up as the buzzer rang and clicked in a middle-aged, plain-looking pair.

"Hope you can still make a delivery tonight," came the cheery voice of the female.

"If it's nearby, I'll deliver it myself on my way home, about nine-thirty," he answered.

"Thank you so much, dear boy. That will be excellent. It's a birthday message for a friend, but today is the day."

"Oh, you sound Russian. Are you here on holiday?" Bobbie prided himself on identifying accents.

"Yes, a short trip to our favorite city, to see a few plays," she said.

"Please fill out the message form and the address information," Bobbie said, handing them a blank page and envelope.

"We have already written the card. Can you just deliver it?

"That will be no problem. It'll be my pleasure."

They wrote down the name and the address and handed him the double-sealed envelope.

"Decktora Raines at the Langsford," Bobbie said, confirming what they had written. "Such an elegant place. The concierge knows me well. We have many deliveries there."

The Couple made no comment.

"That will be twenty pounds. Which credit card will you be using?"

"We'll pay in cash."

"Certainly. No problem," he said, as they gave him the money. He handed them a receipt and asked them to sign it, which the male did with a swift scribble.

"Have a lovely stay here and let me know if Yellowfin can do anything else for you." Bobbie was thorough, and his manager always praised him for that. He was happy tonight. Such a lovely couple.

Bobbie Grey would be delivering the envelope after he closed the shop at nine-thirty. It wasn't a perfect plan for the Couple, but hopefully the delivery would help them spot Raines. Still, the boy had been too curious, asked too many questions. He had their signature and he knew what they looked like.

Thus was his destiny sealed. They pulled out their cell and dialed. Olga answered right away.

The call lasted less than a minute. Olga had a new assignment.

Find Bobbie Grey.

CHAPTER 19

LONDON, JUNE 6

I awoke to the beeping of my alarm after a very patchy night. It was eight o'clock, but I still had to force myself out of bed, the niggling pain over my eye gone for now. I made coffee in the room and drank two solid cups. I had a lot on my plate, and strange as it was, what was unfolding in London excited me. The old case officer in me was coming back to life. I needed to see Perlman, but that would have to wait.

Nigel's directions in hand, I had a yearning for fresh air, so I walked the fifteen minutes to Yellowfin. They had just opened, and I seemed to be their first arrival. Fine for me, given the circumstances. I introduced myself to the young man on duty. He had a slightly Goth look, tattoos on both arms, and a cleanly shaven head.

"I'm Decktora Raines. Just in from the States, staying at the Langsford Club, and I got a bike delivery from your service late last evening. I'm afraid I couldn't read the signature and wanted to know who sent me the letter." I was overly polite, eager to get as much information from him as possible, without his finding me too curious.

"I'm Reginald Talley, the office manager. Call me Reggie."

"Thank you, Reggie." His courteous nature belied his appearance, and I felt mildly relieved.

"We usually don't do this, but if you can give me some ID, I'll check." I showed him my passport, and he turned to his ledger, flipping only the top page.

"Yes, here it is. Bobbie carried the letter. The client signed here, but the writing isn't very readable. Take a look. Perhaps you'll recognize the name or the writing."

I turned the ledger around and looked at the scrawled signature. I had no idea who had sent me the message. Now even more uncomfortable, I asked, "Do you think I could talk to the delivery boy? I can't read this either, but the message was important, and perhaps Bobbie can help."

"He'll be in at ten. Feel free to come back then. He's always on time, one of our best and most reliable bikers."

I thanked him, took a Yellowfin Bikes business card, and left.

The streets were bustling. Everyone was on their way to work. I picked up a newspaper at the closest stand and wandered to the first coffee bar I could find where I could actually sit down and read. I ordered a latte, decaf. I'd already had enough caffeine to feel a buzz, including the hangover from the head meds, and it was possible I might be waiting for Reggie for quite a while.

Amid my mental meanderings, I heard someone crunching next to me and turned my head to see a small, skinny woman who looked and ate remarkably like a rabbit, ensconced in a book. I was aware of everyone around me, but the rabbit clearly had no interest in me.

Another table over, I noticed him, the same man I'd seen getting on and off the elevator yesterday at the Langsford. He didn't look my way, but for me, coincidence does not exist. I discreetly tried to draw his features in my mind, in case I needed to come up with a sketch later.

At ten-fifteen, I returned to Yellowfin.

Reggie shook his head, a frown on his face. "He's not in yet, Miss. I don't understand it. Should be here any time now."

I gave it another thirty minutes, wandered, checked the corner newsstand for headlines, and then phoned Reggie. I was starting to worry about getting to Perlman early in the day, but this took precedence for now.

"No, ma'am, I'm sorry. We keep trying his flat, but no one is answering. His roommate just moved out, and there isn't anyone else we can call. If he doesn't get in soon, we'll have somebody go to his place, but it isn't exactly next door. Islington. And we're busy today."

"Let me give you my cell number so you can call me when he shows up. I'm sorry to be such a bother, but it's really important."

"No problem. This is unusual for Bobbie. Sorry, but we'll get back to you."

A few minutes later, I heard "Fur Elise" playing from my pocketbook. I dug into my purse and pulled out the cell.

"Miss Raines, Reggie at Yellowfin. The police are here. Can you please come in? We need to talk to you—or they do—right away. It's about Bobbie."

It took me less than five minutes to get back to Yellowfin. As I opened the door, a tall, lumbering man with something of a limp moved toward me.

"Chief Inspector Cransford Garvin from the Metropolitan Police," he said, flashing his ID. "This is Sergeant Fawkes."

I looked directly at the chief inspector. His eyes were alert, and he glared at me as though I'd mugged someone's grandmother.

The younger man had a mop of unruly reddish-brown hair and the slightly gawky stature of a teenager, though he must have been in his late twenties.

"What's going on?" I asked.

"That's what I'd like to ask you." His speech was civil yet clipped—the no-nonsense tone of a man who expected to get the results he was after.

"Reggie suggested this has to do with his messenger...."

Garvin interrupted. "We understand you're looking for Bobbie Grey. We'd like to know more about your relationship with him."

"Relationship? I don't *have* a relationship with him, never even met him." I winced, but hoped it didn't show. This officer certainly got right to the point, no time wasted in civilities. "The night porter at the club where I'm staying told me a fellow named Bobbie Grey delivered a message to the club last night for me from this service, and I was following up with Yellowfin to try to find out who sent it."

There you have it, I thought, realizing I had not mentioned the contents of the letter.

"The delivery to you was his last reported activity," he stated, his eyes fixed on mine.

My heart skipped a beat, but I managed to suppress a shudder. "What happened to him?"

"Bobbie Grey is dead."

"Dead?" I glanced at Reggie, whose hands were so tightly clasped together that his knuckles were white.

"I'd like to see some identification, ma'am," the DCI continued, holding out his hand. The tall young man beside him watched me closely.

I pulled out my passport and showed it to him, explaining that I'd arrived in London the day before for a short vacation. I had no intention of telling him anything more about myself. For reasons not entirely clear to me, I was rubbing the officer the wrong way. My mind dredged up the outdated thought that he might not have a high regard for women. Still, there was no sense in irritating him. I softened my stance and waited.

"Decktora Raines, American," he read flatly.

"That's right." I returned his intense gaze.

"Most people don't contact a messenger in person unless they have a reason to," Garvin said, making no effort to give me back my passport.

"My reason? I wanted to find out who had sent him, as the signature on the message he delivered was unreadable. But I assure you I never met this poor man."

He nodded. "Still, it's strange. Suddenly I have a dead messenger boy, one with a stellar employment record, if Reggie is to be believed," the DCI said. "And now I have an American woman who is trying to find that very same messenger."

"This is disturbing to me too, Inspector. I'm staying at the Langsford and spent the night there, which the porter will be able to confirm. As for this morning, I've been walking around Piccadilly, passing time until the messenger surfaced. And now you tell me he's dead."

"Murdered," he said evenly.

"Murdered. When? Why?" Enough words, I told my investigative self. I didn't need to give this man any emotional information about me other than concern for the victim. What the chief inspector did not tell me was how Bobbie was murdered, and I didn't consider myself in a position to pursue the matter further. Better to get out of Yellowfin with as little challenge as possible to the police and then get to Perlman right away.

"I'm very sorry this has happened and even more so if you consider the tragedy connected to me. I can assure it is not and really don't think there's anything more I can add. If you'll give me my passport, I'll be on my way."

I turned to Reggie. "I'm sorry for your loss."

"Not so fast, Miss Raines," Garvin said, slipping my nondiplomatic passport into his pocket and handing me his card. "I'll have follow-up questions. Please adjust your vacation so that you can be at the station tomorrow morning at nine. Does that work for you?"

Noooooo, it doesn't work for me. Garvin's tone indicated he couldn't care less if it "worked" for me or not, but I was between a rock and a hard place. Now I *really* needed to see Perlman.

"I'll see what I can do," I said with a cheeky smile. I could dish out sarcasm as well as he could. I certainly wasn't inclined to give in to his orders, though I probably had no choice.

"The address is on my card," he said.

I headed toward the door. Furious. And without my passport.

CHAPTER 20

LONDON, JUNE 6

Garvin went directly back to the station after the unpleasantness at Yellowfin Bikes. He sank into the well-worn chair at his desk, having ordered his secretary not to interrupt him. His team had already given him their immediate report on the Grey murder. The words "puncture of the jugular" and "white powder" were part of their initial review. The investigation had just begun, but the similarities to two other cases were too glaring to overlook. Three murders with similar markings—the Thames, Cornwall, and now this. And an American tourist—a mouthy female who was pretty touchy about her passport. Understandable, to a point. He needed to check her out. He pushed a button on his phone and put out the order.

He struggled with the pieces. Only a few of his key officers had been briefed on the killings, and they'd been ordered not to share any details with their colleagues. Once the whole business leaked out, it would be impossible to keep it out of the headlines. And Garvin still didn't have the damned report on the mysterious white substance from toxicology.

He considered the possibilities. Garvin himself had viewed the strange cuts on Johnston's neck and the white powder. The idea of a serial killer again popped into his head. Now he had three similar murders. As he mulled over how they might fit together, he began to regret that he'd gotten involved.

Within ten minutes of his return, his secretary suddenly appeared at his door, walked in, and handed him a message. She'd checked out Raines's passport info and managed a little background check. There wasn't a lot, but she had one piece of news.

"Decktora Raines, former diplomat, US Embassy, London."

What the hell, he thought. Was the US government involved in this mess some way?

Now he had to talk to Drake. Immediately. Garvin walked over to his wall safe and opened it. Reaching behind a pile of neatly stacked papers, he felt for the key to his secure phone, which he seemed to be using a lot lately.

He inserted the key and dialed. The strange bass rumblings told him it was going through.

"Drake here," he heard through the tinny connection.

"Jason. Cransford Garvin here, over at Metropolitan Police. Have a question for you."

"Delighted to help. I owe you one."

"There's been another murder," he said, outlining the events at Yellowfin and the death of Bobbie Grey. "But there's an additional complication."

"What's that?" Drake asked, withholding his shock over this news and his desire for specifics.

"A former American diplomat is somehow involved. I think you might be able to help me with the details. One Decktora Raines. Can you confirm that she was or is with the American government?"

Garvin heard the slight pause on Drake's end of the phone. He wasn't about to confirm her identity, if it was even she, until he talked to Perlman.

"Cransford, let me look into this. I'll follow up and let you know anything I can."

"I told her to come to the station tomorrow morning at nine. I need to question her, and as you will understand, I want to do it in my setting. So the sooner you can get back to me, the better. I'm holding her passport, by the way."

Drake hung up the phone, looked in his directory, and dialed Perlman's secure line.

Yes, he knew Decktora Raines. *This changes everything.* Why was the CIA in the picture? The latest victim wasn't a Russian, but now there were three murders and a definite pattern. Drake was almost disappointed that this one wasn't Russian. He realized the possibility of a serial killer would be on the table. Still….

Hopefully, the call to Perlman would clarify some of the mystery. The last conversation he'd had with the COS was about Federov. He hadn't briefed him on the Sempworth aka Karchenko case, but he would now. At the top of his list, however, was Decktora Raines. When she worked in London, they'd coordinated on some defector cases they'd had reason to revisit. She was smart and focused, he recalled, as he keyed his phone secure.

"John, this is Jason Drake. Do you have a minute to talk? I can use your help."

"You've got my attention. What's up?"

"Well, two matters, but first, it seems that one of your colleagues is somehow involved, or should I say, connected, to a very recent murder. It occurred sometime in the past twenty-four hours, and I'm trying to sort out the initial details right now. Is Decktora Raines here in London? The Met DCI wants confirmation of her presence here."

Drake heard Perlman suck in his breath.

"Can you verify that Raines is in London and approve my confirming her CIA connection to the senior Metropolitan Police official involved?" he asked again.

"Jason, you know we don't generally give out or confirm the names of any employee, past or present, to British police, not that I'm saying she is or was one, you understand."

"I do. But this morning she showed up at the workplace of our latest murder victim, a deliveryman with a messenger service. She said she'd received a communication the night before and that it had been delivered by an individual named Bobbie Grey, the man who turned out to be the victim." Drake outlined the Yellowfin events to Perlman, including the suspected murder weapon.

"What the hell," Perlman muttered under his breath.

"I'm not suggesting she was connected to the crime. The DCI overseeing the case checked her name when he got back to the station and got a report that she had been a diplomat with the US Embassy in London. He was quick to try to confirm it with me. Of course, I recognized the name right away, though I didn't tell him that."

The COS had heard enough. "Yes, Raines *was* a CIA officer, currently on a leave of absence. She arrived in London yesterday, to meet a former contact who'd reached out to her for reasons we have yet to determine," he said, now without pause. "I'd prefer not to discuss this further at the moment, but I can assure you she is reliable. She's still undercover, but as long as that sensitivity is handled with care, I have no problem with your informing the DCI involved about her connection. Her name should not appear in the media or any public records. Also, just so you know, her clearances are still in place."

"Thank you for confirming. I didn't think there could be two people with the name Decktora Raines. I'll let the chief inspector know. "Jason, you said you had two matters to discuss?"

"Indeed. You know about the Federov case, but it turns out there was another killing earlier this year in Cornwall, similar profile."

He could almost picture Perlman's eyebrows raise as he proceeded to fill him in on what little he had on Sempworth aka Karchenko, noting the involvement of the Metropolitan Police and stressing that the Met had not been briefed on the Russian connection and would not be until he had a better handle on the situation. Drake then asked Perlman if he could find out if Langley had anything on Karchenko, since Karchenko had had a brief contact with American intelligence before he started working for the Brits.

"I doubt you'll find much, but want to cover all our bases. Mainly, we'll look for similarities in the histories of Federov and Karchenko."

"I'll check it out. Two former Russians murdered. Traitors to their side. I see where you're headed. I'll get back to you."

"Priority, please. I know I don't need to tell you that this is all highly confidential at the moment. The media and all that."

"No worries there. I avoid the media like the plague. You'll never see me or my name quoted anywhere in the public domain," Perlman asserted. "I'll talk to Raines right away and find out what she knows, what she thinks is going on. I'll get back to you."

"Thank you, John."

"Please keep me informed of anything else you hear about my officer," Perlman said, knowing he was giving Decky credibility, but he would deal with her on his own, forthwith.

Drake called Garvin back and confirmed Raines's identity.

"If you don't mind coming to my office tomorrow morning, you can meet the CIA woman herself," offered Garvin.

"I'll clear my schedule," Drake said. He didn't bother informing the DCI that he had worked with her in the past, but he'd certainly like to know for himself how Raines was involved. One thing was for sure…she was.

CHAPTER 21

LONDON, JUNE 6

After talking with Drake, Perlman leaned back in his chair for a two-minute mental replay of their conversation. Then he punched the intercom for Grace, and when there was no answer, dialed her cell.

"Grace, get in here."

"Chief, I'm out of the building, working with liaison all afternoon."

"Cancel the meeting and come back." Click.

Perlman wanted immediate headquarters traces on Karchenko, and that was Grace's job. Three killings in his territory, two Russian defectors, both resettled in England, and now a London messenger to whom Raines was somehow connected. No coincidence there, he was sure, and though he would not let Raines know it, he was becoming concerned about what she had gotten herself into and about his ability to protect her.

Perlman dialed the number written on a scrap of paper on his desk. He had to get her a proper cell phone right away. Damn, she'd barely been here twenty-four hours and she was already caught up in a murder.

"Raines, I need to see you ASAP. You *know* what this is about."

* * *

I was on my way to Grosvenor Square when I saw the phone message from Perlman, telling me to get over to the station immediately. Can't say I was surprised. I'd stopped for something to eat after the unpleasantness with DCI Garvin. I needed a little time alone to sort out my thoughts and think about the whole Yellowfin mess, and I wasn't quite ready for Perlman, who was next on my list. I suspected the good inspector would quickly find out who I was, since a simple check in his office would likely reveal what I hadn't told him directly: that I was CIA. Then he would want to somehow confirm my identity and find out if I was doing anything in London other than vacationing. I admit to trepidation over how Perlman would take the Bobbie Grey story, especially since he barely wanted me in London in the first place. And I had yet to brief him on last night's meeting with Sergei, which would no doubt raise a lot of questions and lead to a virtual cross-examination—of me.

So far it hadn't been a good day.

I did a less than perfect SDR on my way to Grosvenor Square. If someone was pursuing me, they'd guess where I was headed and that should give them pause.

The bronze eagle looked down on me protectively as I walked up the stairs to the main entrance of the embassy. This time the security check was quick. The COS had likely called down to tell the guards to admit me. When I got up to his office, he dismissed the three people sitting in the room and beckoned me in. He seemed composed, not agitated. Maybe this meeting wouldn't be as bad as I'd expected.

"I just got a call from Jason Drake over at MI5," he started, motioning me to sit down.

I waited…

"He told me about a little encounter you just had with the Metropolitan Police. Needless to say, that call didn't make me happy. Is there anything you want to tell me?"

I guess the meeting wasn't going to go so well after all. I could almost see the smoke starting to rise out of the top of his head.

"What the hell is going on here, Raines?" he snapped, now so red in the face his blood pressure must have shot up.

I took a deep breath. No sense in escalating things if I could prevent it.

"First, let me say that I haven't had a minute yet to brief you. It's all happened so quickly, and I'm trying to put the pieces together myself."

Perlman leaned back in his chair and waited for me to spill the story, which I promptly did, all the Bobbie Grey details and my unpleasant encounter with Garvin.

"I've been, uh, how shall I put this... 'ordered' to his office tomorrow morning." I looked down at my hands, then back at the Pear. "He's got my passport, so I suppose I need to go for that if nothing else."

"That's why Drake called me. I confirmed you, so that's taken care of."

He paused, now getting more serious than I'd seen him, his chair cracking as he leaned forward. The Pear had gone from red-faced to calm in a matter of minutes. This man could switch moods at a dizzying pace, unless he was acting, which was a distinct possibility. Now I understood why he was a great case officer—he could manipulate and control. But I was good too. I would let him feel I was controllable.

"I don't like the idea of you being called into Garvin's office, but I've been thinking it over and am of the mind you should go. You'll need to use your elicitation skills, get everything you can from the meeting, especially from Garvin, so we can understand what the Met knows, if they have any hint of a Russian connection. Please tell me you didn't say anything about the real reason you're here."

"Of course, not." *Just how unprofessional does he think I am?*

Perlman shrugged. "Nor should you have. No need to share information on a previous asset with the London police, for God's sake. What I want to know is what they plan to do about you."

"About me?" I all but shouted. Okay, he got me on that one.

"Well, kiddo, you do seem to be in the mix somewhere, don't you think? By the way, don't be surprised if Drake is at your meeting tomorrow morning. This chief inspector invited him. If that's the case, reintroduce yourself. You may need more than one friend, the way things are stacking up."

"Did you perchance tell Drake about Sergei and why I'm here?" I asked.

"Just confirmed your identity. Said you were on a leave of absence. Nothing about Sergei. Besides, you were supposed to get back to me this morning about your Sergei meeting before anything else, but you didn't do that, did you? So what could I tell him?"

No, I went off and got myself involved in a police investigation instead. I looked at him and let out a deep breath.

"Now tell me about your meeting with Sergei."

I briefed him on the whole evening, as concisely as possible. Perlman was a get-to-the-point kind of man. When I mentioned Ivanchukov, his gaze hardened and he leaned forward.

The Pear got to his feet and walked to the window, his back to me. "My counterpart—the Russian Chief of Station, the Rezident. Damn, I need Headquarters to respond to my cable. How long does it take those idiots?"

"Well, apparently Ivanchukov has an assistant of some sort," I said, describing Sergei's call from Yulia aka Olga as best I could with what Sergei had given me. "I'm not exactly happy with the situation myself, and I'm concerned that I somehow led the wrong people to Bobbie Grey."

Perlman turned to look at me as he walked back to his desk. He dropped into the chair heavily. "Stay here and write up everything on your meeting last night, just like the old days. I'll have Grace get Olga-Yulia traces and photographs, if any, from Langley and check the dip list on Ivanchukov's staff here in London. I'll find out what Drake has. Obviously, somebody's on you, or you wouldn't have received the message at the club. That worries me."

His comment jarred me. I'd been so focused on Sergei and Bobbie Grey that I hadn't thought much about my own circumstances, except to take the normal precautions I'd been trained to do. Still, I was not unhappy that the Pear was actually going to check with headquarters. Maybe he wasn't such a cowboy after all.

"There's another piece to the puzzle," he said, his tone somber. "There's been another murder."

I felt my body heat increase as he recounted the tale of the Sempworth, aka Karchenko, case. Lots of loose threads, but all the same color.

"Last night I wondered if Sergei was being paranoid," I said slowly. "As I was walking back to the club, I had the feeling someone was on me, so I stepped up my ditch-the-surveillance moves, where possible staying on busy streets. I got home damned late and wondered if I was just amped up from my meeting with Sergei. But it quickly became obvious someone knew where I was staying. And now that poor messenger is dead."

"This all needs to go into your cable to headquarters, but don't write up the Bobbie Grey business. I'll take care of that. We'll see if

Langley has anything around the globe that indicates the Russians are going after some of their old defectors."

"Let's remember, I have to keep my sights on Sergei," I said. "*We have to*. If Ivanchukov is in London, and Yulia—Olga—is who he thinks she is, he's in grave danger. You need to get someone to watch him." I was pushing Perlman, no way around it, but I was way up there on the worry meter and felt he had to produce some support to keep track of Sergei and anyone who might be pursuing him. As soon as we could get trace results and hopefully photos, it would be easier to surveil.

"One step at a time, Wonder Woman," Perlman said, once again getting to his feet. "I'll get Grace. She'll outfit you with whatever tech equipment you need—concealment device, disposable phones, whatever. No short cuts from here on."

He punched the intercom and in she marched.

"Grace? Decktora Raines. You remember her, right? She thinks she's on leave, but she couldn't stay away and has now gotten herself into a mess of trouble."

I winced as Grace and I exchanged a quick hello.

"Get her some sort of concealment device, proper cells, you know the drill." Grace moved toward the door and I stood, collecting my purse and my thoughts.

"Okay," said the Pear, shooing us off like we were annoying children. "Raines, write this whole thing up and get out of here. I've got other things to do. Oh, and by the way, I think you'll like your new position as an *access* agent."

My head snapped around. "What?"

An access agent? Very amusing. I'd run a lot of those myself and now the Pear was calling me one, using my "access" to Sergei and my potential for providing new intelligence on Ivanchukov and whatever else I could dig up.

Some leave of absence.

"How you doing, Decky," Grace said as we walked down the hall to her office. She'd gained weight since I'd last seen her, but still looked physically strong, as if she worked out regularly. Her boxy figure and tight, curly gray hair gave her a rather sexless appearance that probably made working with the Pear possible.

I liked her and sensed the feeling was mutual, though I'd had it a lot easier in my career than she. Grace was one of those COS secretaries who were never really able to strike out on her own, largely because she'd joined the Agency when women had little chance of getting directly involved in operations, of becoming case officers. "Women can't recruit agents," went the old boys' mantra. Foolish, I thought, since recruiting agents was what I did best. But back when Grace entered on duty, the most she could hope for was to attach herself to a rising star and stay with him as he went up the ladder, his ladder, but not up the pay scale.

I had plenty to be grateful for, and I knew it.

And Perlman did too. He was lucky to have her. She was a workhorse and had the smarts to become indispensable, the kind who helped her chief rise to the top and who knew every detail of his work. Her reward was one overseas assignment after another, and it didn't get much better than that for someone working in the DO, despite the pay.

"What have we got?"

"One burn cell today. You can use it one time, so it's pretty much emergency only. That should suffice until we can get you a proper secure phone, which the techs can doctor and have to me by tomorrow."

"I really have to have one for my defector. He's the reason I'm here, and right now, I have no secure way of communicating with him."

"Sorry, Decky, we need you to have the phone I just gave you. I'll have the techs get me two phones, one for each of you, by tomorrow, with the latest technology. I have nothing else in the office at the moment. We have a quota, you know, budget constraints, near the end of the fiscal year," she smiled sarcastically. "In the meantime, you need to buy a shopping bag at Harrods, one of those big pocketbooks they sell in the tourist shop on the second level."

Grace drew a rough sketch of the bag, noting the approximate measurements. "Get the green one. It'll pop out at you, believe me, standard Harrods fare. If you can do that, we'll reconvene later tomorrow afternoon, and I'll replace it with a concealment device that has a covert section to hide the phones, papers, et al. You'll be impressed at the workings and miniaturizations of our latest field technology. Sound good?"

"All good. I'll get it done."

"So, tomorrow at four at our safe house on Edgware Road," she said, giving me the exact address and asking me to memorize it. That goes without saying, I thought, but I had no desire to be flip with her, as I would have been with the Pear.

Grace left me alone to write the message to headquarters outlining the Sergei meeting. As always, I included every detail I could and highlighted the business about Yulia-Olga. If Langley had anything on her, I would be plenty happy.

CHAPTER 22

LONDON, MAY 22-JUNE 6

Another one down, thought Vladimir Ivanchukov as he sat in his office in the Russian Embassy in Kensington Palace Gardens, looking at the wood-paneled walls and long silk drapes that surrounded him. Ivan Federov, Kamera/3, was dead and he had Olga to thank for that.

This overseas posting had been a long time coming. It was now 2012. He'd arrived some six months earlier, during a cold, gray London winter, but nothing like the freezing Moscow January he'd left behind. Ivanchukov had paid dearly for this, in more ways than one, proving that patience was indeed a critical element for success. Hands clasped behind his back, he strode to the window. It was going to be a good summer, he thought as he looked out, not on the hardy snow-laden fir trees of the Kremlin, but on colorful, wildly growing English flowers in the gardens of the embassy.

There was a special bonus in this assignment, above and beyond the honor of serving in this center of Western power. Ivanchukov would oversee one of the Kremlin's most sensitive covert projects, the Kamera Operation, whose single objective was to eliminate that handful of Russians who had betrayed their homeland while working in the deeply classified Poison Factory, officially known as Department

12. Each had spied for the West. Each had then clandestinely escaped the homeland. Not only had they committed treason, they'd taken with them some of the most tightly held secrets in Russian and Soviet intelligence. Betrayal was the most unforgivable sin of all for the Kremlin's leader.

While he waited for Olga, Ivanchukov stoked the fires of hatred with memories. Clearing his head and his throat, he spun on his heel away from the window. Yes, he, Vladimir Ivanchukov, was head of the rezidentura, the Chief Rezident, in one of Russia's most important foreign posts.

It seemed so long ago now. It was immediately after the Sergei Dumanovskiy spy swap in the mid-nineties that Ivanchukov had been ordered to the office of his senior manager in the First Chief Directorate, why he didn't know, a promotion he hoped. But the news hadn't been good. When he got there, Lyev Vasiliev, the paunchy, white-haired master of the universe, stood up from behind his desk, walked toward Ivanchukov, and shook his finger at him, uttering a string of obscenities that included the word "treason."

"Treason," Ivanchukov yelled back, fists clenched but held firmly at his side. "Why do you say this? Of what do you accuse me?" Ivanchukov stood like a statue, so angry and shocked that he felt frozen in place.

"You know exactly what you've done. You and your friend Sergei Dumanovskiy were working together. We know everything. It started back in the early 1990s, when you both worked in the rezidentura in Washington. When you got back to Moscow, you arranged for him to work directly under you. Very impressive, but a crime punishable by death, as I'm sure you know."

"This is wrong! You are wrong. He was my enemy." Ivanchukov's face turned white as a sheet, his fingernails digging into the palms of his hands. "I had him arrested, sent to Lefortovo. You must know that!"

"But you got him off. You had him sent to America. Were you planning to be next?"

"No, no, no," Ivanchukov blasted back, explaining his history with Dumanovskiy, the fact that he barely knew him when they both served in Washington all those years ago. Once he started talking, he couldn't stop. But he had no proof to save himself.

"Enough!" shouted the deputy director. "We'll see, but if you survive this, and I mean 'if', you will be given a new assignment, far from Moscow."

Ivanchukov gasped. Neither choice was good, but, of course, staying alive was the better of the two. His stomach churned as he waited for what would come next. He knew he could convince no one once they'd made up their minds.

"You're going to Lefortovo, just like your friend, and then we will see. Didn't you realize that Dumanovskiy might betray you in the end? It was you, after all, who had him arrested…."

"That cannot be!" Ivanchukov spat. Was it possible that Sergei tried to destroy Ivanchukov? Of course, it was, he slowly realized. A mortal enemy who has nothing to live for will do anything. Ivanchukov's head fell into his hands.

"We had a very complete debrief with him before he left."

Sergei had turned the tables on him, at the end, as he was leaving for Washington. The treasonous bastard. Don't worry, he thought, I will find you. And you will pay.

With that, Ivanchukov was sent to Lefortovo, a payback he could never have imagined. His stay in prison was bitter, but brief, less than two months. He was then reassigned to the Fourth Directorate and sent to Yakutsk, deep in the eastern part of the USSR, to work on transportation security for the railroad. It was a devastating demotion, but he was alive, as he told himself repeatedly. His wife, Vladlena, had refused to move with him or to send along his two boys. They had remained in Moscow.

When he returned four years later, she was living with another man, and their sons were with her, having all but erased their father from their lives. Yet another hardship he had to bear. Anger was etching into his being, an anger that could not be kept under control forever. But after Yakutsk, he was finally being recalled to Yasenevo for a position overseeing the prison system. He had proven himself in Yakutsk, his own personal gulag, and he was thereafter viewed as rehabilitated and having been falsely accused of treason.

During all this time, chaos and change reigned in Russia as it struggled its way into its post–Cold War identity. By the end of the nineties, the unpopular Gorbachev and Yeltsin periods were over, and the new head of the Kremlin was bringing in his own people, those who, like him, hated what had happened to the USSR and who wanted Russia to be the power it once was. Ivanchukov had survived, transforming into a more devout Russian intelligence officer than ever. His personal crises and the unacceptable changes in his country drove him. Fierce determination and an urge for revenge were steeped into his character.

It was 2006 when Ivanchukov received the job that would change his life, a senior assignment in the Department 12, the Poison Factory, near Moscow. He was suddenly being praised for the courage he'd shown during his time in Lefortovo, then Yakutsk, as well as for his now well-tested loyalty to the service. His achievements in this latest position were winning him accolades from the top of the Kremlin. Assassination by poisoning was in the Russian DNA, from the long-ago killing of the Grand Duke of Moscow via an arsenic-laden chicken dinner, to Lenin himself, who opened a poisons laboratory after an attempt on his own life. It was known as Kamera, "the Chamber," eventually morphing into the more benign-sounding Department 12, the laboratory that developed poisons for the Kremlin to use against enemies of the state. Ivanchukov had finally demonstrated that he was up to the darkest of tasks. There would be more political assassinations, and a proven soldier would be needed for them. Moscow had its man.

He glanced back out the windows of his still new office. The Kremlin had chosen wisely, he thought. And they had let him take his special cadre with him, five of them: Olga, his assassin; the Couple, the husband-and-wife surveillance team; his longtime secretary; and his special security guard, all of whom he had worked with and assessed at the poisons lab. Their loyalty and skills were solid and had been honed over the years. They knew his ways and carried out his orders without question.

He would have to bring in more operatives. Ivanchukov didn't like going outside of his well-tested cadre, but the workload for his special five was suddenly getting too heavy, and the newcomers would have to be trained in and agree to his principles. He would cable Yasenevo today. The prison would have some good candidates.

Ivanchukov's brilliant organizational invention, DTGK, the acronym for its four elements, would, he firmly believed, someday be used throughout the intelligence services. He employed it in every operation he undertook, compelling those who worked for him to learn and systematically carry out its four stages—Disciplina (discipline); Terpenie (patience); Gotovnost (readiness); and Krov' (lethality/ blood)—and work through them step by step. Lethality was always the final chapter of a successful operation.

All good, he thought, and now the pièce de resistance, Ivanchukov was close to the man who had been the cause of so much pain in his life—Sergei Dumanovskiy. Ivanchukov would find Dumanovskiy, and when he did, he would tell him how successful his pathetic attempts at vengeance had been—accusations of treason, suffering in Lefortovo, the demotion to Yakutsk, the end of his family life, and then the good news that he had been rehabilitated and sent to Department 12. He would watch Sergei take pleasure in that. And then he would kill him.

A smile came over his face as he thought about that. Then he leaned forward in his chair and tapped the buzzer on his desk.

"Have Olga come in."

CHAPTER 23

Olga had proven herself to Ivanchukov from her prison days and her subsequent work in Department 12. She'd been his pet since he took her from Matrosskaya Tishina Prison and trained her in some of the dark arts of the old KGB. He'd shaped her into the exact creature he needed, a perfect fit for the Kamera Operation. Many who had worked in the Poison Factory left in disaffection. They dared not speak of the work, and some suffered severe psychological distress as a result of it. Not Ivanchukov. And not Olga. They were inured to the implications and use of certain poisons in political assassinations: Olga because she did not suffer from a confining morality and Ivanchukov because he had already seen and experienced death and torture in some of their ugliest forms. All of this was paying off in their new assignment in London.

He was ready for her latest report.

"You have outdone yourself, little one," Ivanchukov praised. "You will get your rewards when we have completed our work. But now tell me everything."

When Olga related how she had killed Federov, K/3, she could see his pleasure in what she had done. It made her happy that he wanted to hear all the details, even about her grandmother's gift of the *Celem*. Ivanchukov knew she'd been surveilling Federov for over four weeks, observing his patterns, looking for the best place to eliminate him. On the chosen day, she told him, she'd gotten up before sunrise to prepare the claw her beloved Babuyla had given her when she was merely twelve, not knowing that her granddaughter would later use it for anything other than self-protection.

The rarely indulgent Ivanchukov smiled as Olga once again described how she used her weapon and the special meaning it had for her. It was yet another sign of her talents, her unique worth to him.

The camouflaged weapon, she reminded him, appeared to be nothing more than a colorful piece of jewelry that sat on her bureau like a piece of art. When she picked up the *Celem* on the morning she would kill K/3, the peacock feathers were as fresh and vibrant as if they had just been plucked, and the red ruby brooch they surrounded shone like new. A tap of the finger on the stone, and the claw emerged, barely noticeable amidst the feathers. Olga told Ivanchukov how careful she had been, slipping on a pair of rubber gloves, then opening the tightly sealed cosmetic container on her dresser and dipping the talons of the claw into the white powder. The talons were sharp enough themselves to be lethal, but the toxic white mixture ensured death. She shook the talons above her latrine, she said, and let the loose powder fall off, then gently pushed the claw back into its feathered bed and tucked it into the deep pocket of her running gear. It was still dark when she headed out for the Thames pathway to find her K/3.

Olga didn't care about financial or other rewards. Her payment was his approval; the look he had just given her on hearing the story and her strict attention to his tight organizational plant was payment.

"You have done excellent work, my dear, once again. Now, sit here and rest while I read the latest from Yasenevo," Ivanchukov said, handing her a mug of tea from the pot on his desk.

Olga sat back in the chair, confident that her presence was welcome, and sipped the black Russian tea that Ivanchukov took with him everywhere.

After all this time, Ivanchukov and Olga were now in what people like them called a target-rich environment. Britain held all the remaining Kamera targets.

Back in the Motherland, when Olga was working for Ivanchukov in Department 12, she understood that some labeled her a sociopath, but he insisted she was a savant, his savant. Whatever the term, she knew her value to him and his to her. He allowed her to have a life, and to live it on her terms—except when she was on assignment with him. He'd provided her with a purpose and she had no intention of betraying that gift. Killing was something anyone could do, to be honest, but to do it with enough skill and finesse not to be detected was an art. Olga knew she wasn't particularly attractive to men, certainly not without some cosmetic adjustments, but that worked to her advantage. She could fade into the background with relative ease, and that could be useful in her line.

At the special lab in Department 12, she'd studied an array of poisons and performed experiments on gerbils, mice, frogs, even small crocodiles, using a variety of combinations. She could spend hours a day doing this work and not want to stop and go home when the workday ended. Ivanchukov watched her grow. He liked her enthusiasm and her brains. Yes, he had been right to take her on.

Most of the time, she worked in the bowels of the lab. She hardly noticed what would be too bleak a working environment for most, and was one of the few who could stand the odors emanating from its dankest corners. She just continued working, working, working, until she came up with her own sublime formula.

When she first shared it with Ivanchukov, himself an expert in modern radioactive toxins, he was skeptical. But he eventually conceded to Olga's urgings to go back to the basics, to old poisons. The killings would not get the same public attention, she'd argued. No one would suspect the Russians of assassinations using such primitive elements. No one would even consider the current work of Department 12.

She'd never imagined it could be so simple, almost in front of her eyes. Ornithogalum umbellatum, an exquisite poison not deeply toxic in its flowering stage. One would hardly be aware of it until the bulb dried out, was crushed, and turned to powder. Like magic, she had created a virulent toxin, one that was very difficult to trace and that seemed so benign that it would not attract attention. The plant produced a beautiful six-petaled flower that came to be called Star of Bethlehem for the likeness it held to its godly counterpart. The irony was not lost on her, though she viewed religion as nothing but myth.

The second ingredient, curare, was as old as time. Olga had only read about it, and for some reason Kamera had none in its stock, but she quickly got Ivanchukov's approval to purchase it. By now he gave her everything she wanted.

So he had one of his people go into the Amazon to find the deadly poison used by primitive Indians in South America to kill their prey. When its most toxic form, calebas, was added to Star of Bethlehem, it would cause instant paralysis and a quick death. She changed the dosages and combinations, testing them as she progressed, on small animals at first, and then larger ones comparable in weight to humans.

When she was ready, Ivanchukov came down to observe her testing it on a large monkey, with a body similar to that of a human. The speed of the paralysis and death were so striking that it was unlikely anyone would suspect there had even been a poisoning. With the *Celem*, the claw, and the white powder mixture, she would have her own signature when the time came to use it. And only one other person would know that signature.

Once the product was fully tested, Ivanchukov sent Olga on a mission to Thailand, where one Kamera defector had been spotted and identified by the SVR officer assigned there. She went in the darkness with more than one carefully prepared dose of the poisons. And on that assignment, she performed her first human poisoning. The body was found the following day. The news barely made it to the local police. In that part of the world, another body did not create much more than a raised eyebrow. This success was followed by a mission the next year to Australia, where another turncoat was living in exile and was quietly eliminated. The killer was never found, in either country.

Now Olga had eliminated K/2 down in Cornwall. There had been almost nothing in the press about that, but he had been killed far from London, and the media and police hadn't even been certain he was murdered; mauled by an animal, they'd concluded.

K/3 had been done away with. Ivanchukov agreed with Olga that the reports of his demise would fall to the back pages of London tabloids, just another death, until they figured out the entire mystery, which she doubted they ever would. And indeed by June, there was little mention of the Thames murder in the newspapers.

K/1 was now in her sights.

CHAPTER 24

Garvin was glad to get home.

The day had been exciting—a little too exciting—and a whiskey sounded good to him. He wanted something stronger today than his usual ale. He went into the kitchen, poured a stiff drink before even saying hello to his wife. The television was already on, Wallie sitting comfortably in front of it, a cup of tea on the table beside her. The one and only newsreader he liked, Charlton Stern, had just come on the air.

"Good evening, London. We start off tonight with grim news, the story of a chilling murder, one that will most certainly frighten normal Londoners."

Garvin put down his drink and turned up the volume.

"According to sources at Yellowfin Bikes, a company messenger was killed early this morning. Eyewitnesses said the body was spotted near the front door of the victim's residence, partially hidden by overgrown bushes. An elderly lady noticed it and screamed, thus drawing the attention of the neighbors, who immediately contacted the police. Though the police tried to discourage the media, the woman who discovered the body was so upset she became overly voluble, stating that she saw odd cuts on the man's neck."

"Goddammit," Garvin yelled.

His wife quickly appeared at the living room door. "Cranny, what is the matter?"

The reporter continued on, "The police held to a 'no comment' position, stating that the family of the victim had not yet been notified. We will let you know as soon as we have anything more on this macabre development. Now, back to you with more news of the day, after this commercial."

"What the hell! No one told me the media was there," he fumed.

"Settle down and tell me what's happened," Wallie said, trying to calm him.

Garvin picked up his drink again, took a deep gulp, and told his wife the broadest details of the murder, not mentioning the killings of Robert Johnston and the Cornwall fellow that he was still trying to figure out.

Well into his second whiskey of the evening, he announced, "I'm going to have to make a press statement tomorrow. Dammit, dammit, dammit!"

CHAPTER 25

LONDON, JUNE 6-7

It was well after five by the time I'd finished my write-ups and was able to leave the Station. Meeting Sergei over in Chelsea was next on my list. Ch—rist, I had to cancel. I had no secure phone for him, nor any updates I could share with him, and I wasn't about to mention the Bobbie Grey matter.

I pulled out my burner phone and dialed. He answered on the second ring.

"Has something come up?" I heard the tension in his voice.

"I have to cancel our meeting today. I know it's late and I apologize, but the day has gotten away from me. Nothing special," I lied. "Shall we try again tomorrow?" That meant one hour earlier tomorrow, same place.

"That's fine with me. I was just heading out. Tomorrow then."

He got it. I clicked off. So much for that phone. I had a lot to think about and looked forward to being alone for the night—and to getting some rest. I needed it to keep my head clear.

Back at the Langsford, I opted for a quick bite in the club restaurant, and more important, a glass of wine. The heavily beamed room and antique fireplace in what must have once been the family salon were comforting, insulation somehow from the events now swirling around me.

There couldn't have been more than five other people in the room, two couples, another single, and me. And then I saw him, the man from the elevator and the coffee bar. He walked into the club room, spoke momentarily to the maître d', glanced around, briefly catching my eye, then left. I didn't like that. In my business, paranoid equaled prudent. I shouldn't have allowed eye contact, even for a split second, but I had, all of which made me feel slightly off my game.

Staring into the fireplace, I started turning over the pieces. What linked these murders? The claw, the white powder, the history of the victims. And me.

I would wait for the traces and feedback from Langley just to be sure I had everything I could possibly get my hands on, but by now I was certain there was a connection among the Russians—former intel, defectors, and now residents of England, each with a new identity. And then there was Ivanchukov, and Olga, both assigned to London. Those defectors were traitors in Ivanchukov's eyes, and betrayal is not kindly looked upon by the Kremlin.

When I got back to my room, I fell into bed and into what must have been a deep sleep, because the buzz of the telephone early the next morning jolted me out of a REM state. I flipped my hair out of my eyes and picked up the receiver.

"Ms. Raines, Cransford Garvin from Metropolitan Police headquarters confirming our nine o'clock appointment." I recognized his gruff voice, though he sounded tired.

"I plan to be there," I responded, a little surprised that he'd called me directly.

"Have you have seen the news?"

"I'm afraid not."

As Garvin told me about the terse media announcement on Bobbie Grey, he sounded less aggressive than he had at Yellowfin Bikes. Maybe the confirmation of my identity had helped, and perhaps now I would learn something from the police. I could hope.

We ended the call civilly. It was going to be another long day, hopefully without any more dead people on the agenda. I headed to the bathroom, took a shower, then pulled myself together at an impressive speed.

I had one more thing to do before leaving the Langsford. I pulled the bit of paper out of my wallet and once again dialed the only phone number I had for Bredon Aberforth. A husky female cigarette voice answered.

"I'd like to speak with Bredon Aberforth?"

"He's no longer here."

"Please, can you give me his forwarding number," I said.

"No, Madam, I cannot, but I will try to get a message to him."

Okay, he was alive and she knew his name. I hoped I was getting a step closer to finding him, but prayed he was not on assignment in some faraway land.

After coffee, orange juice, and an unhealthy muffin, I headed out. The minute I got to the first newsstand, I saw the bold headlines announcing the murder of Bobbie Grey glaring at me. Three daily newspapers in hand, I looked forward to the meeting. Inspector Garvin wasn't the only one with questions.

I caught a cab and headed to the Metropolitan Police Station. The guard at the security entrance waved me through as soon as I gave my name.

"Room 112, ma'am. Through the main doors and down the hall to the left."

Once there, I saw the young police officer who was at Yellowfin the day before, as well as Chief Inspector Garvin. Jason Drake was standing beside them, looking as dignified as I remembered him, his black hair now silver, an unlit cigarette in his hand. We nodded knowingly to each but didn't exchange words. There would be time for that later.

"Everyone take a seat," said Garvin, clearly aware that Drake knew me.

I was vaguely uneasy as I waited to see how the meeting would unfold, and most particularly, how I would fit in and to what degree Garvin would question me. I wondered if everyone in this room had clearances, given the possibility the session could take a turn into classified territory. It seemed insecure to me. But I had to leave that up to Drake. I myself would share nothing I viewed as classified, no matter what questions were asked of me. That "nothing" included anything Perlman and I had discussed yesterday.

"Ms. Raines, the senior CIA officer in London confirmed your background and identity yesterday with Mr. Drake. I understand that you're on leave and in London on holiday?"

As I said, "insecure." No need to know. Garvin had just confirmed my identity, and that there was a CIA presence in London, and that he had contact with its "senior" officer, which I assumed to be the Pear. If accused, Garvin would have said it was an "open secret," but there was no such thing in my world, and I didn't like sloppiness. File that away, I told myself.

"I'm glad you were able to clarify my situation." I hoped I didn't sound as insincere as I felt. Garvin resumed his comments as if I hadn't spoken.

"Which is why I'm going to provide you some additional details before getting to the point of today's meeting. I was assured you were a responsible officer and therefore accustomed to secrecy and the necessity of keeping certain information out of the media."

Ah, that slightly condescending tone again, but I was ready to hear what he had to say. How much did he know that I already knew?

Garvin reviewed the details of the three murders, noting the signature claw markings on the neck in each case. He made no reference to the true names of the victims or to any Soviet or Russian connection. Then, barely pausing for a breath, he turned to me.

"Ms. Raines, my immediate concern is how you fit into all of this. Somehow on this vacation of yours, you have stepped into something of a mess, one that seems to be growing around you." He glanced at Fawkes, then Drake. "As quickly as possible I must determine if you are a possible target or have some other role in all of this."

I straightened up in my chair as he said the words "target" and "role."

"I don't know what else to say beyond what I reported yesterday. At the moment, I'm as mystified and concerned as you over the Grey case and the timing of my arrival. Seems like a dreadful coincidence to me."

"I'm not so certain 'coincidence' is the right word," Garvin said acidly. "There are some clear links in these killings, and right now, you appear to be Link Number One. What is it you are not telling me?"

Ouch. His tone carried an edge that meant business. I forced myself not to show any reaction, but "Link Number One"? Really?

"Inspector, suffice it to say that I had planned to be in London for a short vacation. Now that I'm on leave from my career, I have time to travel and grabbed the opportunity to visit with old friends here. That's it. There's nothing more I can tell you," I concluded with a slight shrug.

I did not mention Sergei, and I wondered what Drake was thinking, especially since he, unlike Garvin, knew of the Russian connection. The DCI nodded and shared a small smile. "Well then, Miss Raines, you'll be happy to extend your vacation until all of this is cleared up, in the spirit of cooperation and all that. You see, you've become a key player in it all. Among other things, you may be our best hope of drawing out the perpetrators."

Now I understood why I had been invited. They weren't looking for my expertise or additional details. They planned to use me as bait. But even if I was linked to the death of the messenger, and, of course, he could see I was, how could he possibly think I was connected to the others?

"Inspector, wouldn't it be better if I just left? I'm afraid my intelligence affiliation is now bound to leak out and all that would do is make for tabloid news, which will do nothing to help solve your murders," I said, stressing the word "your." Of course, I had no intention of leaving, but I was curious how Garvin would react and was all too willing to provoke him.

He shook his head quickly. "No. You must stay. There's no reason to expect a leak from anyone here."

He must have seen my eyes start to role.

"I'm sorry to put you in an inconvenient situation, though I imagine this is nothing new to you, given your former career. We at the Metropolitan Police and MI5 will be close by to make sure you don't get caught up in anything too dangerous."

Sure, what the hell. I could only end up dead, that's all.

I cleared my throat. "I don't like the prospect of someone else being victimized just so I can get another unpleasant message."

"I doubt it will unfold that way," Garvin responded confidently.

"I'll discuss it with my colleague."

"Miss Raines, let me be clear. I'm not giving you a choice. I will keep your passport, and in your current status, you're not under diplomatic immunity. Until Bobbie Grey's murder is solved, you will stay in London."

I liked this man less with every sentence he uttered, and I couldn't help but note that Drake made no effort to intervene.

"Back to the matter at hand," Garvin continued. "No additional details of these murders can get to the media, so if you are approached, please refrain from making any comments."

"Surely someone in the media is going to make the connection," I said. "The claw marks, the jugular, these are pretty unique facts."

"I understand that, Ms. Raines, and I will be grateful for any time we have before those vultures put the pieces together. I'm only asking you to remain here and will assure you that we can keep you safe. Now that we have three victims dead with the same pattern, we cannot rule out the possibility of a serial killer. But I need as much time as I can get to try to beat the media at their own game."

I listened intently, avoiding Drake's gaze. Scenarios raced through my brain. It was a serial killer, all right.

We called them assassins.

CHAPTER 26

LONDON, JUNE 7

Garvin was about to call an end to the meeting when a slim, angular young man in uniform appeared at the glass door to the conference room. He looked eagerly over at the chief inspector, who motioned for him to enter.

"Judging by your expression, you have some information for me?" Garvin said as he turned to face Drake and me. "This is Tommy Hawkesworth. He's been tasked with dogging the labs."

"I didn't realize you had anyone with you, sir," he said, looking questioningly at the visitors.

"It's all right. This is Decktora Raines. She's with the US government and working with us on the Bobbie Grey case. I believe you know Jason Drake from MI5. They're appropriately cleared and can stay," Garvin said, nodding to the others to leave and signaling Tommy to get on with it.

"It's about the powder, sir. We just got the final report back from toxicology." Tommy paused and glanced at me and Jason, still appearing uncomfortable at the presence of outsiders.

"Carry on," Garvin said gruffly.

"Very well, sir. Forensics has concluded the substance is a composite of at least two sources of poison, put together, they believe, to mask the ingredients and to assure lethality. One of the compounds is curare. You know what that is, sir?" he asked, a shock of blond hair falling over his left eye the more animatedly he spoke.

"Of course, I know what curare is! Go on."

"We've rarely heard of its use in the developed world, certainly not in modern times and not in Britain, which is why Forensics eventually determined it had to have been combined with something else. The thing about curare is that it causes almost immediate paralysis of its victim's respiratory system, which means that the victim shuts down."

"And the other compound?"

"That's the tricky one. The inspectors had to go outside of our lab to get their hands on other toxins they were considering as possible companions to the curare. They studied traces and mixes of a wide variety until they found the culprit. It's a miracle, sir, an absolute miracle," Tommy said excitedly.

"Yes, Tommy, that is indeed excellent news. I'm well aware that we do good work here. But what is the other poison? Do tell."

"Ornithogalum umbellatum,"

"You got me on that one. What is it?"

"Star of Bethlehem is the vernacular name. It's primarily found in Syria. Whoever thought that one up...," Hawkesworth grimaced. "Only a monster could devise such a horrendous toxin. Nasty work."

"Thank you, Tommy. I will be sure to commend everyone involved," Garvin said, well aware it was time for praise. "I assume they and you have looked into the history of this mixture to see if it had ever been used before?"

"Yes, of course. They found no other cases involving this precise mixture, but one thing is for sure. It wouldn't be difficult to obtain supplies of either one. This is not like ricin or any of the restricted radioactive poisons."

"And the forensics and biochem experts are still working on the take from yesterday's victim, the Yellowfin fellow?"

"They are. They have a much better sampling than we got from the Johnston case, and they've already determined it looks similar under the microscope. But they're just starting the analysis."

"Keep me posted, but remember, Tommy, no one besides those directly involved can know anything about this. Absolutely no hallway discussion. None. Is that clear?"

"Right, sir."

Garvin knew he aroused enough fear and respect in Tommy to keep the younger man's enthusiasm under control. Tommy was like a favorite nephew to Garvin, always eager to learn, and to please, but excitable. There was something about him that reminded him of himself back when he had just started with the Met and was excited and eager to learn everything. Not the man he was today, he thought, as he shooed off his younger self.

"Things should move faster now that our biochem people have something good to work with."

Tommy smiled, nodded at us, and went out, closing the door gently behind him.

"Well, it looks like we *do* have a serial killer in our midst," Garvin announced. "Hell, I hope I can keep this out of the media. I will have an hysterical London on my hands and I don't need that."

He thought to say more but glanced at his watch and quickly ended the meeting. Time was moving too quickly, and he didn't know who was holding the hourglass, but it needed to be him.

Drake and I gave each other a "let's talk" glance as we exited the conference room. We both knew that Garvin's serial killer was probably a Russian—and a diplomat. It surprised me Garvin hadn't excluded me from the conversation once he saw where it was headed. I suspect it was the US government connection that kept me there. Still, I was plenty glad to have been included, in spite of his linking me to the Bobbie Grey business. And now, thanks to Tommy Hawkesworth, I had a solid piece of intel on the poisons to add to the story, which makes someone like me very happy.

Once we were out of Garvin's building, Drake and I chatted superficially but we both knew this was no place to talk about sensitive intel, and we also knew where we wanted the conversation to go.

"Decktora, I'd feel more comfortable having this discussion over at my headquarters. Do you have time to go there with me now?"

I didn't, but I wasn't about to miss a chance to hear more from Drake. We grabbed a taxi and headed to Thames House, the MI5 offices at Millbank, and went directly to a secure conference room.

It didn't take long before I dug into one of my bêtes noires. "I've always been mystified why your people let Litvinenko's assassins get off so easily." I spoke as politely as I could, but I wanted Drake to spill the inside British version of the story, what his people were really thinking when they were first handling the case, and why they let the two assassins go.

"Ah, I remember now, you're a woman who gets right to the point," he smiled. "That cursed tragedy has been a thorn in my side since it happened. I argued with everyone about it. Nobody wanted an international incident, not when we were all supposedly getting along so well, Cold War over and all that. The outcome didn't sit well with me or with a number of my colleagues. I'm hardly leaking a state secret in telling you this. Still, the last thing we—or you—need is an international frost-up with the Russians."

"Since I'm currently a bit separated from the Agency, I have more interest in seeing the Russians held responsible than in dealing with international politics. But now, we have these new murders…."

Drake jumped in before I could finish the thought—the thought we were both having.

"They have Kremlin written all over them," he said. "But the claw marks, white powder? Why so primitive?"

Good news. We were in basic agreement. I didn't know how far he could, or would, go with me from an MI5 perspective. I did not have a clearance in British intelligence, and he had his own obligations and commitments. Thankfully, he continued.

"If the Russians are behind these latest murders, it's possible they're trying something new—or rather, something very old. Harder to detect, maybe? Do we know if they still have an actual poisons laboratory? I've been of the mind that their latest killings were just a series of one-offs, but there's really no reason to think the poisons activity of their intelligence service doesn't go on. Still, curare mixed with another compound? These are antiques in the world of toxicology," Drake said. "Hardly the radioactive poisons they've been using of late."

"No one seems to be paying much attention. It's not just Litvinenko who was assassinated. Remember Anatoly Trofimov," I said, "the former KGB'er who handled Soviet dissident cases and was a mentor to Litvinenko? He was killed in Moscow about a year before his friend, gunmen not identified. And Anna Politkovskaya, the Russian journalist and human rights activist, shot in her building's elevator, murder still unsolved. Jason, with all of this history, and now the Russian connection to these new victims…." I was building the case, almost unwittingly, but the pattern was evident.

"I think you're onto something, my friend. Glad you're on our side," he said, flashing a handsome, slightly roguish smile.

"We're going to figure this out," I said, not sure why I was so confident. "A serial killer on the loose in London. Old poisons, nothing that would smack of state sponsorship, like ricin or polonium-210. No radiation traces. Why would anyone suspect the FSB or the SVR in these cases?"

"And it would avoid an international confrontation," Drake said, finishing my thought. "Worth considering. Very clever."

I liked the way our conversation was going and felt my first vague sense of relief, of having a comrade, since this whole mess had begun.

"And the poison, this Star of Bethlehem, Garvin's man said that it comes from Syria. How convenient for the Russians?"

I stopped speaking for a moment, weighing my next words, which would move into an area where he might not want me going. "It would help if I knew what you have on Federov and Karchenko."

Drake paused. "I'll work on that, but we have to deal with your clearance status first," he said, as I winced.

Our procedures in this touchy area were different, specific to our own agencies. Though I still had mine, I had no idea how sensitive his old cases were and if my level of clearance would meet MI5 requirements.

"In the meantime, I have a colleague here at MI5, Stanley Brewster, who's an expert on Russia and a brilliant analyst on top of it. You two should talk."

It was time for me to tell him about Sergei and the real reason for my trip to London. He had earned that.

"This adds another layer to the story," he said, obviously quite surprised at what I'd shared. "On top of everything else, I have to handle the matter of not briefing Garvin. There's no way I can give him the true identity of the two defectors until we know exactly what we're dealing with. I suspect I'm going to get grief from some seniors around here who thought that most of this squirrelly business with the Russians was over and who don't have much interest in revisiting the issue of Russians poisoning their former countrymen in London. Nobody will want to stir that up again."

"Awkward about Garvin," I said. "I'm glad I don't have to deal with that, but then I have the problem of being Link Number One in the eyes of the good inspector, who has not taken kindly to me for some reason. He's been annoyed with me since our first meeting."

"I wouldn't lose any sleep over that, but it's clear that someone has their eye on you, I'm sorry to say. And I suspect he's not angry with you, Decktora. He's probably worried for you."

"I don't get that! Maybe he's just a classic case of being a cop too long. Women don't belong in these jobs, etc., etc." I looked at my watch. The day was flying by and I still had to get to Harrods.

CHAPTER 27

LONDON, JUNE 7

He always chooses pretty women. In fact, this new one looks like Katya. Based on her pictures, younger, of course, but she had the same look, slim, pretty, pale, blondish. She wondered what it was about men that drew them to certain types, as she observed Johanna in the playground with young Georgie.

The whole thing offended her. Olga wasn't jealous, not the least bit. Who wanted to be bothered with marriage and raising a family in this world? She'd learned long ago that sex was a release. She could pick up a man and have sex that same night, never see him again, and she knew she was lucky to feel that way. Most women suffered in relationships. Not her—she was careful never to get involved.

On the rare occasion when Olga was tempted by someone in particular, she reminded herself that she already had a serious relationship with a man. And that was the only one she needed—Ivanchukov. She would do whatever he wanted her to do. And right now that involved pursuing Sergei Dumanovskiy and the other Kameras.

From her surveillance perch on a bench just across the street from the playground in St. John's Wood, she could get a pretty good feeling for mother and son. That boy is going to look just like his father, she thought. If he grows to adulthood.

She was doing what her boss called collecting information. The operation was in the preparation phase. He had ordered her not to take any action for now against the wife and son. This part of the mission was about Sergei Dumanovskiy.

"Each Kamera asset will be different," he'd told her when the program began. "You must make a study. I can tell you where each one is located, but you have to determine the best way to get to them and to dispose of them with absolute efficiency. But this one, Dumanovskiy, this is the big one, and everything must be perfect."

CHAPTER 28

LONDON, JUNE 7

It was half-past twelve, and I had to get to Harrods, then to the meeting with Grace at the safe house, and later, Sergei. The taxi dropped me off a few blocks away from the store, which allowed me the opportunity to walk and observe my surroundings. I was back in the flow, and my sixth sense was alive and well.

I entered through one of the back doors of Harrods across from the Café Rouge and walked through the quiet men's department. The crowd thickened as I got to the popular food court and headed straight to my favorite counter to buy a package of turquoise, blue, and silver-glazed chocolates. If anyone wanted to hang around there and watch me, they were welcome to. I was waiting for them.

I lingered, looking over all the colored chocolates, as if I couldn't make up my mind, then chose the package of blues. As I was about to pay, I turned slightly and noticed, almost felt, a short person in a hoodie and a casual gray sweat suit, a hint of glasses, also peering at the candies. She, or he, did not appear to be someone who would be interested in high-end chocolates. And the individual didn't need to stand so near me in such an uncrowded area. My antennae rose, but I wasn't about to twist around and stare. Had I seen this individual since

I'd arrived, and not noticed? I paid for the chocolates, then turned to leave. My head down, I got a good look at the shoes. Neither of us could see each other's face. I was sure of that, but I would be watching for those shoes, the one disguise that often didn't get altered during a surveillance detection route.

Next on my list was the tourist shop on the second level. It might be difficult to spot any surveillance in this well-dressed crowd, a majority of women in hijab. Still, I would be as alert as possible for eyes directly on me. In the shop, I rummaged through memorabilia—bears, piggy banks, cookie tins, scarves, everything decorated with the Harrods *H*. An array of large pocketbooks was displayed on the wall shelves. The one I was to buy jumped out at me. They carried the exact same bag in black, maroon, and that army green that I hated. Double-handle straps and a gold logo emblazoned across the side. Yes, it would indeed make an excellent concealment device, large enough to hide a camera, some papers, and my normal purse innards.

My new bag in tow, I indulged in a window-shopping SDR along Brompton Road. All good so far. When I got to Harvey Nichols, I paused to look in the first large display window. In the reflection, I saw just behind me a twosome in decidedly unchic clothes. I thought I'd caught a glimpse of them in the tourist shop at Harrods, busy as it was. Something about the woman's outfit had caught my eye. It seemed unfitting in that dressy part of Harrods.

What I didn't know was where this couple had picked me up, if, in fact, they had. I dreaded to think it was outside of the Langsford, which would mean they knew where I was staying, and they, or a colleague, had had me under observation since I left for my morning appointment at the Metropolitan Police. But then again, *someone* knew I was staying at the Langsford. The same people?

The twosome was middle-aged and very average looking, both good qualities in the surveillance business. The woman was wearing a flowery pale green skirt, an unattractive, dated style suited to certain working-level women from the former Soviet Union or Eastern Europe.

Just as I went into the store, I saw the hoodie again, standing just inside the front entrance. The shoes. It had to be the same person. Similar stature, same gray running outfit, eyeglasses. The hoodie quickly turned and started to walk away from me, but in that brief moment, I got a glimpse of the face. It was a woman, and the eyeglasses were prominent. I couldn't get anything else, but the wiry female frame felt familiar to me. This was no coincidence. Now I was certain I was being followed.

I walked into the cosmetics department to see if the couple would reappear. There were lots of mirrors in that section. After checking a few counters, I saw that the woman was still with me, minus the man, who was wise enough to stay just at the edge of a woman's department and give the appearance of waiting impatiently for his wife. I wanted to get rid of them, so I veered toward the special elevator just outside the front door of Harvey Nick's and took it up to the restaurant on the top level. I thought I'd lost them, given that little maneuver, but within a few minutes, I saw them again. They weren't new to this game, and they weren't going to drop me. But what their reappearances told me was that they didn't know I'd spotted them.

At that point, I considered dropping the meeting with Grace, but I really needed to see her and to get the CD and the phones. There was too much at stake to delay any further, so I decided to take my chances.

I needed a little time in a private place, and that meant a trip back to the Langsford. I doubted they would follow me there, wait, and then pick me up again—too obvious and too open in front of the club. They could, of course, call in another team. I had no idea what their capability or numbers were, but I knew I could get out of the Langsford via a different exit than I'd used before, and hopefully that would suffice.

I left the club at three fifteen, noticing none of the characters I'd seen on my shopping expedition earlier in the day. I walked over to the Green Park station and caught the Piccadilly Line, then switched at South Kensington to the Circle Line for Edgware Road, about a forty-minute exercise in all. I knew the Edgware Road exit would open to a busy corner where I could be surveilled, but could easily counter if I felt the need since the area was full of shops and eateries.

At the newsstand on the corner, the headlines leaped out at me: "Serial Killer Loose in London." I leafed through a couple of the tabloids, until the cashier gave me a "buy one or leave" look. Garvin would be tearing his already-thin hair out by the roots, though it was a break Perlman, Drake, and I needed.

The safe house was eight blocks from the station, and after a few intentional twists and turns, I reached my destination just after four. I was never late to these meetings, but it was only Grace and me and I suspected she would understand. There was hardly anyone on the streets. Feeling secure, I rang apartment 4A, and after making sure it was me, Grace buzzed me in. When she opened the door, it was clear from her eyes that her day had been as stressful as mine.

"Rough day?" I asked, sweeping quickly inside so we could get the door locked behind us.

"The usual. Mr. P's been on a rant over this Russian stuff and has me running all over the place."

She noticed me glance around the room.

"Don't worry, it's been swept. No one will hear our conversation. How'd it go at Harrods?"

I nodded. "I'm quite sure I was under observation in Harrods, and then at Harvey Nichols, and possibly back to the Langsford, perhaps two or three surveillants. I don't know where they picked me up," I said, describing in as much detail as I could the couple, the hoodie, and all that had transpired from Harrods until I got to the safe house. Grace needed every detail for Perlman. Now that I'd identified surveillance, we'd entered a new phase, and the chief would have a fit if he wasn't briefed right away.

"No problem, Decky, he would never let me loose this early anyway."

"I'll give the station a complete description of the couple. If you have any photos of Russian embassy employees and intelligence officers, we should take a look at them. Maybe Perlman could have MI5 send their profiles and pics over as well."

"Okay, let's see your new bag."

I pulled it out and handed it to her.

"I couldn't look more like a tourist," I said sarcastically, unfolding the army green patent leather Harrods bag. It had magnetic fastenings and two side zipper pockets inside.

"Perfect. That's the one. Now, let me show you the latest in high-fashion concealment device design," Grace said with a smile, revealing a virtually identical knockoff of my new purchase. "A tiny camera is hidden in the side pocket. There's a Harrods monogrammed handkerchief sticking out of the pocket, but the camera is tucked in behind, in its own magnetized inside compartment. If you have to reach in, you will feel the handkerchief, then the small, flat protrusion behind it, a little thicker than a credit card and designed to look like one, except for the tiny button. If you need cover, you can fake a sneeze, or not, and pull out the handkerchief, taking your photos first. It's wide angle and produces excellent quality at amazing distances.

State of the art. The pictures will be automatically transmitted directly to the station and to my special smartphone," she said, displaying it to me.

I'd handled a lot of these cameras in the past, but this one was indeed a beauty. So small and flat that my fingers seemed almost too large to click a button. But no worries, all I had to do was touch once against a certain spot on the fabric of the concealed pocket to activate it, point the purse toward the target, and touch it again.

"Once you get used to the pocketbook, you'll find that you'll be able to connect with the button by pulling your elbow into the purse," Grace said, showing me the exact spot where it would have to connect with my elbow, just above the "a" in the Harrods logo. We tested the handkerchief version together a few times to make sure I was comfortable with the click site and the aim. Our sample photos, which we could see on the smartphone, were good, as was my aim, which was really my only concern. Then I tried to take some photos with the purse closed, by clinching my arm close to the "a." We determined exactly where the shoulder strap should be for me to make this connect. It was easy. I played with it until we both felt I'd got it.

"Impressive," I said, as I transferred all my purse items into the new bag. "Especially the wide angle, which I'll need since there's little chance I'll be able to get directly in front of my target. Let's hope I have a chance to use it."

Knowing there were more treats to come, for both me and Sergei, I said, "I can't wait to see what else you have for me."

Grace then gave me another device, a wristwatch that I was to give Sergei for emergency use only. It contained a minuscule button that, when pushed, activated an alarm that went directly to Perlman's secure phone as well as to the one she was about to give me, each relaying Sergei's precise location. Sergei was to wear the watch 24/7.

"It's beginning to look a lot like Christmas," I hummed, but Grace wasn't finished.

"And the phones," Grace said, handing me two cells. "The first one is for you. The number sign gives you emergency contact capability with us if you should need it for any reason, at any hour. You can use the phone normally otherwise. It has advanced technology that should block interception. Sergei's is the same model, excluding the ability to contact us directly, but he can call you. Still, we recommend minimal use. I'm putting everything in this little box for you to hand over to your friend, gift-wrapped in case you have an audience."

"Is there anyone better than you, Grace?"

Now to meet Sergei. It was just after five, and I needed to get to him by six.

I took the tube to Chelsea and got to our meeting site ten minutes early so I could scope out the place and, hopefully, get a quiet corner table. It was close to teatime, which meant the café could get busy in the next hour. Sergei arrived spot on time.

"Sorry about the change of plans yesterday. A lot to fill you in on," I said quietly, watching his face grow animated in expectation.

The waitress came over. We ordered tea and scones, and waited till she was out of hearing distance.

"Sergei, you were right. I can't put it all together yet, but I want you to know what's happened since our meeting Tuesday night.

"I'm more than ready," he said, not sarcastically.

"First of all, I've learned that another Russian defector was killed down in Cornwall a few months ago. I don't know much about the case, but MI5 is looking into it."

"What? Who was...."

"That's all I know. I have nothing more," I said strongly. "Nothing, and I will tell you when I learn something."

I relayed the rest of the events in sequence, telling him I'd received a threatening message when I got back to the club after our meeting, but I included only the barest facts surrounding Bobbie Grey and made no mention of DCI Garvin. Sergei kept trying to interrupt me with questions, but I kept my answers brief and wasn't about to give him too much detail. I watched him as he absorbed what I was saying and tried to figure out how it all came together.

"You're being followed, Decktora. It's my fault…."

"It is not! It was my decision to come here. And I want to get to the bottom of this with you. We're in it together now, and we'll figure it out as long as we trust each other and share what we learn."

Sergei listened silently, though I could see anxiety building in him.

"Okay, Sergei, enough about me. It's your turn," I said, smiling faintly and toasting him with my cup of tea.

"Decky, I had to tell Johanna about you and our get-together."

"Tell her what?"

Was Sergei getting loose around the edges? His defector contacts, now Johanna. Talk, talk, talk.

"Johanna's easy. She doesn't ask me about the past, rarely has since our early days together. I don't think she really wants to know more. Decky, you of all people surely understand that I had to urge her to be more aware of her and Georgie's surroundings. That, of course, led to some questions as to why I was suddenly worked up. So I mentioned the murder of Federov, but said it likely had nothing to do with his past. She got it, and that was the end of the discussion. As I said, she doesn't make life difficult."

I stared at him a long minute. He wasn't a novice and I believed him. "Okay. Now, have you sensed any unusual activity, any possibility of surveillance? Did Johanna mention anything odd on her side?"

"Nothing."

"On a more pleasant note, happy birthday, Sergei," I said, handing him the small gift box.

He opened it, observed the two items and looked back up at me, expressionless, waiting for my explanation.

"The cell phone is easy to use and will block interception, state of the art. The watch is appropriately masculine but needs a little explanation, which I think we can manage without your handling it here." I described the activating element and its direct connection to me and the COS, and we discussed where and when he would use it.

"You seem to believe my story now," he said, "more than you did at the Forum." His gaze was fixed on me. "Is there anything you aren't telling me?"

Yes. "No, but you gave me a lot to think about, and I need to learn more about some of the players, find out if MI5 has anything."

"Decktora, I've accepted that you had to tell your chief over at Grosvenor Square, but I don't want the world in on this. That's why I contacted you. MI5 will be furious that I didn't go directly to them. You know that," he said, understandably irritated.

I nodded and hoped he understood, because I still needed to wheedle out of him everything on the defectors he'd mentioned having contact with, and I didn't want him to hold back because he thought I was reporting to the others. Kind of a tit-for-tat situation. It seemed we each had gone further in spreading our stories than either of us expected or wanted. Never good in the intel business to have a big audience. And, I admit, ours was growing.

Still, the warning note sent to me and the death of Bobbie Grey had elevated my concerns about possible threats to Sergei and his contacts and I didn't want anyone else exposed, or Sergei's situation made more dangerous, until I got a better hold on the situation.

"I can only ask you to be very careful until we come to an understanding of all that has transpired. Or, do I need to say, 'beg' you?" I asked pointedly, watching his eyes. "Why don't you wear the watch? Sort of a test run. We can go over it tomorrow if you have any problems with it. One o'clock at the girly café in Fortnum and Mason. Watch your back."

He reached across the table and covered my hand with his. "It's been very quiet. I'm not expecting to hear from anyone. Trust me."

Right. I don't trust anyone, and my concerns were not assuaged by his justification for that network business of his.

CHAPTER 29

LONDON, JUNE 7

When I got back to the club, it was after seven. I studied my new pocketbook again to make sure I was comfortable handling the camera from inside and outside the purse. I didn't have access to the photos I'd taken, but the whole process felt comfortable to me now. Things could move fast when an operation was active, and I had to be certain I didn't miss anything—or mess up. After doing my homework, I threw in enough personal accoutrements to fill up the bag.

Suddenly I was starving. I'd been so focused on my conversation with Sergei that I hadn't touched the scones. I didn't have any dinner plans and was in no mood tonight for the solitude of the club. I leafed through a few pamphlets on the bedside table looking for tempting spots, then remembered a quaint little Lebanese restaurant somewhere off Piccadilly. The name evaded me, but I decided to find it.

It was a cool night. I threw a navy pashmina over my shoulders, careful not to cover my fabulous new bag, specifically the camera site, all well-positioned under my right arm. I had time to do a little street work, take some photos, before dinner.

It was hard to get my mind off Sergei and the meeting we'd just had. His "trust me" comment gave me no comfort, nor did the fact I'd chosen not to tell him about the dreadful developments of the day—the murder of Bobbie Grey, and then Fawkes's report on the poisons—all of which probably related to him in some as yet undetermined way. Aside from the unlikely possibility he'd seen it in the news, Sergei knew nothing about the strange murder of Bobbie Grey and certainly nothing about its connection to me.

Berkeley Square was crowded with people heading to dinner or home from work. I passed through the narrow John's Place and emerged near the coffee shop I'd stopped in the night before. As I got closer to it, I noticed the woman in the flowery, pale green skirt sitting alone at a table, appearing to read a newspaper.

She didn't seem to see me, and I remained confident she didn't know I'd spotted her and her partner during my shopping expedition. There was no way she'd be so unprofessional as to show up in my neighborhood if she had. That was the good news. The bad was that they were on me and obviously had me at the Langsford. Since her compadre wasn't with her, and I hadn't seen him around Berkeley Square, I had to conclude that one of her colleagues, someone I'd not yet identified, was closer to the club and she was sitting by as emergency backup.

I kept walking in the same direction, looking straight ahead. As I passed by her, I clicked the camera repeatedly. Good thing I'd done a little practice. I hadn't expected this opportunity and prayed the images would be clear enough to enable us to identify her, assuming she was somewhere in any of our records. I was already fairly convinced she worked over at Kensington Palace Gardens with the formidable Mr. Ivanchukov.

Finally, my eye caught the red awning of the restaurant. I recognized it right away and was happy there were few patrons inside at this still early hour. My stomach was crying for a plate of Lebanese tapas—hummus, baba ghanoush, and feta—and my mind for a moment of quiet and sanity before going back to the club.

"Red or white, madam?" asked the waiter, assuming I would want wine.

"House white," I said, but my mind quickly flashed to Alex. He only drank red, and I only white. It was a joke between us that we could never order a full bottle of anything, so we had long agreed to stick to our own preferences in this one little concession to the success of our relationship.

The sun had not yet set when I got back to the hotel, but I was now ready to collapse. The minute I opened the door I saw the flashing red light on my phone. Aberforth had returned my call. Good news. He left a contact number but said to call back in the morning. I listened to the message several times to see if the voice sounded familiar, and though I didn't know him all that well, I convinced myself it was indeed Bredon Aberforth.

Settling in for the night would be difficult, with all that was roiling around in my head. I had to get some sleep, so I took a swig of melatonin and somehow managed to drift off into that sort of doze state between worlds.

It must have been two o'clock when my eyes popped open. I bolted upright, wide awake. It wasn't possible!

Elena? The hoodie I'd seen twice today. Elena Radzimova, my lost agent, the one whose disappearance had tormented me all the years since Tallinn. That small, slim creature *felt* like Elena. Was that possible? She had been such a part of my life. In my mind, I knew her so well.

Either she is alive, or my brain is playing nasty tricks on me. I got up out of bed and poured myself a glass of water.

It was my first overseas assignment, Tbilisi, Estonia—and Elena my first target. With her recruitment, which took many months, I was off to an impressive career start, receiving kudos from my chief and headquarters for my "skillful development of our relationship." Recruitment was the name of the game. Within the first year of my assignment, I had one under my belt.

My initial ops plan had been to accept every diplomatic invitation I got until I could spot and sidle up to Elena. The chief gave me most of his invites and those of some others in the office as well, hoping that Elena's and my paths would cross.

All I needed was one contact.

It was at my fourth dip reception that I finally encountered her, a challenge mostly because we were working without photos. Elena was too low level to appear in the diplomatic books and Langley had nothing on her. Fortunately, one of my male colleagues had been introduced to her at a function and said he could identify her. This meant he would thereafter be my "date" for all events that might include her.

On our third office date, my colleague saw Elena standing at the bar of the reception we were attending. Two men were chatting with her in Russian, presumably friends from their embassy. I waited until they left, then wandered over to her and tried to strike up a conversation, introducing myself as Carolyn Shaw, an alias I used extensively in my ops work in Tallinn.

The initial contact proved easier than I'd anticipated. We quickly began speaking Russian, since her English was very limited. I attributed my language skills to parental expectations. We agreed to meet at a café a week hence, where we could discuss our lives as "females" working in a foreign land. She was small, slim, not exactly pretty, but I could see why a man would be attracted to her—trim body and big, brown eyes even though covered by old-fashioned horn-rimmed glasses, and a slightly Romanesque nose.

Our social contacts continued, on a carefully planned but infrequent basis, and I rigorously wrote everything up for Washington. Elena complained about her terrible hours and a boss she described as moody and sometimes tyrannical. The minute she mentioned his first name, I knew whom she referred to, the Rezident, a man of great interest to us. Elena's and my meetings were now all outside of diplomatic circles, but for some reason her office either hadn't noticed or had allowed her to socialize with me. The thought niggled at my brain. There was, of course, every possibility she was targeting me as I was her.

As our conversations grew more personal, Elena revealed to me that she was "involved" with her boss, that he'd maneuvered to bring her with him on the assignment as his assistant, wife left at home. We shared stories of our romantic lives, mine fabricated. I even told her that I had suffered a terrible heartbreak not too long ago because of a married man, the reason I escaped to Estonia, I said. Those soap operas became the basis of our relationship, two female diplomats living single in a foreign country. When the Rezident suddenly decided to call his wife to Tallinn and temporarily put a lid on their affair, it was me in whom Elena confided.

She was bereft, and I was a person on a mission. It was the first time, but not the last, that I would have to deal with the issue every case officer faces—manipulating and lying to a target in the guise of friendship. I told myself all along that I was helping her, and that I would be able to offer her a better life—and I almost convinced myself, too.

Over the few months we had together, I managed to elicit intelligence from her about her boss, his work, their mission, all things she should never have discussed with me. There were a lot of hangovers, but I was on a roll, and headquarters liked what I was sending in.

Then she disappeared. Totally vanished.

The COS, headquarters, and I reviewed every imaginable possibility as to what had happened. In our after-action reports, we concluded the most likely scenario was that Soviet surveillance had seen her with me, having already figured out who I really was, and then accused her of espionage. We had no other agents in the rezidentura to help us fill in the missing pieces.

We never learned what happened to Elena, and I never got the whole matter out of my mind, despite all the support I received from my superiors, who basically said, "You have to live with it. That's the business we're in."

I wandered into the bathroom, wet a facecloth with warm water, and held it to my tired eyes. In a moment I felt myself begin to relax. Still, I doubted I would get much more sleep tonight.

CHAPTER 30

LONDON, JUNE 8

I wanted to speak to Bredon Aberforth before I went out. Elena was floating around my brain as well, though I was less certain about my sudden insight than I had been in the middle of the night. It might have been due to an overactive imagination or awakening during a dream. I dialed the number he'd left. A man's voice answered.

"Bredon?"

"Decktora."

"You recognized my voice?"

"It was a good guess."

I could feel the smile in his voice, which seemed familiar to me, even though it had been several years since we'd had any contact.

"So what brings you to London? And how's Alex?"

There it was, the question I wasn't about to answer.

"It's a long story," I said, realizing I'd told Sergei the same thing. "Is there a chance we could meet for a drink later? Somewhere easy for you?"

"Sure. What about the Olde Ship in Shepherd Market at six. Do you know it?"

I assured him I'd be there. Yes, I knew it, though not well. I'd been there once or twice in the past. A tiny place run by a woman who had a cat named Rodolfo after the character in *La Bohème*. Don't know why I remembered that, but I did.

I was surprised to see Nigel at the front desk when I got downstairs. He looked as if he'd been struck by a thunderbolt."

"What's happened, Nigel?"

"We've had an emergency, ma'am. Some shocking news."

Oh no. "What's happened?"

"Lionel died early this morning." Nigel looked as grim as he should have.

"But I saw him just yesterday. He seemed healthy, in good spirits," I said, stunned.

"They think he was murdered, attacked right in front of his home in Brixton. We're all in shock. I was with him late last evening when his shift finished, and he didn't seem to have anything on his mind but getting home." Nigel stopped, as if he'd already revealed more than he should have.

"And…?"

"The police are on their way. The whole staff's been called in. They want to talk to everyone here."

"I'm so sorry, Nigel. Is there anything I can do? I've known Lionel for years and consider him a special friend." I wanted to ask more but sensed I should tread lightly until after the police visit.

The news hit me doubly hard because I knew instantly that my presence had contributed in some way. I felt the twinge of a migraine suddenly hovering over my right eye. I ran back to my room, slipped a pill under my tongue, and prayed it would work, because I didn't have time for a headache today.

The phone rang as I was about to leave again. It was Drake, asking if I could come to his office right away. This had to relate to Lionel. I said I'd head over, wondering what Drake had.

I really didn't want to discuss the Lionel matter with Drake before I talked to Perlman, but I was going to have to. I would try to find Perlman right after Drake.

The police arrived at the club just as I was leaving. No one looked familiar, thank heavens, as I didn't have time to waste. I grabbed a taxi. In all this chaos, if anyone wanted to follow me to Vauxhall, they were welcome to try it.

A security guard insisted on escorting me up to Drake's office. He met us at the elevator, dismissed the guard, and walked me down a dimly lit, undecorated hallway to his office, where he introduced me to his secretary, Evelyn. It seemed obvious they'd had a long professional history, probably both overseas and at headquarters. She was to be trusted.

As Drake directed me into his office, he told Evelyn to get us some tea and then contact a colleague named Stanley to have him join us.

"You look distressed," he said, but didn't ask why. He had something to tell me first.

"I know about the incident involving the Langsford doorman. Garvin has already been in touch with me, up in arms. Told me the victim worked at the club where you're staying, that a claw mark and white substance were found on the neck at the site of the wound. This time Garvin said the mark was well delineated. He's now quite convinced that London has a serial killer." Drake let out a breath.

Of course, he was upset about his situation with Garvin, especially now that the serial killer verdict had etched itself into Garvin's brain. Drake and I both inhabited a world in which holding back the truth was sometimes essential. Some called it "lying." I called it a necessity.

"To add to the saga, Garvin's now even more certain you're connected to all of it in some way."

I winced, then opened my mouth to speak.

"Don't worry," he said, raising his hand. "I calmed him down, told him I'd discuss it with you and get back to him. He's uncomfortable, doesn't know what to make of your presence here."

"I still don't get the man. He took my passport but let me sit in on Thursday's meeting. Darned strange behavior."

"I think he needs you to stay in London until the Bobbie Grey matter gets resolved."

"Resolved, but I had nothing...."

"I know you had nothing to do with his murder, but the case is pending and you're part of it. To be honest, I think he's relieved to let me 'handle you', as we say. I should be able to keep him off your back for a while."

"Perlman's going to have a fit when he learns about all of this, but you called, so here I am. That'll be my excuse anyway."

I told Drake exactly what Nigel had reported and what I could add about Lionel, concluding with the bad news that he was the one who received the Yellowfin message meant for me.

Drake swore under his breath. "Decky, it's a good thing for both of us that Garvin is preoccupied keeping the lid on the press. Now that the serial killer story has taken hold—between the public and a few higher-ups in the government—he's got his hands full."

"If he stays focused there, we may have time to give the killers a false sense that they're safe," I said optimistically, then looked at Drake as if to ask, what else?

"There's another reason I called you. We located the records on Federov aka Johnston and Karchenko aka Sempworth much more quickly than I'd expected. I've had only a few minutes to glance over them myself but will dig into them later today. In the meantime, Stanley Brewster, our intellectual-in-residence on things Russian, is coming up. I mentioned him to you when you were here on Thursday. You'll want to talk with him. I've told him and Evelyn to speak freely with you. We need everything we can get our hands on, but I think we're headed in the right direction. We just have to pick up the pace."

I paused and swallowed hard. I had more to tell Drake.

"The Russians know I'm here," I said, giving him a truncated version of my surveillance problem and my view that it was connected to the rezidentura. "I just wish I knew how much they have on me and Sergei, why he contacted me, all that. The more I learn, the more worried I get about him."

"And I, my friend, am worried about you. I'll talk to Perlman about countersurveillance for you. But for now, take a look at the files. I've settled the clearance issue." He didn't say how, but I assumed it was due to the "special relationship" we had with the Brits and perhaps an additional check with the Pear.

Before I could begin reading, Stanley Brewster and Evelyn appeared at the door. Drake invited them in and told them about my background and my reason for being in London. A hard-working staff, I thought, but realized Drake viewed my appearance and all that surrounded it as something of an emergency and must have called them in.

"Stanley, I've given Ms. Raines the files on Federov and Karchenko to review. Once she's finished, you two should put your heads together on the three defectors, one of whom is still alive—Sergei Dumanovskiy. If you find a thread—any thread—we'll discuss it right away. The two most recent murders are obviously not defectors, but there is a conspicuous link to our friend here. Let's figure this out."

I felt my stomach wrench when Drake said the words "still alive," and hoped like hell that Perlman had put surveillance on Sergei. In the meantime, a three-inch stack of papers sat in front of me, and it was clear I'd need more time than I had to review it all. I could feel Perlman breathing down my neck and hoped something would jump out to me in a fast read.

Drake continued talking with Evelyn and Brewster but sent me off to do my homework. I was well aware that I had a one o'clock appointment with Sergei, but figured I could at least do a quick read-through and come back if I needed more time.

I settled into a chair and opened the file on Federov. The first thing I wanted to know was exactly what assignments Federov had had in his KGB career. The brief bio sheet showed he was married before he began his clandestine life, no children. Spoke French, Polish, and German, along with his native tongue, and, of late, English. Overseas assignments primarily in Europe, with the requisite between-tour years in Moscow. Pretty much like us.

I was skimming over the portions on his Moscow time when my eyes fell on a document that said Federov had worked in Department 12 of Directorate S. According to the report, he left after only about six months, having completed the "required tour of duty." A short assignment. Why? I stopped reading and started thinking over what I knew about *that* department. These damned directorates could be hard to keep track of, especially with the post–Cold War rearrangements and name changes.

Suddenly the light went on. *Department 12, Institute Number 2, the poisons unit, once known as Kamera,* the idea Drake and I had tossed around yesterday, questioning if such a unit even existed these days.

A poisons factory in today's Russia? This would be something from another era. I sat back and thought. Yes, there had been some British media reporting suggesting the existence of such a place after the murder of Litvinenko, and there was a recent book by a former GRU official about a so-called poisons factory in or around Moscow. And, of course, there was the dated tale of the 1978 murder in London of a Bulgarian dissident, who was killed when the tip of an umbrella delivered a lethal dose of ricin into his leg. The story was lore in the annals of intelligence. Everyone knew the KGB was behind it, even if the act had been carried out by the Bulgarian secret police.

I stopped thinking and turned full tilt into the file on Karchenko. A loner with no immediate family, who had handled illegals for the Soviets and defected in the late 1980s before the Iron Curtain fell. His story read like that of the stereotypical KGB hack who was involved in support operations for senior officers. Not many assignments abroad, but one full two-year tour in Department 12. Oh my God. I tore through the file looking for more. There was nothing else, just a job with a boring-sounding office called Department 12.

I suddenly remembered something Sergei had once reported. It was before my time and never came up in the later years when I dealt directly with him. By the time I met Sergei, the debriefs had been mostly completed, and I had taken him on because of his psychological issues. I vaguely recalled having read in Sergei's files that he'd had a very brief stint with a component called Department 12 early in his career. He'd hated it, and though eager to get out, left because the KGB needed him in Washington. I knew little about this department when Sergei and I first met, and was with him for other reasons than to further debrief.

A link to two of the dead defectors. This I had not expected. I didn't know whether to laugh or cry.

Drake and Brewster stared at each other as I relayed what I'd uncovered. The Department 12 thread was thickening into a rope, and Ivanchukov's hand was on it. Now he was a diplomat serving in London, which put him on Drake's turf.

Drake walked over to his bookshelf, pulled out the latest Blue Book, the list of foreign diplomats assigned to London, and started leafing through its pages.

"There he is," Drake said, pointing to Ivanchukov's name, "just below the Russian ambassador." Brewster's eyes widened.

Drake waved the book at him. "I want you to find out if there were any other defectors in Britain who might have had an affiliation with Department 12. If you can come up with connections to Ivanchukov, all the better. It may be daunting, but we need to search each and every name where there might be a link—*any* connection. This could go beyond our Caesars, but start with them."

"One more thing," Brewster said as Evelyn packaged some newly arrived files for him. "It's about the claw. As I was reviewing these files, I remembered something, somewhere in Russia years ago, maybe two decades back, about murders involving a claw. I think they found the guilty party at some point, but that's all I can recall. The story must have tucked itself into my tattered old brain because it was so unusual."

"Sounds preposterous. One might even say too good to be true. And as for your 'tattered old brain', I could use it myself," Drake replied, patting Brewster on the back.

Brewster continued undaunted. "I'm digging through old files to see if I can find anything on this. Not much on computers back then, so the search is challenging, but I'll give it a try."

I had to get to Perlman. Langley needed to review Sergei's old reporting to see what they had on this. Fragments mattered.

And I needed to talk to Sergei about Department 12.

CHAPTER 31

LONDON, JUNE 8

I gave Grace a quick call to tell her I had to see Perlman but couldn't make it till late afternoon. I definitely was not comfortable with the thought of meeting both Drake and Sergei before updating Perlman. Worse things had happened, I thought, but I wasn't sure he'd agree.

I had little concern about choosing Fortnum & Mason as our meeting site since it would be difficult for anyone, particularly a man, to surveil me and Sergei at midday at Fortnum's, a place for "ladies who lunch." Plus, the high-decibel chatter would allow us to have a conversation without being easily overheard. I was now prepared to tell him more about what had happened to me since our meeting the night I arrived.

The cafe's atmosphere—shades of pink and yellow, aroma of peonies—contrasted with how I was feeling and what Sergei and I had to discuss. They wouldn't seat me until we'd both arrived, but I made sure they'd save the little table along the back for us. Sergei got there shortly after me. We gave each other a kiss on the cheek and then set-tled down at our table.

He took a deep breath and dove right in. "I've been wondering if you would find anything more on Ivanchukov after what we discussed yesterday."

"We're moving as fast as we can. You know better than anyone that this can take more than two or three days. But Sergei, I may be onto something. Didn't you once work for Department 12, or Kamera, as I think your colleagues called it, early in your career?"

He was clearly surprised by my question. "My God, Decky, that was so long ago, and I got out as fast as I could, saved by an assignment to Washington, which at the time, I thought was good," he said with a sad smile.

"Do you remember any details? Was Ivanchukov connected with that group? Sergei, think, think, think. What do you recall? Were you on specific projects? Do you remember the personnel? Anything?" I was now speaking in as low a voice as possible and trying to look as if we were having a happy, perhaps romantic conversation.

"I hated the place and have tried to wipe it from my mind. It wasn't a fit for me, so they certainly didn't involve me in any delicate operations. And as for Ivanchukov, no, I have no memory of him until years later when he became the head of our unit in Moscow."

"What about Olga, aka Yulia, her latest persona?" I didn't mention that I thought she might have yet another persona, one I'd known long ago.

Sergei paused, rubbed his forehead. "No, she wasn't there either, certainly not that I can recall, though there's no reason I would have noticed either of them at that time. I hadn't yet come to know them."

"I've been back through the records of Federov and the man killed in Cornwall. Both of them had experience in Department 12. And then suddenly I remembered that you'd had an early connection with it as well."

I kept pushing him, and though he simply couldn't recall much, we agreed that our conversation would probably trigger something in his mind. The jewel for me was that he confirmed he had worked there. Now I had something that linked the three defectors, but I still had to get to the bottom of Sergei's network. I hadn't really buttoned that down, and there was a distinct chance that the Kamera thread might weave into that group, so I asked him to explain.

Sergei groaned, "I'm sorry I mentioned it. It's not a club, rather a handful of individuals, former Russian-Soviet defectors, who contact each other if they learn something that might threaten one or more of us, as I've already told you. And I might mention that no one has brought up anything about the Cornwall fellow, or whoever else might be targeted."

"I need to know their names," I told him. It's possible that some of them had a Kamera affiliation, and if I can get into their files, I can uncover that."

"I'll handle that," he said. "I'll find out if anyone had a connection to that criminal lab."

He wasn't letting me into that club. Still, I gave it one more shot.

"I'm trying to save your life and perhaps some others' lives as well. Do you know if any in your group worked for the poisons unit?"

He shook his head. "I don't know. For a while in the early nineties it looked as if some of the worst parts of Soviet government activity had disappeared, but now I wouldn't put anything past them. This new group is as treacherous as the Soviets. That poor Litvinenko. I knew who was behind it the minute I saw the tragic pictures of him in the news. And now these others."

We both sat back for a few minutes. Neither of us touched our tea, and then we both laughed. "We're paranoid people, Sergei, and we should be. But I promise I didn't poison your tea, and I'm pretty sure you didn't poison mine."

So we drank the English tea and ate their lovely little sandwiches quietly, both in our own thoughts for a few moments.

Suddenly Sergei perked up.

"I just thought of something. There is one fellow, someone I met only once, in the presence of another defector. He's at Oxford now. I don't know how he got defector status since my understanding was that he worked somewhere, midlevel at best, in the administrative part of the SVR, post Cold War. It's never been easy to get defector status, but he managed to do it not so many years ago, so he must have been involved in something sensitive enough to be of interest to British intelligence."

"Do you remember his name?"

"He goes by Misha Murphy, a little too close to the bone, I think, but apparently he wanted to keep 'Misha'. He's involved in Russian language or Russian studies at Oxford. That's about all I know."

"I'll find him," I said, giving him what I thought was a reassuring smile.

Sergei groaned and clasped his head in his hands, "That sounds like a very bad idea."

We finished up. Sergei left before me. I loitered over my tea, using the time to check my phone messages. The cafe was busy, full of chatter. A few people had come and gone since we'd arrived, but I saw no one who resembled my surveillants from my shopping expedition.

CHAPTER 32

LONDON, JUNE 8

I checked my cell again and saw that I had a message from Grace. Perlman couldn't see me until four o'clock. Good news since he'd have less excuse to go ballistic over the fact I'd discussed the Lionel matter with Drake before him. Now I needed Drake again, this time to see if he could give me anything on Misha Murphy. Thank heavens I had my new cell, the one Grace had assured me was untraceable, because I was too pressed for time to go over to Vauxhall.

I dialed. Evelyn picked up and buzzed me through to Drake right away.

"Didn't expect to hear from you so soon. What's happening?"

"Jason, a quick question. Do you know Misha Murphy? Teaches at Oxford."

"Not offhand but will look into it and get back to you. We're not on a good line."

"It's better than you think, but I'll explain that later. Call me if you can find anything."

No further comments from Drake. I knew he got my point and would understand why as soon as he identified Murphy.

Now I would spend a few minutes on my new project—finding Misha at Oxford. I searched for the main Oxford campus number, found it easily, then dialed.

"Oxford University. If you are calling for…," said the recording. After several button punches, I got through to the Department of International Studies, the most likely place to find him, I thought. "I am looking for Professor M. Murphy," I said evenly.

"We do have a Michael Murphy here. He is not actually a professor. He teaches Russian language skills three times a week."

"Thank you, that's the gentleman I'm looking for. I'd like to contact him about a translation project. Perhaps you can tell me where and when I could find him."

"He teaches at University College every Monday, Thursday, and Saturday afternoons from four until six o'clock in Room 103. I'm afraid I can't give out his home address."

"No, of course, not," I said, not entirely surprised.

I'd get that from Drake.

I was feeling uneasy and decided to walk back to the club from Fortnum & Mason. It would do me good. I reminded myself I'd been away from this part of my ops life for a while. The streets were crowded, especially as I got closer to Piccadilly and Berkeley Square. In the melee, it was impossible to assess whether I had anyone on me or not.

No one was at the front desk when I got back to the club. Strange to me they didn't have enough staff to cover for Lionel. As I headed back to my room, I realized how much my perspective had changed. When I'd first arrived, all I wanted was a quiet, secluded location, and now, in midafternoon without a soul around, I found the atmosphere unsettling. I quickly pushed my key into its slot and just as quickly closed the door behind me.

The red light flickering on my telephone immediately caught my eye. There was only one message, garbled words and then a quick hang-up. I had no idea who'd tried to call me and no way to find out. Maybe it was a wrong number. I could hope. I checked with the hotel operator, but she was unable to help me. I had way too many unsolved mysteries on my plate already. I'd have to ignore this one for now.

I'd only been back a few minutes and wanted to freshen up before I dashed out again. I heard the flush of a toilet in another room. I wasn't alone after all, which wasn't an entirely comforting thought either. I wondered if that man I'd seen a few times was next door to me and why he was there in the middle of the day.

The developments with Bobbie Grey and Lionel had amped me up. Being in the rear of the building meant I couldn't look out a window onto Berkeley Square and check for my new friends. It was unlikely the couple or the hoodie would be there, but it would have been comforting to have a glimpse from my room to see if there was anyone below worthy of my attention. When it was time to meet with Perlman, I felt oddly reluctant to leave my room. This was not the "me" I was used to.

"Where have you been?" Perlman barked at me, walking toward me down the inner corridor that led to his large corner office. There was almost no one in the office today.

"You couldn't see me until now," I flipped back. I wasn't in the mood for a lecture, especially since I knew he'd ream me out when I told him the mess of activity I'd been involved in since our last talk—and that I'd already briefed Drake.

But I could see he had something on his mind, something he seemed eager to tell me about because he was virtually pushing me into his office. Perhaps that would distract him from getting worked up about my latest ventures.

"I've got some information for you, and after I give it to you, we need to discuss how we move forward with Drake and Garvin. This has gotten very complicated."

Yes, I know that.

"We've gotten back some of our traces and have identified two of your surveillants."

"What? Tell me!" I blurted out. Oh my God, what if they'd found something on my phantasmagoric Elena. Still, no need to mention my middle-of-the-night revelation to the Pear right now. I didn't want him thinking I was losing it.

"They're with the Russian Embassy. Headquarters has cabled with everything Langley has on these two, including past assignments and two rather blurry photos. Apparently, they're an actual couple. Husband is midlevel in logistics, and the wife a secretary or clerk of some sort."

"Right. You mean ops support officers," I said sarcastically.

He gave me their names, which I didn't recognize. I must have let out a breath I didn't realize I was holding.

"Raines, you okay?" he asked, looking at me closely.

I nodded. "Yes, I'm fine. I was hoping I might recognize the names, but I don't. What about the third one?"

"Nothing else, and no known intel affiliation on this twosome," he added.

"Until now," I said. "You'll be pleased to hear that I was able to get some shots of the female using my new CD."

I asked to see the photos from headquarters, but he said I'd have to wait. He had one of his people going over them to look for links in London. Damn.

Now it was my turn to raise his blood pressure. "Chief, there's something else we have to discuss."

His eyebrows rose. I didn't know how he'd react to the news of Lionel's murder. But all he said after hearing me out was, "I'm not happy about the connection to you." His voice sounded uncharacteristically solemn. Obviously, he already knew about Lionel.

"I wish there were *no* connection to me."

"Wish again, my friend. There are no ruby slippers in this game, as you well know."

"I met with Drake at his office this morning." I waited for the Pear's reaction, but to my surprise there was none. He was taking this all in and apparently in no mood to harass me.

"After the meeting with Garvin yesterday, Drake and I spoke privately about the Russian connection. I went to his office this morning and reviewed some of their old files on these defectors. Good thing you verified my clearances."

"And… ?" he prompted.

"I've found a link between the Russian cases—perhaps *the* link," I said, telling him about the connection each had to Department 12.

"Holy … I haven't thought about that group in years. Except for the polonium-210 case, which I concluded was a single poisoning. I'd hoped they'd gotten out of the business of political assassination." I decided not to bring up the Misha Murphy fragment that Sergei had given me. I'd do a little more research on that on my own before raising the Pear's blood pressure even higher.

"We just haven't been looking at that area. We're all friends now, right? Everyone plays nice."

The Pear let out a low whistle. "I never thought that, Raines, but I agree that Russia has slipped down on our targets list," he paused, rubbing his hand on his chin. "I need to think about this. I'll have headquarters review everything we have on these defectors and see if Department 12—or anything like it—surfaces. I'll get back to you. This is a big story."

Now it was time for me to go private. To do something completely on my own. I only hoped the Pear didn't have his own surveillance on me, to make sure I was safe, of course.

CHAPTER 33

LONDON, JUNE 8-9

I recognized Bredon the minute I saw him. I'd forgotten how handsome he was, dark blond hair, built like the classic British SAS intel officer, but in a gray tweed suit and dark, faintly patterned tie, à la MI6. We gave each other a British air kiss greeting and walked into the "wee" pub, as he called it. The inside of the front entry was the shape and size of an old nineteenth-century sailing ship, which Bredon said had been installed by the original owner, an old Navy captain who had been loath to give up his command. We walked up the rickety antique stairs directly into a small bar, all wooden but clearly separate from the ship. There were only a few tables, and but a handful of people inside. A middle-aged woman stood behind the bar, a bit ragged looking but very much in charge. Then I saw Rodolfo peek out from behind her.

"Hello, Rodolfo," I said to her British Blue show cat.

"You've been here?" Bredon said with a surprised look that matched that of the woman behind the bar.

"Long ago," I said. The pub was all but hidden on a tiny street in Shepherd Market, one of the old red-light districts of London, where the Tyburn River once flowed through, all of which made it romantic and quaint to me.

"Then you've met May, the owner?"

I hadn't. A fellow was behind the bar the last time, but I recalled that the owner was a woman, somehow related to the old owner, now long gone.

"Decktora, meet May," said Bredon as May pointed to a table in the corner that was meant to be ours. Bredon had certainly been here before. We ordered drinks, then sped through the chitchat and quickly turned to why I'd called him.

I took a sip of my wine and started talking. I hadn't really told the Alex story to anyone outside the Agency.

"He was involved in a highly sensitive operation," I began.

His face went appropriately solemn as I unfolded the tale. I knew he had clearances, but this was not an approved briefing and I was at the wrong end of the pool. I held back some details but was very blunt about the timing, what I knew of the location, and the probability that one of the men in Alex's cadre was a Brit.

"Probably an SAS officer," Bredon said, adding that he would try to find out if they'd lost anyone in the Syrian war zone. He shared with me that several Brits, not all military, were still in captivity somewhere in that godforsaken region, but he wasn't working that area at present.

"Was he in alias?" he asked quietly.

"I don't know what it was," I responded, upset that I had cut my last call with Alex short and hadn't even tried to pry his operational name out of someone at headquarters. I felt myself starting to tear up as I thought about the hang-up and the little spy routine we had if we couldn't see each other in person before he had to leave. In those cases, Alex always ended our calls with a phrase like, "If James Deering calls, let him know I expect to be back in three weeks." I learned his alias and when he would be back.

But now I was upset with myself all over again. There had been no pre-hang-up message, not this time, and it had ended up being the only one that counted.

"It's okay, Decktora. Let's see what we can figure out without ruining both of our careers," he said, hinting that he might dig a little deeper for me than perhaps he should.

"Bredon, the only shred of information Alex gave me in our last telephone conversation was that he would bring back 'a better rug' than we had got the last time." I didn't want to mention the unpleasant last words I'd had with Alex, or that our very private tradecraft MO re time and location had not taken place, thanks to me. "If I were to surmise anything from it, I would say he was referring to Turkey since that's the only place where we actually bought rugs."

I told him Alex had disappeared in or around Syria, and we agreed to put our heads together to figure out what might have been the locations of tactical interest to both of our governments when Alex was lost. Bredon knew the area well, and I said I'd spent so many hours on it in recent months that I was nearly an expert myself. I gave him what little info I'd gotten from colleagues in Langley. I hoped that he'd worked with Alex enough that he might have insights into this part of Alex's life that I didn't.

Bredon appeared to veer off into his own thoughts.

"If I had to guess, and I mean guess, I'd say he was somewhere in the Idlib area, in northwestern Syria, probably on a capture-or-kill op. Idlib is on the Turkish border and a place we've sent people before, in part because it's well located for us."

"But, President Gul, Prime Minister Erdogan?" I interrupted.

"Erdogan gets Gul to look the other way as often as he needs to. Not one of our best friends, but not eager to make enemies of either of us. Idlib has been something of a safe haven, though it's full of hostile groups who've staked out their own areas, from Syrian rebel factions to the Al-Qaeda affiliate Ahrar al-Sham. In my opinion, the area is likely to go the way of Aleppo, which means it's a place we watch as closely as we can. But Decktora, I can't go too far with you on this. We're getting into highly sensitive territory."

"My clearances are current. Don't you think there's a way they can pass with MI6?" I pushed.

Bredon smiled. We both knew clearances didn't really work that way. They weren't interchangeable. And I doubt I would have moved the envelope for him, but it was worth a try. Any shot at finding Alex was worth a try.

"Let me see what I can do," he said, giving me a shred of hope that there might be some flexibility on the clearance issue.

As we got deeper into the conversation, I was glad I'd spent so much time studying the Syria situation, most of it nightmarish. I'd seen and heard a lot in my profession, but what was going on there was as bad as it gets—beheadings, torture, biological and chemical weapon attacks. Dark. And my Alex was there.

As I'd hoped and suspected, Bredon confirmed to me that he'd been in Syria numerous times and had a good understanding of infiltration areas we'd used. He didn't spell it out, but he was letting me know he understood the region and might have some access there.

It was, for now, the most I could hope for.

As we finished our drinks, Bredon gave me a questioning look and asked why I was in London.

"I assume this is not a vacation, Decky."

I shook my head. "It is sort of a 'business matter' and a bit sensitive at the moment, so let's leave it at that. I'm working with an officer called Jason Drake of MI5."

Aberforth played by the book when it came to the rules of intelligence, and that meant coordinating with Drake. He suspected Decktora Raines would not be surprised at his move, though she'd obviously gone around Drake and her own Chief of Station in London to find him. If Drake confirmed that Raines was indeed in London on a proper mission and working with MI5, he would find a way to help her and hopefully keep them both out of hot water. Damned shame about Alex.

By now, it was the middle of Friday evening. Aberforth called Drake's office number, got a night duty officer, and left a message asking Drake if he could meet early Saturday morning at Thames House. A call back to his cell within the hour from the duty officer confirmed the meeting.

Bredon went directly over to Thames House the next morning, aware that he'd probably upset Drake's weekend. He showed his badge and the guard lifted the phone and then told Aberforth to go to the fourth-floor conference room.

"Bredon, a surprise meeting. Good to see you, I think," he smiled.

"Sorry to interrupt your weekend, Jason, but I have a story to tell you, and then I have a question."

Drake nodded and Bredon proceeded to tell him he'd been contacted by and just met with CIA officer Decktora Raines. He explained his relationship with Alex, that she wanted his help in trying to find him, and had given Drake's name as bona fides.

"She probably didn't think I'd immediately come to you, but I want to know what and whom I'm dealing with here. I've got to say, her news about Alex is distressing. I'd like to help if I can."

"She's legit. That I can tell you, though on some sort of a leave of absence from the Agency. Frankly, I'm surprised she didn't raise this with me. We're working very closely on a highly sensitive operation."

"She went off the books on this, which I concluded from the way she talked and the limited references to anyone in Langley. Jason, I worked with Alex and consider him a friend and an outstanding professional. I came to know Decky only through Alex and a few get-togethers for dinner in London, four of us. I can tell she's suffering, somewhat desperate, much as she tried to hide any emotion."

Drake nodded. "The chief over at Grosvenor Square did tell me that her significant other is missing somewhere in the Middle East. Apparently Langley had warned him she was mightily upset over how they were dealing with the case. He thought this could explain why she took a leave of absence. Still, I'm surprised she gave me no indication she'd try to contact someone else in our service. Did she mention her COS?"

"Not a word."

"So she is indeed doing this alone and hoping you can help her," Drake said, rubbing his chin. "I'm not against your trying, but we're in the midst of a serious operational matter ourselves and I don't want, or need, any problems with the Americans."

"I too was surprised she didn't mention coordinating with our American counterparts," Bredon said, "and I didn't push it, but will if we go forward. She's really out there on her own, trying to solve this without her own headquarters. Not good, but we'll see how it unfolds. The question is how to proceed, given the clearance issues and the way she's handling this. Not to mention the fact that he was working in alias."

"She suggested to me that he was using the alias 'James Deering'," he continued, "but I can't be sure that's the field alias they would have used, more likely a contact name for her with Langley."

"Let me know what you find, if there's anything we have that might be of help," Drake said, "and then we can figure out how to proceed with her and Grosvenor Square."

"I'll keep you in the loop."

Aberforth returned to his office at MI6, ready to dig into recent clandestine activity in and around Syria. Could he get to some of his colleagues covering the region now, he wondered, and find out if the Syrians—or the Russians—were holding any captives? That had to be his first quest.

Truth was he'd enjoyed meeting with the very attractive Decktora Raines, but the news of Alex, his colleague on black ops in the worst war zones of the Middle East, was unsettling. They'd carried out enough dangerous missions together, successful ones, that he was disturbed to learn this man was in trouble.

CHAPTER 34

LONDON, JUNE 8

Alastair Sinclair-Jones was a happy man. His journalistic career was back on the upswing. And now he had a front-page article. He'd been looking for a big story for over two years, and today he had one, all because he'd had the good luck of being on call the night that Lionel Whitestone was killed. The two desperate middle-of-the-night phone calls from the night desk at *The London Hour* went directly to him.

His first report appeared on the top of the page of the early evening edition, far right column. "Grisly Murder of Night Porter at Langsford Club" read the headline. The newspapers were on all the major newsstands in time for the morning commuters.

The macabre murder of a gentleman porter at the Langsford Club was reported by the police early this morning. A couple on a late-night stroll in the quiet neighborhood of Brixton saw the body of Lionel Whitestone in front of his apartment. They walked through Mr. Whitestone's front gate, thinking he had fallen and hit his head. It was immediately clear that he was dead, as there was blood on the ground under his head and a deep mark on his neck. The police arrived within minutes and cordoned off the body, identified the victim, and said they would have to consider the possibility of murder, though adding typically "it was too soon to tell." The police are now questioning neighbors and delivery services that cover the area. They said they have no suspects, nor an identifiable motive, and with that, offered the usual "no further comment."

Sinclair-Jones wanted accuracy in his report, but throwing in a little spice wouldn't hurt, he thought, as he seasoned his article with as much blood, gore, and mystery as he could appropriately include.

The locals told the press they were shocked. They called Mr. Whitestone an ideal neighbor who worked nights and kept to himself. "Who would want to kill that nice man?" one commented. "It's impossible to imagine that gentleman having any enemies," said his elderly female neighbor, who said she was now terrified herself.

The article concluded with the bland information that the police were urging neighbors not to panic, stressing that this was a single incident and the area had no history of criminal activity. They said they would be watching the case until the matter was fully resolved.

While Sinclair-Jones was beginning to gloat, DCI Garvin fumed. He could not interfere with the press, but he could renew his efforts to contain the story, he reminded himself as he perused the latest reports.

He felt his blood pressure rise and his face redden as he read on. He could hear his wife's voice warning him to relax. Garvin knew the tabloids would soon be competing to get the best headlines and the most riveting version of the latest events, but it was Sinclair-Jones who worried him. The man was one of London's most widely read journalists, a ruthless one with contacts in every notable walk of life. His name under a headline guaranteed a big audience.

Today the chief inspector would give the officers involved a reaming for saying so much to the press, especially suggesting that murder was involved, even if it was. Damned if he wouldn't remind them that they should have told any witnesses that they were seriously jeopardizing the police investigation if they talked with the press. It was time for a heavy hand.

And then he would call a brief news conference and give the media a benign overview and an unprovocative comment they could quote.

But by late evening, in the day's final edition, a second article by Sinclair-Jones hit the front page of his newspaper, and this one reported that both Whitestone and Bobbie Grey had been killed by clawing to the jugular vein, and that a mysterious white powder was involved.

Is a serial killer on the loose again in London? Is Jack the Ripper back? What are the Metropolitan Police doing to protect our safety?

The murder of the night porter has become macabre. According to a bystander at the scene of the crime, whose name will remain anonymous, the police said the man appeared to have been clawed to death. But, readers, there was yet another claw killing. At the time, it barely surfaced as a murder. You probably did not even notice the story of poor Robert Johnston, whose body was recently found along the Thames.

London, we have a serial killer on our hands, and all we have from the Metropolitan Polices is this, and I quote Chief Inspector Cransford Garvin: "I am deeply concerned about all the leaks to the media." He urged citizens not to panic, noting that his people were working day and night in pursuit of the murderer or murderers. He said there was no reason to suspect a serial killer despite the seeming coincidence of the markings. Well, if you believe that, dear readers, you are naive. We expect more from our police. I intend to follow this story until we get to the end. I disagree with the good inspector, because I believe we do indeed have a serial killer on the loose in our beloved city. Our newspaper has been flooded with calls from citizens asking for more information about these killings. It is clear a sense of panic is beginning to develop, and we encourage the police to do everything they can in this case. Londoners, we are on your side!

Garvin steamed. He clenched his fists and crushed the tabloid in his hands. Sinclair-Jones had tied the three murders together. He was tempted to call the flamboyant journalist to urge him to lay off until the police could get a handle on these murders, but he knew this man would take anything he could get from Garvin, off the record or not, and write as colorful a story as he could.

No, he wouldn't call him. He was far too angry to trust himself in a one-on-one conversation with the man.

Garvin felt strongly that keeping the media informed was appropriate, but only at the most superficial level, and he would not give out more details until he was absolutely certain what he was dealing with and was near to solving the case. That was the way things had always been done.

Maybe his wife was right. He was getting too old for this business.

CHAPTER 35

LONDON, JUNE 9

I was still in bed when my phone rang early the next morning. It was Drake, calling to report that Garvin was up to his ears in the media headlines and that I had slipped down on the DCI's list of concerns. The good news for Drake and for me was that, as far as the media was concerned, the story was about Robert Johnston, not Ivan Federov. The Russian connection was not yet in the public domain. Still, Drake asked if he could drop by the club later in the morning to give me more details.

I wanted to know everything he had, so, of course, I said yes. I didn't feel the least bit guilty about depriving Garvin of this special knowledge. It was, after all, a national security issue, and it didn't hurt that the city's chief inspector was focused on identifying a "serial killer."

Nigel was at the front desk when I got down to the lobby. He looked and sounded exhausted. When I mentioned that he seemed tired, he nervously told me the police had been in and out of the club all day yesterday, questioning the staff. The Lionel matter was taking a toll on him.

"Don't worry," I said. "They're just making sure to get anything that might help them solve this wretched thing."

"Thank you, Ms. Raines. Oh, there's a message for you. Apparently it was found in Lionel's locker with a few other papers. Don't know why he didn't leave it in the mail slot. He must have been planning to put it there and forgot or else wanted to deliver it to you himself. Hope it's nothing pressing. We try to do our best here." His hand shook slightly as he handed it to me.

Again? A chill raced down my spine. "No problem," I said, trying to appear calm as I opened the envelope and pulled out the plain white sheet.

You have been told to go home. This is the second time you've been asked to leave. Consider this your final warning.

Typed in a plain, widely used format, probably untraceable, no ink or personal markings. My heart was beating so hard Nigel could probably see it. I wasn't too keen myself on getting killed, and at the moment there was no one around who could help me. Why had Lionel been holding the note?

"Nigel, can you tell me who delivered this envelope? I can't make out the signature, and it's an invitation I need to respond to," I lied.

He pulled out the log and checked several pages of delivery items.

"Ah, here it is, ma'am. Appears to have been delivered about five o'clock in the afternoon two days ago. I can't read the signature either, very much a scribble, and Lionel didn't write anything down beside it. I'm afraid that's all I can tell you."

I doubted the sender would have used Yellowfin Bikes again, not after all that had happened, and there was no marking on the envelope.

I had a pretty good idea who'd sent the message, and while decidedly unpleasant, I had a brief good moment of thinking we might be on the verge of pulling down some very nasty people. Hopefully, before anyone else got hurt—including me.

I needed to get this news to Perlman. At this point, I had no desire to go back up to my room. I stepped out into the front of the club and looked around. There were enough people in Berkeley Square that I felt comfortable, so I went across the street and sat down on an empty bench. I pulled out my secure cell and punched the number sign, the emergency connection Grace had given me for her or the Pear.

Perlman himself answered, and on the first ring.

"Thank God, it worked," I said, referring to my high-tech phone.

"Of course, it did. What's going on?"

I told him the contents of the note and that it was found in Lionel's locker. He said he didn't know what to make of it but was worried, specifically about me, which was not reassuring.

"Decky, you're not alone. We've got somebody watching you."

"What?"

"He's been near you at the Langsford since the night you arrived. I didn't tell you because I knew you'd resist, but when you briefed me about your reason for being here, your plans with Sergei, we had to put someone on you. No way you were going to handle this all on your own. It was impossible to assess the danger with what you gave me. So you have a neighbor."

Now I knew who the man in the hallway was, the man I had seen off and on since I'd arrived at the club. Perlman, and presumably Drake as well, had worked fast.

"Really! So what's the deal? Where is he?" I was a solid mix of angry and relieved, not to mention concerned about my unauthorized contact with Bredon Aberforth. "Is he staying on my floor?"

"You might start with 'thank you'," he said. Today's Perlman was getting under my skin. "He's right next door."

Ah, well, one problem was now solved. My mysterious neighbor was not the enemy. Perlman was right. I would have made a fuss if he'd said he was putting someone on me, though now I was glad he had. But I didn't see myself thanking him. I wasn't used to being second-guessed, or should I say one-upped?

It was cool and slightly foggy, the sun barely peeking out from behind the clouds. I just stayed put on the bench, my brain hashing over everything I knew about Lionel. It was still hard to accept that he was dead, and the thought that I was responsible wouldn't go away. I recalled briefly mentioning the content of the first message to him when I got it and sensing his obvious concern. I'd been so taken aback by the message that the words had just slipped out of my mouth.

Did he get too close to something, see something or someone he should not have?

Drake arrived at eleven o'clock. We went inside and directly into the dining room to a corner table, my usual habit. I told him about the message Nigel had just given me. He in turn apologized for not advising me about my tail, which Perlman had coordinated with him, but said it was now more important than ever.

"I've got some good news for you, Decky, not that anything in this whole matter qualifies as good news." He paused and straightened his shoulders as if about to make a major announcement. "I was able to get the background on your Michael D. Murphy, formerly Mikhail Marenovsky, nickname 'Misha'."

I leaned in closer to him, my heart racing.

"We discovered that our Misha has a middle name, D for 'Decius'. So, of course, I knew immediately he was one of ours. Better yet, he worked for Department 12, and that's the *only* reason he got defector status. Apparently, he was a midlevel techie and occasional communications operator, never a full-fledged ops officer, but overall, he had access to highly sensitive information. He knew the players in the supervisory chain in Kamera and was aware of some of the department's darkest projects. The few documents I've been able to review described him as 'quiet and introverted', the kind of person who fit that unit in terms of temperament. Further, he was in the assignment for a full two years before they rewarded him with a softer position at Yasenevo."

Drake pulled a notepad out of his vest with illegible-looking handwritten. His, presumably. On the top was a copy of a passport photo of Murphy, taken some years ago, but enough to give me an idea of his appearance. The address showed him in Oxford.

I glanced at the passport, noting the address, easy for me to record in my brain.

"Guess who the senior manager was when he was there?"

"It can't be."

"It can be, and it was. Ivanchukov."

"Oh, my God," I almost shouted, then quickly dropped my voice. Drake smiled, then nodded.

We mulled over the facts we had. Drake had orders out to retrieve all the retired files, which he expected to have in his hands within twenty-four hours. His next step, with Brewster's assistance, would be to review Marenovsky's history meticulously, along with whatever intel he had provided as part of his defection agreement. In so doing, Drake hoped to learn more about Kamera and Ivanchukov's tenure there.

I knew what my next step had to be.

With the fragments of info I now had on Murphy, I went back to my room and started researching Oxford and the college where he was teaching. I was able to check an online map for the proximity of his residence to the train station.

I knew it wasn't a great idea to head off to Oxford without telling anyone, much less alone, but the more I thought about it, the more determined I became to go. I would have an eye out for my neighbor, who hopefully would not tail me, but if so, fine. I was a tourist in England, after all, and deserved a few hours of vacation in historic, beautiful Oxford. Plus, with my now tested cell, I could get to Perlman instantly if I needed to.

An exploratory trip, I told myself, and if I found Misha, maybe I could figure out the direction the Russians were taking. Waiting for more information out of a bureaucracy, even MI5 under Drake's orders, always has delays in spite of his quick response on Misha.

As always, I had Sergei on my mind. I still didn't know exactly where he fit into what was unfolding. I was certain the Russians had him in their sights, but had no idea how close they were to doing him harm. I wanted to find out if Perlman's people had picked up any information from their surveillance of him, which I prayed was well in place, as the COS had promised.

The trouble was, we had no reporting assets inside Ivanchukov's camp, and I didn't see any golden opportunity for recruiting anyone therein. Would the Russians move when the opportunity was right? If so, what and when was "right"? I had no idea, but it had to be soon.

CHAPTER 36

Stanley Brewster sat alone in the windowless cave that was his office. Saturday was just another workday for him. It had the look of an over-worked professor's lair, full of books and papers, a general mess. He'd begun to start plowing through the pile of old documents and newspapers he'd pulled for Drake. His Russian was good enough that he could skim for key words, and it helped that he knew what he was looking for. Now he just had to find it. The few claw references he spotted in the open source material were stories of animal attacks. Keep digging, he told himself, his way of thinking so analytical and academic that he was not easily discouraged by the slow process. He was looking for the proverbial needle in a haystack.

Hours later, his third cup of Twining's cooling down, a tattered document caught his eye. Small bits of the pages were missing, but he could see enough to spot the words "claw" and "murder." His Russian–English dictionary beside him, he dug into to this specific document, knowing he had a complex read ahead of him.

It described the arrest in the 1990s of a Belorussian girl who had been apprehended in connection with a chilling set of murders. As he pieced the pages together, he saw the name "Olga," followed by the letter "F," the rest of the name a small hole in the page. Because of the bloody claw marks on the necks of the victim, it was initially thought that a wild animal had been responsible. Of the incidents reported, all but one resulted in death. The last attempt, the one that proved a human was involved, failed, and the victim survived long enough to finger his killer. In police custody, the girl confessed to the other three killings and the attempt on the fourth victim.

They were called the "Claw Murders" when the story came out, but, as was typical of Soviet media at that time, the details were limited. The perpetrator was described as a very young woman, viewed by the head of her school as brilliant, but withdrawn and with a spotty attendance record. The police took it a bit further, calling her "insane" and "criminal in her actions." Because of her gender and age, Brewster assumed she had been sent to a state mental institution, a sure road to nonexistence in that society.

He worked his way through the rest of the documents he'd found, but there was no further mention of this girl. He would go over those pages again and see if he could do a better job of piecing the tidbits together. It was always good to review key documents more than once. He sat back in his chair and closed his eyes, willing his mind to relax. He could find what Drake wanted, he just needed to breathe in deeply and take his time.

When it came to him, he bolted upright in his chair. There it was.

Brewster dashed up to Drake's office.

He announced to Drake and Evelyn what he had uncovered and then pointed at the Blue Book, the diplomatic list, in Drake's office.

"We need to find out if there is anyone with the name "Olga F," or "Olga," working in Ivanchukov's group. If not Ivanchukov, I'll go through the whole blasted Russian Embassy list to see if there is an "Olga F," Brewster said.

Drake went into his office and picked the Blue Book up off his desk. He hadn't touched the dip book this much in a very long time. He opened it to the Russian section, pulling his finger down over the long, complex names. Suddenly his eyes widened.

"My God. Could it be the same woman?"

"Yes, indeed," Brewster said, looking at the name with him, his smile turning into a broad grin.

Evelyn clapped her hands together, and the three looked at each other as if they'd just won the National Lottery.

"Brewster, I want any background you can find on Ivanchukov and Olga before this assignment, and photos, any photos. We need to figure out exactly who is on his team, and I know they won't be listed in a neat package directly under his name. We'll have to dig."

CHAPTER 37

OXFORD, JUNE 9

Misha Murphy loved Oxford and his adopted Anglo-Saxon surname. He especially liked teaching the class in advanced Russian. He had the best students, all in international studies, the serious ones, who would go on for postgraduate work. His course gave him a chance to speak his native language and to carry on full conversations, since they were all at the fluency level required for an advanced degree. To top it off, he felt respected in his new position, something he had not experienced in his past life.

He was at heart a techie, but his Russian background had landed him the job at Oxford. His students thought he was a white Russian, an émigré descendant of one of the old aristocratic families who had managed to escape Russia when the Bolsheviks were rampaging in 1917. That image suited him just fine.

But Misha no longer felt completely secure in his new life. It was after the poisoning of this Litvinenko fellow that the worries began. When he first heard the news, then saw the gruesome photographs of the man dying in his hospital bed, he knew who'd done it, and from the appearance of the man as he declined, how. Misha had, after all, once worked in the poisons laboratory, which was most certainly the source of the toxin used against Litvinenko. No one was ever apprehended, and the Brits had averted their eyes.

The Russians were back in the business of eliminating the enemy using poison. Misha knew plenty about this work. Low level as he was when he worked at Kamera, he had been an observer, and as a tech, had been called to many parts of the lab when his services were needed. As he put the pieces together in his mind, a chill set in, an unrelenting edginess. Did he know too much? His students had begun to notice the change and asked him about it, not mentioning that they saw him at the pub more often than in the past.

Misha had been using his original first name, Mikhail, and had told some of his students that he had "another name," much like this one but a little different, more Russian. He thought he might be a little more cautious about that in the future.

Misha liked two things—computers...and men.

By the time he defected in Prague in the late 1990s, he was fed up with the Russian way of life, even with the post–Cold War changes. He'd never really gotten over the arrest of his father. On a bleak, ferociously frigid winter night when Misha was only ten, the police knocked on the door of the family apartment in Yaroslavl, not far from Moscow. He woke up when he heard adults arguing in the main room, but he quickly fell back to sleep as only the young can do. When he arose the next morning, his father was gone. That was all there was to it. He never saw him again. Perhaps his mother intended to talk about the tragedy one day, but she never did and was herself dead by the time he was sixteen.

Misha was unschooled in politics, something of a country boy with a fascination for computers. When he moved to Moscow and got his first government job, it was as a computer operator. In his midtwenties at the time, he was one of the few knowledgeable employees in the emerging field of digital technology. It was the GRU that had snatched him up, a fact he didn't know initially. He became a popular figure, in the sense that seniors increasingly relied on him, on and off the record, to fix any problems that involved technology. One result of this was that he began to travel overseas, mostly to conferences, always accompanying higher-ups who needed his expertise. His quiet nature helped, and his travels became extensive.

It was at a British-run scientific conference in Kuala Lumpur that he met a Brit about his age, Nathan Edwards; a young academic who claimed to be studying international relations at Oxford. Nathan was handsome, dark-haired and muscular, and though Misha had never been open about his homosexuality, Nathan was a temptation—a big one. But Nathan was in fact an MI6 operative officer with a reputation for spotting and recruiting hard targets. Misha had drawn his attention because of his tech skills and who he was traveling with. MI6 intel officers always needed help on technology, and Nathan knew the Russians were no different. All these old guys, the ones in senior positions, were the same. They couldn't do anything on their own, digitally.

So Nathan courted Misha, pursued him but always put off the final act, while making sure he was invited to the same semiannual academic conference, where they could, as he put it, "continue their relationship." Misha's unfulfilled crush on Nathan had grown into a kind of longing. In the third year, after meeting five times, Nathan told Misha he wanted him to join him in England. He promised the opportunity of a lifetime, a teaching job at Oxford, along with himself, of course.

Initially shocked by the invitation, Misha insisted he couldn't accept—the repercussions in Russia would be too severe, too dangerous. But Nathan didn't give up on the offer, and the more they talked, the more the vulnerable Misha took to the idea, despite his fears. He increasingly thought back to how his father had been treated. He had no loyalty to the government that had killed his father.

When he got to the semiannual in Prague, Misha was excited to see Nathan and readier than he had ever thought possible to accept the offer, if it was still on the table. Was it change, resentment, his lack of personal ties—or Nathan? All Misha knew was that his will had weakened and his outlook had changed.

Nathan patiently observed that transition, watched the ripening of his target. It was time to make his pitch. On the last day of the conference, he told Misha to meet him for dinner with a couple of others from the group at the small Papi Oliver restaurant in downtown Prague. Whatever initial resistance there had been, after the dinner Misha left for England hidden in the trunk of a car driven by Nathan.

He never returned to his hotel. His colleagues looked for him at departure time the next morning, but by then he was in Dover, England, with Nathan, whom he soon learned was not a potential romantic partner. At first he was hurt when Nathan revealed the truth about his sexuality and his job, but it was too late. But Misha now had Oxford in his sights. Being admired, taken seriously, would be another kind of reward.

After his debriefings, for security reasons he was initially sent to Liverpool to live, but once the Cold War was well over, the Brits decided it would be safe for him to move to Oxford, under his new identity, of course. In this, Nathan kept his initial promise to Misha.

"Anyone for a lager at the KA?" asked Misha, smiling, pleased that he had adjusted so well to his life in Oxford that he could call the popular pub, the King's Arms, by its colloquial name.

"Sorry, sir, but it's the end of the term. We have to study. You remember those days, don't you?" said one of his students, speaking for all of them. The small group nodded in agreement.

Misha had gotten used to pub outings with the students, but he knew these young academics were too serious to join him for their usual after-class drink this late in the term. He decided to grab a lager at the King's Arms anyway. He didn't need the company, and he enjoyed people-watching. It would be an early night. He was tired, and it looked as if rain was coming on this cool and breezy night.

Until Oxford, Misha had met few real foreigners. Only at the international conferences had he had that exposure in the past, but when at home in Moscow, opportunities had been limited, especially in his sensitive job. Now he was teaching young people from all over the world. He was finally contented, after so many trials, and even had comfortable, if infrequent, relationships with those of his sexual orientation. His English was excellent now, only slightly accented, and he even used British words with confidence. Look how easily "ale" fell off his lips and how well he had settled into the academic world of Oxford, he thought confidently. As he sipped his drink, he mused, life could not get much better.

He finished a second ale, then left the pub, and started his well-worn trek home. He meandered down Mansfield Road, onto Holywell Street to Broad Street. He wasn't really in a hurry. A mass of gray clouds crossed the half moon, darkening the sky. The absence of light didn't bother him. He knew the winding streets so well that his mind was able to wander into daydreams of the brilliant academics who had walked these same paths over the centuries. Oxford was like Moscow in that way, but much more charming—and benign.

Fifteen minutes into his walk, Misha reached Mill Street, where he turned left and headed toward his comfortable little row house. He didn't even mind passing by Osney Cemetery. It was large, gray, and mystical, he thought, not scary, though he reminded himself that most people would find it so. He could feel the leaves dancing in the breezy sky.

Moscow seemed so far away and so long ago. Maybe he would be able to visit again one day, now that the world had changed. He might even teach a course there in global realignments since the fall of the USSR. Wouldn't that be a nice new chapter in his life?

The thickness of the stones beneath him told Misha he was getting close to home. He wished he'd set up a timer for the light in his living room, so it would look inviting when he returned home alone. He should do that. The small attached house had been chosen for him by Nathan. It was perfect, in a quiet neighborhood, old, and very private. Nathan had treated him well.

As he got near the front door, Misha reached inside his vest, an Oxford affectation for him, pulled out his key, and walked through his front gate. The slightest crack of a branch caught his attention. He looked behind him. No one there.

Of course, not.

He turned the heavy bronze key in the slot, pulled it out and opened the door.

It happened so quickly that Misha felt little pain. Someone shoved him inside his apartment and pushed something into his neck. He slumped to the ground, grabbing his throat. He felt a sharp pain. What was it?

He would never know. Misha was dead within two minutes, his body lying in the small foyer of his house.

CHAPTER 38

I taxied over to Paddington Station and bought a ticket for the four o'clock train, which would get me to Oxford in about an hour and a half, enough time for me to find Murphy's classroom and hopefully the man himself.

I'd thought over what I would say to him, what I wanted to elicit. I'd done this so many times in the past I was confident I could draw him out, if I could actually get in direct contact with him.

As the train sped beyond London, I looked out at the beautiful countryside, rich and vibrant looking, and hardly a telephone wire in sight. Such a small country, and yet within minutes of London, I was traveling through lush green fields and pastures full of aged trees and flowing streams. No, Decky, you're not on a vacation, I reminded myself.

An hour into the trip, the train lurched to a stop. Everyone looked nervously around to figure out what was going on. Then a voice came over the loudspeaker to announce there'd been a major accident on the M40 with a car smashup that pushed one car onto the railroad tracks. They didn't know how long it would be before the train could proceed but insisted the police were on top of the situation and moving fast.

209

Damn. Holy damn. This was all I needed. I was on a schedule with very little wiggle room. I looked at the GPS on my cell phone to check again where Misha's house was vis-à-vis the train station. I'd expected to find him at University College near Carfax Tower, an area I knew fairly well from the past and one that I could easily get to. My goal was to locate him before he left the university. I had no idea what his schedule would be after that.

It was more than an hour before the conductor announced that they were proceeding. After reading through the whole newspaper, I turned to the crossword puzzle, keeping myself as distracted as possible from the latest screwup in my plans. The train finally pulled into Oxford Station at almost seven o'clock. I quickly disembarked and decided to head directly over to University College, hoping Murphy might still be there talking to students.

When I got there, a few students were mingling and chatting in front of the entrance to the classroom, but there was no sign of Murphy. Now I had no choice but to find his home and hope he was there. Not my preferred plan, but I was in Oxford and all I needed was to get Misha alone for a few minutes.

It took me at least fifteen minutes to find a taxi, which I had drop me off about a quarter mile from Mill Street. I intended to walk part of the way since I didn't want to arrive in a taxi and catch the eye of anyone in the neighborhood. I sure as hell hoped he would be home, as I had no intention at the moment of spending the night in Oxford.

My map showed the few turns that would get me to the house. I walked past an old cemetery, which gave me a creepy feeling, but I told myself it was atmospheric, especially considering my mission. Misha's place was small and tightly wedged between two larger houses, all of which had an aged Oxford look, crooked windows, and slightly slanted roofs with small chimney stacks. No light. Damn. I refused to entertain the possibility that he wasn't inside. I opened the gate and walked to the front door, tapped on it, waited a minute, and then tried again. Nothing.

"Mr. Murphy?" I called, as I rapped on the door a little harder.

It opened under my touch, just slightly.

"Misha," I said, lightly nudging open the door, which I now realized was not securely closed.

I pushed it wider cautiously, repeating his name.

There was a dim light, probably in the back of the living room, which I hadn't noticed from the street, enough that I could make out a rug and desk inside. I prodded the door further.

And then I saw Misha Murphy. His body lay inside the entry-way, not far from the front door, a small trickle of something shiny and moist looking beneath his neck. It didn't take much for me to realize this was blood, but I wasn't about to touch anything.

I resisted the immediate urge to run, pulled out my cell, and took three quick photos. Then I turned and fled, having no idea if the killer was still there or nearby. I wasn't afraid as much as unequipped to handle whoever might be lurking in the house. On a busy block, I checked my map and headed to the train station. As soon as I saw a small cluster of people and the station directly in sight, I punched the number sign on my phone. Grace answered immediately, but I wanted the Pear this time, and he was in a not-to-be-interrupted meeting in the SCIF, the station's Sensitive Compartmented Information Facility, for at least another half hour. So much for my "direct access" phone. I hung up and dialed Drake's number.

"Thank God," he answered. "Decktora, I can't believe you went there," he said when I told him where I was.

"No sense in getting upset with me, but I need to make sure I'm reporting this in proper channels ASAP. You can get Garvin more quickly than I, so please do," I said, telling Drake the details of my Oxford venture.

"You're in the bad spot of leaving the scene of a crime."

"I know, but there's no way I can be seen here. I didn't touch anything except the front door, and I left it exactly as I found it. Garvin will just have to deal with it. If I hadn't appeared, Murphy would probably not have been found until tomorrow or later. There's no way I'm going to stay around for the Oxford Police and a repeat of the Yellowfin episode."

"Not good, my friend. What did you tell Perlman?"

"Couldn't get him, so called you. By the way, I don't see my tail. Did he take the night off?" I realized I sounded sarcastic, but where was the damned fellow when I needed him?

"He's at the Langsford. He wasn't set up to follow you to the train station and then Oxford. Frankly, I wouldn't have suspected that action from you." He sighed. "We really should sit down and talk. *Before* you get yourself killed, that is."

Okay, Drake wasn't pleased. I'd have to deal with that later, along with Perlman. I cringed thinking about Garvin. He did, after all, have my passport. I felt the pinch in my head, right behind the eyes.

All I wanted now was to get on the train and back to London.

CHAPTER 39

OXFORD AND LONDON, JUNE 9

Olga had felt Marenovsky's pulse. He was dead. K/4 had been eliminated. Now she would turn at last to Dumanovskiy, K/1, the prize. She knew Ivanchukov would be ready.

She'd crept out of Misha's cottage and tried to secure the front door as she left, but it stuck. Too bad, she'd thought, rushing from the scene as quickly as possible.

She was grateful for the overhang of the heavy, ancient trees and the gray sky surrounding her. There was no reason to think anyone had seen her, but it was always good to be out of sight. She knew exactly where she was and had already plotted out the walk back to the train station. This was an easy one, she thought, a smile creeping across her face as she considered how skilled she'd become at her art and what an excellent choice she'd made in combining Star of Bethlehem with curare. Who would ever unlock that combination?

Olga had learned the hard way that the slightest movement by the victim could cause the claw to bypass the jugular. She had rarely missed in all these years—when she was young and vengeful, she'd used only the claw, no toxins. Unfortunately, for her, the victim survived, and she'd ended up in prison. But it was there that she met Ivanchukov, who changed her life. So it had all worked out for the good.

Strange how unemotional, even guiltless, she felt after each of the assignments. And yet, for Ivanchukov she had feelings—fear, loyalty, and something close to adoration. Not love, but, yes, a strange and secure kind of commitment. She knew he would protect her. And she understood now that he needed her. It was a good relationship. It was her only relationship.

After all these years, she was developing a slightly messianic sense of herself, correcting the ills of those who had worked against her, and against her country. She wasn't religious, not at all, but she liked the ring of moral authority that her special formula and weapon gave her as she eliminated the treasonous Kameras, one by one.

Near the train station, Olga stopped at a Pret a Manger and headed directly into the restroom and double-locked the door. She pulled out the claw and sterilized it with a small container of drugstore antiseptic gel. Once home in London, she would go over it again with her special fluids. For now, she slid it into its feathery casing and pinned the brooch back on her jacket. She removed the cheap rubber gloves she was wearing, folded them inside out, and tucked them in her bra until she could dispense of them. There would be no evidence of her at the crime scene, no DNA, no litter, nothing.

Olga went out of the loo and bought a sandwich, ham with heavy mustard, something to eat on the train. She allowed herself to be a little messy since she wanted the mustard to drip into the sandwich bag. She would have a use for it later.

Fortunately, the station was quiet, only a few people there waiting for the train, in part because she had just missed a train and rush hour was over. She saw no one of interest. Several chatty students and an elderly couple, all wrapped up in their own conversations. It was always better to have a little human traffic around. A woman alone at a train station at night was a tad too noticeable. But she wasn't alone, so now she would sit calmly and wait.

It had been a successful night.

The train was late. Olga secreted herself in a corner and took out an old newspaper. She didn't like waiting but was glad to see more and more people coming into the station. She hoped to grab one of those single seats on the train at the entrance to the car. As was her way, she watched everyone.

Then she saw someone she had not expected. Keeping her head low, Olga nonetheless got a good look at the face. The woman was wearing the same coat and wrap as the person she'd surveilled with Dumanovskiy in St. James's. Her clandestine photos hadn't come out well enough to identify the face, but it seemed so obvious now. This had to be Decktora Raines, the CIA woman, the Sergei connection. What the hell? Why hadn't she put it together sooner? She felt herself gasp and lowered her head to make herself less noticeable.

Elena Radzimova's life had not unfolded as Decktora Raines had thought. Elena didn't even exist. Never had.

She had indeed departed Tallinn suddenly all those years ago, but she had not been arrested, much less executed. In fact, she went home to a promotion. Elena had targeted the American CIA officer just as she knew the American was targeting her. It was all part of a carefully planned operation by Ivanchukov and the chief of the rezidentura in the Estonian capital, with whom she had pretended to be having a love affair. Ivanchukov insisted she take the assignment, which meant temporarily disconnecting from him.

"You must learn, Olga. You have to have the training before we can move to the next stage."

"But aren't you coming?" She rarely felt this kind of dependence, but it was a reminder to both of them how important he was to her, which was exactly what he wanted.

"It will only be for a few months, and we have a target for you to work, a female. Her name is Carolyn Shaw, a first-tour officer in the American Embassy. That puts you on equal footing, and common social interests will bring you together. There aren't many female spies in the American service, so this will give you a chance to hone your skills. The Rezident in Tallinn will give you tidbits of disinformation to feed to her, and then, after you've developed a relationship with her, you will disappear quite suddenly. This will alarm her and present problems for her and her office."

Elena had learned a lot on that assignment, even enjoyed Tallinn, but she was happy when it was over and she could go home, now to a special job with her mentor, who was moving into Department 12.

She was glad to be Olga again. Elena Radzimova had gone back to her real self, just as Carolyn Shaw had returned to her own identity, Decktora Raines.

She watched Raines holding her phone tight to her ear, talking in a low voice and looking very serious. Carolyn Shaw had barely changed after all these years. And now she was in Oxford. There could be only one explanation.

Like Raines, Olga did not believe in coincidence. Maybe she had found a dead man. Well, what if she had? Just another serial killing. Still, Olga was shaken. Deeply shaken. She had not anticipated seeing Shaw. Ever again. Now she had to get back to her apartment, clean up, gather her thoughts. She would make no move against this woman, but would report to Ivanchukov immediately.

Fortunately, for Olga, Raines was focused on a phone conversation and probably never saw her. When the train arrived, Olga watched where Raines entered and went back two additional cars to make sure there was little chance of an encounter. When she disembarked in London nearly two hours later, there was no sign of Raines. Olga went into the restroom and lingered some fifteen minutes, hoping Raines would have exited the station long before. She had no reason to think her enemy had spotted her. Then Olga walked rapidly out of the station and headed in the direction of her apartment. A few blocks along, she paused to fold her sandwich bag tightly, allowing the mustard to spread a bit. Then she reached into her bra and pulled out the rubber gloves, opened the bag, and pushed them inside the sandwich bag. She massaged it as she refolded it, careful not to break it or create any holes. A few blocks later, on a busy street, she stuffed the bag into a corner bin.

The evidence was gone. There was no way the police would find that tiny, messy package, she was sure of that. And even if she was being followed, a possibility she now had to consider, who would open a discarded, pungent sandwich bag?

It was late when Olga got home. She opened the door to her small, sterile apartment and looked around, as she always did, before walking all the way in. The shades were still closed from the morning.

After she washed and stored the *Celem*, she headed for the shower, eager to cleanse herself of the detritus of the day. She turned the hot water on to create as much steam as possible, and as the water fell over her, she meditated on the day's events. Dismissing Raines from her thoughts for now, she started to feel a sense of excitement. All the newspapers were talking about the claw murders. Tomorrow it would be even better. To think, she was the "serial killer in London."

CHAPTER 40

It was midmorning when Alastair Sinclair-Jones got the call in his office at *The London Hour* that one Misha Murphy had been killed the previous night in Oxford and that he may have been clawed to death.

Sinclair-Jones had all the phone numbers he needed already filed, waiting for the perfect moment. Within an hour, he had a quote from the Oxford police, two of Murphy's students, and the next-door neighbor, an insomniac who said he thought he had seen Murphy come up his walkway midevening and might even have caught sight of the killer. In spite of Sinclair-Jones's pushy question, the neighbor said he couldn't expand. The police had asked him not to.

All this would make a major news story, but Sinclair-Jones needed more to make it a great one. He decided to head to Oxford and track down some of those sources himself. The neighbor would be a little skittish, but Sinclair-Jones could be very persuasive. He was a fast writer, and though he needed time to get to Oxford, he figured he would be the first major journalist to report the latest murder. Incredible, he thought, now the serial killer had moved beyond London. Oxford couldn't possibly have seen anything like it in years.

The story out of Oxford was not entirely what he had expected. It was not a well-kept secret that this Misha Murphy was in fact a Russian émigré. Though his profile was unlike those of the previous victims, Robert Johnston, Bobbie Grey, and Lionel Whitestone, the method of killing was the same, a claw to the jugular. Sinclair-Jones's intuition told him the Oxford hit was not a copycat. There was something else, something important that the police either weren't getting or weren't divulging.

As he dug more deeply into the story, he became fascinated with Misha's background. Why was he in the UK? Why did he leave Russia?

The students told him what they knew, but they also said they'd often wondered the same about Misha. Maybe he had been a really important Russian. Maybe he had left under desperate circumstances. Murphy was such a common name, and they suspected he'd changed it for good reason.

Yes, this was something bigger than another Jack the Ripper. Sinclair-Jones had covered too many international dramas to see the murders in such a small way. He'd even written about the murder of that Litvinenko fellow and the suicide of the victim's mentor, Berezovsky.

Was it possible the current story involved the Russians? If so, he would have to tread carefully. He didn't want them on his back, but he intended to dig deeper, and he would publish the story tonight before anyone else could get on it.

If he was right, he could well be up for Foreign Affairs Journalist of the Year.

CHAPTER 41

LONDON, JUNE 10

Perlman was furious when I told him about my trip to Oxford and Marenovsky's murder. I let him lecture me for fifteen minutes and winced at some of the names he called me, though I didn't really blame him.

He had a CIA officer on his turf, and now she'd stepped into a murder scene, without his or headquarters' knowledge or approval. I'd created a mess for him, but I didn't regret going to Oxford. If that blasted train hadn't been delayed, I might have caught Murphy at the university, and maybe he wouldn't be dead. On top of that, now I would never learn what Marenovsky could tell me about Kamera, about Ivanchukov.

Sergei remained my biggest worry. I couldn't figure out why the Russians hadn't yet moved on him. The only reason that came to mind was that they were setting the stage, and that scared me. With my arrival in London, the murders seemed to have shifted to people who had had some contact with me. There'd been only one meeting between Olga and Sergei at Antiquarian before I was called to London, but nothing since then. Why? The rezidentura was waiting for something and we had no agents inside to tell us what that was.

Perlman and I hashed the whole business over once again. We even discussed the Cornwall murder, which had gotten so little attention that it hadn't added to public anxiety, but nonetheless had the pattern we'd now identified. We added this case to Ivanchukov's portfolio, concluding that it was probably the first murder the team had carried out in England, perhaps even a test case to see what would get into the media.

Our summary was persuasive. What we knew and agreed on was that the Russian rezidentura in London was directly involved in the claw murders, that they were using nonradioactive poisons, and that there was a "high probability," as we call it, that all of this was linked to the Russians' poison laboratory—and to the Kremlin.

It was time to move, time to create a plan of action against the rezidentura. Perlman agreed and, with that, picked up his secure phone to call Drake.

"We're on for tomorrow at 0900, MI5 headquarters. The three of us and Drake's assistants," he said as he hung up the phone.

And Garvin? He would have to be brought in, since we were about to run an operation that would cut into the business and purview of the Metropolitan Police, who were, after all, working on the murders themselves. Giving Garvin the facts—and the real identities of the Russians who had been killed—would be up to Drake. I wondered how Garvin would react when he learned the truth, which he had not yet been told because of the significant classified details involved. He was about to get a major shock about the true nature of these crimes. Hopefully, he would understand that until now he'd not met the requisite "need to know" level. I didn't envy Drake.

"Are you and I are done for today? I hope so because you're exhausting me," Perlman said, not smiling.

Likewise, I thought.

I needed a break. I headed back to the Langsford and into the main lounge where I sat down and ordered tea. From my corner table, I could see a few couples scattered about, nobody of interest to me. I had so much on my mind that I didn't even pick up a newspaper, as I compulsively do. I watched some of the Horse Guards go by, but mostly just stared off into space and sipped on my tea. I don't even remember what kind they served me.

When I got back to my room, I saw the red flashing light on the phone and called in for the message. It was from Bredon, wanting to know if we "might meet for a drink at our favorite place around six o'clock?"

My heart raced as I dialed his phone, which thankfully he answered.

"Are we on?" he asked without a pause, and several hours later I was once again saying hello to Rodolfo, sitting on a bar stool waiting for Bredon, and pleased we were meeting in this discreet little pub. I was comfortably early and had a glass of white wine in my hand when he arrived.

We sat at the same corner table—repetition did not seem a security concern in this tiny place with this well-trained man. We took a shortcut directly to the purpose of our rendezvous.

"Decky, you need to know that you have stepped into a very clandestine operation, a true black op, and I am limited in what I can say to you," he said in a near whisper.

"I suspected it was black, and, of course, I respect how compartmented those ops are, but--"

"Let me start with one thing I can tell you," he interrupted. "I think we may have some news about Alex and his unit, but it is just a fragment at the moment, and it is not bad news."

I nearly leaped out of my seat, but said nothing, clenching my hands and waiting for him to fill me in.

"A British SAS officer working in southern Turkey has been following developments in northern Idlib and just reported that the Russian-backed Syrian forces were holding three "hostiles," all of whom spoke English. He said one of them had been injured and was moved to a hospital in the area, which could be in Ma`arat al-Nu`man, a city close enough to Turkey that we may have some access."

I didn't know whether to scream or cry, and I had no idea whether this was really good news or bad.

"Do you have any descriptions, any details?"

"Stop, Decky. I know your questions, so let me go on. We're updating Langley on the SAS report, and asking if this region is where they sent Alex and the other American. We know the identity of the Brit, of course, and have the technical capability to keep track of his movements. I understand you don't want Langley to know you've contacted me, but there's no choice at this point. They've gotten active on this again, even redirected some enhanced satellites over the region we identified. We need to learn the location of their mission and what aliases and disguises they were using."

"I understand, but are they alive? I have to know that."

"We have little HUMINT, few human assets on the ground there, so we rely heavily on reporting from this particular officer. As soon as Langley gets our update and fills us in on their latest, we'll coordinate and move to the next phase. I wish I could tell you more, but I can't, and I felt you deserved to know this much. Decky, there is hope, there is definitely hope. And if Alex is there, we will find a way to get him."

I lowered my head as tears came to my eyes. I didn't want Bredon to see me get emotional. I could usually control myself, but I was stunned by what he had just told me.

"I'm grateful to you, Bredon, I really am, and I know this is all you can say. I suspect you will also have to tell Grosvenor Square."

"I will, but I'm telling you first, so you can be prepared. I promise I'll give you what I can when I can, but I'm confident you do not have to start wearing a black mourning dress." With a cheeky wink, he added, "Maybe a white bridal dress instead?"

I drew in my breath at what I can only call relief. He was so affirmative that I suspected he knew a little more than he was telling me.

I hugged him as we parted. Yes, I was grateful. I was also terrified. There were no good questions racing through my mind. But there was a chance Alex was alive. It was the most I could hope for at the moment, more than I'd been able to hope for in all the time since he'd disappeared.

CHAPTER 42

LONDON, JUNE 11

When the Pear and I got to MI5 the next morning, we were directed to Drake's office. As we walked down the long hallway, Perlman gave me a knowing look.

"I've spoken with Bredon Aberforth," he announced.

I just kept on walking and looking ahead.

"I'm not happy that you went outside of channels, but I understand, and we are going to do everything we can to get to the bottom of this."

His response was more concerned and respectful than I would have anticipated in my wildest thoughts. He was indeed a complex man, not totally bad after all, but I had nothing to say at the moment.

"You look very tired, and I guess that you haven't slept well."

"Maybe fifteen minutes," I said, a faint but emotionless smile on my face.

"I see. Well, we have another mission and it's going to need your total concentration. Are you in?"

"Of course, I am. Who do you think started all this?" And I meant it. I had to keep my focus on Sergei. There was nothing I could do about the other matter. Nothing.

225

Drake was waiting for us in his office, smokeless pipe in hand, Evelyn and Brewster in attendance. He started the meeting by announcing that he now *had* to involve Garvin. No surprise to me.

Still, I cringed when Drake mentioned yet again that Garvin continued to stew about why and where I fit into this mess. With the Oxford murder, Drake said Garvin was beginning to suspect that I might *be* the serial killer. Perlman drew in a sharp breath and glared at me when Drake told us that.

The immediate challenge, and the one likely to evoke some histrionics in Garvin along with most of London, was that the Met had been pursuing a serial killer, a so-called lone wolf, while those of us sitting in Drake's office knew that we were really dealing with political assassinations, committed on British turf by officials from another country, a hostile one. That one's hard to swallow, as bad as it gets in our world.

Just as Drake was finishing his summary of developments to date, our mutual conclusions, and when to brief Garvin, his phone rang.

We watched his face tighten as he listened to his caller.

I held my breath. *Please, don't let it be about Sergei.*

When he hung up, Drake turned back to us. "The body of Alastair Sinclair-Jones has just been found in the alley next to his office. Garroted. No claw. No white powder."

In the shocked moment of silence among all of us, I knew immediately what had happened, despite the absence of the signature. I'd read Sinclair-Jones's latest fodder in last night's press, and realized he had been headed, naively, down a very dangerous path. He'd gone a step too far in his last piece, suggesting a nefarious element, "beyond our borders, possibly in Moscow," words that would instantly have caught the attention of the Rezident and of the Kremlin. Our *friends* realized Sinclair-Jones was onto something.

"The Russians," Drake said, a statement, not a question. We looked at each other in agreement, though we would, of course, have to wait for the evidence, which meant Garvin. The Russians could not possibly have known how much Sinclair-Jones actually had, but his murder reconfirmed their involvement in all of this. His was meant to look like a normal murder, if there was such a thing.

"We have to move now, Decktora. It's time to get Sergei directly involved," Perlman said as he looked to Drake for a gesture of approval.

We were, after all, on Drake's turf, but he was in accord and nodded to Perlman to continue. I was glad to get Perlman's buy-in, because I had every intention of trying to get Sergei to draw Ivanchukov out as soon as possible. I had been sure I could convince Drake it was time, but wasn't as certain about Perlman, until now.

"With this Oxford murder and now the journalist, the Russians have to realize we're onto them, or mighty close. Probably good that the word out of Metropolitan Police, and the earlier media, focused on a serial killer, but with the garroting of Sinclair-Jones, something has changed." Perlman turned to me. "Have Sergei arrange a meeting with this 'Yulia', the one involving her so-called business lead. I'll put money on it that it's Ivanchukov and he wants to get right to Sergei. There's every reason to think they'll kill him at the next contact. At least we need to work on that assumption. It's worth the risk. If I'm wrong, Sergei will get a further look at Olga," Perlman stated, not open to an argument.

All good, but I felt uncomfortable trusting anyone else to take the precautions needed to secure Sergei's safety, not in the midst of a potential intelligence coup of this magnitude.

Drake must have read my mind. "We'll put heavy security on his meeting, which will be in a public place, one of our safe sites. I'll give you a location for Sergei's invitation to Yulia Semenyova, the name he'll continue to use for her. My people will be on-site, and when Garvin is read in, there'll be police coverage as well. At least that's what I hope, because if we do grab Ivanchukov and his girl, we will need the help and concurrence of the MPS."

"I'll get to Sergei. I suspect he's ready to move this thing on, even if it's dangerous for him," I said.

Drake made a few quick phone calls while the rest of us went over the facts once more. Yes, we were dealing with assumptions, the biggest one being: was Olga's "friend" Ivanchukov? We were all on the same page. Russian intel, guilty. Ivanchukov and Olga, guilty. Others, not sure yet. Time to take a chance, well calculated as it would be.

Drake hung up and announced the plan.

"The White Dolphin Pub in Islington, at four o'clock tomorrow afternoon," he said, showing us its precise location on a map. "Evelyn will give you the exact details. The place is small and slightly run down. We like to keep it that way so that there is little traffic. The bartender is ours, and I'll have two other men sitting at a table near the front of the place. I'm not worried about outsiders who might be there, but we'll deal with that if or when we have to."

"That's a tight schedule, Jason. Let's hope Olga bites, and her 'friend' as well."

"If Sergei can't pull it off with Olga and the person she wants to introduce to Sergei for that time slot, we'll choose another. If she turns down the option for tomorrow, he needs to secure a time when she's available. But there is no wiggle room on the site."

"Jason, if I may say something…," Brewster interjected.

Drake gestured his consent.

"I think we all know now that Olga has the weapon, the claw. With what I learned of her history, we should assume that she will have that weapon with her, but we still don't know anything about how she conceals it or exactly what it looks like. It would be good for Sergei to know all of this, so he can watch her movements."

"Glad you brought that up, Stanley. I can't imagine she carries an exposed claw with her, and, of course, Ivanchukov may bring a weapon himself. So there's plenty for Sergei to think about, for all of us, in fact."

"Agreed," I said. "I'll brief Sergei on everything and see what he thinks she might do, since he's the only one who's actually seen her in person, observed how she moves, her quickness, all of that. And he is, after all, a trained intelligence officer himself. I'm somewhat loath to give him too many directions."

The biggest question for me—*What if Olga pulls out her weapon?*

"If all goes as we now hope, Ivanchukov and Olga will sit down with Sergei. If you, anyone of you, senses a need to abort, lift your right hand and run it through your hair. This should be enough to be viewed by any of us. If there is, in fact, a call on our side to abort, tell Sergei to wait five minutes before he leaves. He's the one most likely to be in danger, and we want him out if something goes awry. Decky, you leave at fifteen minutes. The rest of us will fall out randomly after you depart. Worst-case scenario, if the situation gets completely out of hand, we create a rumble and get Sergei out—or if Sergei feels threatened at any point, he should signal you with his watch, and we'll create the rumble and get him out of there. Everything will be in place for that, and Garvin will be part of it.

"Decky, you're the sole point of contact for Sergei. Advise him you'll signal him if any of us sees a problem. We'll all have earpieces and can signal each other at any point if necessary," Drake said. "Agreed, John, Decky?"

Fortunately, I agreed. John Perlman was, after all, the Chief of Station here, so it was ultimately his call, at least with regard to me.

"We can reconvene here at nine o'clock the following morning. No contact amongst any of us if and after we depart the pub," Drake said, trying to wrap up the meeting.

"And, Decky, I want you to get another room at the club. If possible, closer to the front and in a more populated section. You know the place, think it through, but change. You're not safe in that isolated back area, even though it seemed a good choice initially. I don't want to send you to a safe house or take any other action that would give Ivanchukov any hint that we're going operational."

I was surprised and not displeased at Perlman's sudden concern for me. I agreed about changing my room, and I knew just where I wanted to be.

"I'll be fine. I'll work this all out with Sergei. If he has any problem arranging the meeting on this short notice, I'll get back to you. If not, assume we're on. This is all about Sergei now." I couldn't help saying it, but I wanted to keep the focus on the man who'd called me to London, the man who'd brought us all to this point. "Sergei will wear the watch. If anything happens that concerns him, he'll activate its communication device, only one click required. And I'll get the signal and alert everyone from there to abort.

"We'll be within view. I promise you that, Decktora. If you sit in the location at the pub that we map out, we'll know it's you even in your disguise, which I presume will be notably unglamorous," Perlman said, holding back a grin. "You can handle that, right?"

"All good," I said back to Drake, adrenalin surging.

We had just over twenty-four hours, and a lot of pieces had to fall into place. Time for me to see Sergei. It was already eleven.

CHAPTER 43

LONDON, JUNE 11

Drake drew in a deep breath as he thought of the immediate challenge facing him: briefing Garvin. He picked up his phone and dialed the number, which he now knew by heart. Garvin answered on the first ring.

"Drake?"

"Cransford, we need to meet right away, in person. A sensitive matter has come up that needs immediate attention."

"Can you get over here? I'm anchored to my desk for most of the day, but I have a secure room we can use."

"I'll be there within the hour," Drake replied as he picked up his briefcase.

If the White Dolphin operational plan was to take place as the group had just devised, Garvin and his staff had to be briefed. Drake would restrict the full details of the Russian connection just to Garvin, hoping he could get his people involved with their knowing only that they were working against a Russian target, preferably of a criminal, not an intelligence nature.

The chief inspector was waiting in the secure room when Drake arrived.

"Am I to hope that we have some good news on our case?"

"Perhaps, perhaps not. I have a rather long story to tell you."

"I've asked Fawkes and his partner to join us."

"No, please. Just you."

Garvin waved off the other two officers and signaled Drake into the room. As he closed the door, Garvin looked at Drake. A frown now replaced the CI's usual dour expression.

"This will be a classified briefing at the Top Secret level," Drake announced, as he did when he started any intelligence briefing.

He watched Garvin's face change in color and effect as he unfolded the story, starting with the name of the Thames victim, through the Oxford murder.

"You don't mean to tell me...." He stopped and stared at Drake with a mixture of anger and shock.

"I do. Cransford, I deeply regret that we couldn't bring you in on this sooner, but I'm sure you can understand that what we've been in the process of uncovering was at the highest classified level of national security."

"Surely you could have given me some sort of a heads-up before I let this serial killer business take over my staff—and the media," he said, still furious.

"Until I was certain of our analysis, I simply could not discuss it externally. Let me add that we can never be one hundred percent certain of our analysis until we get the last piece, and that's what we're after right now. There's always the chance we're wrong, but I don't think so. We're near the end and you need to be part of it."

Drake let Garvin ruminate, giving him time to adjust to the stunning news.

"Very hard to accept, Drake," Garvin said, now more calmly. "I hear you—even understand you—in theory, but still bad form from my point of view. This serial killer, lone wolf, whatever you want to call it—the story is all over the place, and I have a restless, jittery London on my hands. Calls are flooding in."

Drake nodded. "I hope you can accept this once you've had a chance to digest the whole thing. I'm briefing you on all of it today, including the reason Decktora Raines is in London."

Garvin's eyebrows raised as Drake explained that Sergei had contacted her and asked her to come to London right away.

"You can see now why she is not the perpetrator."

Garvin harrumphed, clearly not eager to let Raines totally off the hook so easily. At a minimum, he said, she had caused a lot of problems for him and his people, not to mention for the two men who are now dead as a result of her association with them.

"As a civilian, she should have come to us. Maybe those two would still be alive."

Drake shook his head. "Cransford, I'm not prepared to blame her for those deaths. She had no idea they were in danger and is herself extremely upset about both—and still deeply worried about her former asset and his reliance on her. The bottom line here, what you already know, is that intelligence can be a nasty business, and with the Russians involved, as we are now convinced they are, a lethal one. There's no good news in this—except perhaps that London doesn't have a new Jack the Ripper running around."

Finally, he reviewed the links to Department 12, the Kamera connection that each of the murdered defectors had, the most highly classified piece of the story.

Garvin let out a gasp. "Holy Christ! What the hell is going on here?" Garvin wasn't asking a question that needed an answer. He leaned back in his chair, grumbling to himself as he processed what he'd heard.

"Can we get them?" Garvin then asked, with a deep sigh.

"A question that brings me to my next point," Drake said, relieved that Garvin had not ejected him from his office, a possibility Drake had considered.

Drake outlined the operational plan to lure Ivanchukov and his aide to the White Dolphin, describing the whole scenario, the players, and the hope that Ivanchukov would, in fact, appear. He said the mission, once underway, would be aborted if Sergei, Raines, or anyone of the group sensed an immediate threat. Then he reiterated the request for MPS support but asked that those brought in be told only that Russians were involved, no further details.

"I understand the degree of secrecy now. It's a tight deadline, Drake, but we'll pull it together."

Garvin had come around.

CHAPTER 44

Thank God, Sergei was available to meet right away. I told him to come to the food court in the basement of the Marks and Spencer on Oxford Street, a distinctly inconspicuous spot, as soon as he could get there. I was already sitting at a quiet table in the back where I could keep an eye on the surroundings when he arrived. We were virtually alone, only a smattering of shoppers, but I didn't know for how long, so got right to the point.

He winced visibly at the mention of Murphy's death, insisting that since he'd given me the information on Misha, he was responsible for the murder. Of course, that wasn't the case, but now we both felt guilty, and there was no bandage that would instantly take away the pain for either of us.

Then I had to tell him about the session with Drake and Perlman and the plan to bring in the Metropolitan Police. We argued on that point, but Sergei lost that one, so all I could do was apologize and tell him that the situation had grown beyond me.

"The bottom line, Sergei, is that we've decided to take action now. I'm very concerned that you may be the next target." I saw Sergei frown at that remark, appropriately so. "You were right about everything, but what that now means is that we're ready to confront the Russians, your specific enemies, the ones who threaten your life." I was getting intense, but I needed his complete buy-in, with no alterations on his side. The plan was firm.

He took a deep breath and then indicated he understood.

"Next steps?" he asked, sitting back in his chair and downing the rest of his tea.

"Set up the meeting with the woman. Tell her you have some additional information on her family background, some items that surprised you. Weave into the conversation that this might be a good time to bring along the friend she had mentioned to you at your meeting. Suggest the information on her family is not highly personal and that perhaps her friend could learn something about how Russian Antiquaria does its business." I didn't say her name out loud. I gave him the time and the info on the White Dolphin, and we discussed the details of who would arrive when, and where each of us would be located.

"What if she can't make it or suggests alternatives?"

"We're flexible on the time. But not location. You'll have to play that out. Maybe you can say you're going out of the country for an extended vacation or some such, anything to make her show up tomorrow. If she doesn't take the invite, we'll replan, but we hope she'll bite."

I glanced down at the special watch on Sergei's arm, glad to see that he was wearing it.

"Make sure you wear the watch to the meeting tomorrow. It's the key to your connection to me. Don't do anything with it, unless you sense, or know, something is wrong." I started to review how to use it, but Sergei gave me a harsh stare as if to remind me he was a professional too, and he was already on top of this.

"We have two scenarios for aborting the mission once we're all in place. First, if you, only you, sense that anything is going wrong, signal me. I'll move it from there. As soon as we've all communicated, probably a matter of seconds, there will be a rumble in the pub. Someone in our group will grab you. Everything is set up to look like a bar scuffle to disrupt the meeting. We're preparing for various options even though we don't know for certain if Ivanchukov will show. That's the big 'if', but we all believe he's the one she will bring, if she bites. And we hope she will.

"Where will you be? I'd like to know that, my friend."

"I'll be in a fairly ugly disguise, sitting toward the front of the pub, alone at a table, reading a newspaper, and hopefully looking very ordinary. The second scenario is if I or anyone of us other than you senses that something is amiss, I'll run my right hand through my hair, which will mean we must abort.

"You mean if Ivanchukov and Olga don't show?"

"I mean *anything* that looks off. If that happens, you pay your bill and leave within five minutes. I'll follow fifteen minutes later, but if this situation unfolds we will have no contact until the following day."

"When we meet at…," Sergei interrupted with faint smile.

"The Pret a Manger across from Marble Arch at eleven-thirty. I want a busy and popular place for that meeting. *If* we have to have it."

"Back to the good old days," Sergei said, no longer smiling.

"Yes, I seem to be choosing all the hot spots, don't I? Don't worry, if we get through this, I'm taking you to a fancy dinner at Rules. In the meantime, if I don't hear from you this afternoon, I'll conclude you've been successful in arranging the meeting, and we'll proceed exactly as discussed here. Any questions or further thoughts, concerns?"

"None."

Now it was up to Sergei. A sense of foreboding had crept over him in the past day, as if he intuitively knew he was sitting on the edge of a precipice about to crack. He knew he had to be near the top of the rezidentura's hit list, probably at the top.

When Raines told him about Murphy, he was certain. As he walked back to his office, his senses on high alert, he got angry with himself for not forcing Johanna to take Georgie down to Cornwall for a few days to stay with her parents. All in the scheme of things, a routine family visit, he said. But she'd refused, insisting she would not be cowed by these people, whoever they were, and she would not leave Sergei alone in such a state of stress. She ended the argument by saying she could handle their son, and she knew how to find police in an emergency. This gave Sergei no consolation. He had never seen her so worked up.

Back at Antiquaria, he checked his alarm system once again, made sure everything was active and functioning properly. Then he picked up his office phone and dialed the number Yulia had given him.

"Hello, yes, so nice to hear from you."

The voice sounded breathless, unthreatening, but she had been waiting for his call. Her quick response told Sergei that.

"Miss Semenyova, I think I may have good news for you. I did some more digging since we last spoke and found three additional references to a man who matches your description of your grandfather." There it was.

"Oh, thank you, thank you, Mr. Devlin. I am so excited. When can we meet?"

"Would you be available tomorrow at around four?"

"But, of course," she answered, her Russian accent deepening.

"I'm afraid we'll have to meet elsewhere. My office is being painted, but I didn't want to delay getting these updates to you," Sergei said, telling her where and when they would meet. She seemed to have no objection to either detail.

"I will make myself available," she all but gushed, "and perhaps I can bring the friend I mentioned to you earlier."

The words he'd been waiting for and he didn't even have to ask.

"Of course, madam."

CHAPTER 45

It was a long night, and I hadn't heard from Sergei, which, from my perspective, meant the operation was a go. I, in turn, made no follow-up calls to anyone, holding to our operational agreement of yesterday. I prayed that Garvin and his people were as adept at clandestine behavior as we were. Now it was a matter of waiting, always one of the hardest parts of an operation, especially for someone like me, who liked being in control and couldn't exactly be commended for my patience. It wasn't my best trait.

At one-thirty, I left the Langsford and started a long but carefully planned SDR, Harrods bag slung over my shoulder, camera secured inside. The next two hours were spent wandering in and out of shops and traveling the tube, where I made a stop at Cheapside. I'd located an H&M nearby, where I would change my appearance. In the lowest cost women's section of the store, I went into an unoccupied dressing room, no salespeople around to watch me, and pulled out the painfully unattractive outfit and wig Perlman had provided me. The drab running suit was perfect, dull enough to match the short wig, which fell just below my ears. My own clothes fitted neatly into the Harrods bag. I changed in a matter of minutes, made the final adjustment to my wig, and took a final glance in the three-way mirror. I couldn't possibly have looked less attractive. But most important, I didn't look like me.

The scent of stale smoke swept over me as I entered the White Dolphin. In a way, the dank setting wasn't bad for what was about to happen. I spotted the two MI5 officers, in perfect lager lout disguise, sitting in the far front corner of the pub, looking like regulars. One of them seemed familiar, and though I couldn't look directly at him, I knew he was my neighbor at the Langsford.

The ops plan called for one of the MI5 officers to take photos with a CD pen; the other would handle the audio, using the latest in clandestine miniaturized receptors. The technology was advanced enough to cut out extraneous pub noises, which Edward, our recruited bartender, would help keep to a minimum.

Though I hadn't sighted them, I was confident that outside the pub, Drake sat with one unit of the surveillance team and Garvin was with a small contingent from the Metropolitan Police somewhere nearby. We were all stationed in our designated locales, waiting.

Edward was well enough trained not to give me any notice when I entered the pub. I'd been assured that a glance from me was all he'd need as recognition of who I was. I took my seat at the small table at the front section, several tables over from where Sergei would be sitting, and angled so I could see him. Even though I'd be able to hear the conversation, I wanted to be able to watch Sergei's face and the action at his table. I felt confidently unnoticeable in my garb. My earpiece was securely hidden under the wig, and the mottled gray-brown bangs covered my forehead down to the upper rim of my nonprescription eyeglasses.

I ordered an ale and opened my newspaper, allowing just enough space between the tabloid and my brow line to observe what was going on in the rest of the pub.

As planned, Sergei arrived alone, shortly after me. His apparent calm was as solid as mine. But I knew what he was feeling underneath that controlled exterior.

Now we would wait for Olga and her friend to surface, to find out if this was a wild-goose chase or the heinous plot we'd all envisioned. If Ivanchukov didn't appear, we'd let Sergei carry out his meeting with Olga as if normal, then redeploy. All eyes would be on her, watching for any movement that could reveal the weapon.

But it wasn't Ivanchukov I saw next. It was the twosome who'd followed me at Harrods. In they walked, hand in hand, hopefully, unable to identify me and certainly not aware that I knew who they were. Not put off by the sleazy nature of the pub and the absence of a crowd, they went directly to the bar, grabbed two stools, and ordered drinks. I hadn't expected to see them, the first unanticipated twist in our planning.

We all held our places for the next forty-five minutes, the time we had allowed to give the targets time to show up. No one else appeared.

We had to abort. I raised my hand and passed it through my hair. Sergei saw me, beckoned Edward for the bill, paid it, got up casually, and walked out of the pub, all within the requisite five minutes. No reaction from the couple, though I saw the woman take a quick glance at Sergei as he reached the front of the pub. I stayed in position, head in my newspaper, waiting my fifteen minutes before departing. No one else came in, and the couple remained, drinking and chatting.

The tension I felt must have been shared by each of us. Something had gone wrong, and that meant they were onto us. Mission *not* accomplished.

I got up and exited when my time came, went to the closest tube station and headed to Henley, which was nearly vacant when I came out. It seemed a good place for a change of clothes, so I went into the station loo and redid myself. No one was in the waiting area there when I emerged, once again Decky Raines.

After my long, professionally convoluted subway travel, I reached Piccadilly Circus Station where I exited the tube and headed into the melee of late rush hour in one of the most crowded parts of London. I hated crowds in situations like this. There was just no way I could spot surveillance or identify any of the few players I knew might have an interest in me. Not to mention that, according to our plan, we were each on our own.

My caution did not, however, serve me well. Someone suddenly bumped up hard against my right side. My first thought was that they wanted my purse, the one with the secured camera, which I'd already used to get a few photos in the White Dolphin. No way could I lose it, so I pulled it tight to me and jerked around but couldn't see who had so rudely banged me.

Then I noticed the blood on my arm and felt my legs go out from under me, as everything turned to black.

CHAPTER 46

LONDON, JUNE 15

My head felt as if it had been hit with a mallet. A nurse was leaning over me checking a tube, which I quickly realized was coming out of my mouth. Nausea rose in my throat, worsened by the sulfuric odors in what was obviously my hospital room.

Christ, what the hell had happened to me? Maybe I was dead.

"Don't move. You're okay," the nurse said calmly, pressing her hand on my shoulder as I attempted to sit up.

We stared at each other as I tried to bring my brain into focus.

"Where am I?" I asked, noticing the raspiness of my voice and feeling the dreadful lump in my throat from the tube.

"Can you tell me your name and your date of birth?"

I came to my senses very fast and answered her question. Correctly, thank heavens. I'd been in hospitals enough in my life to know that was the first thing they asked you in any emergency.

Oh my god, how long have I been in here? My mind immediately flew to Sergei and our aborted op. I wiggled in bed. I had to get out of there and find Sergei.

As the nurse left the room, after poking me in various places, Gladys entered, the Pear not far behind.

He actually looked upset, which unsettled me further since I had rarely seen him in anything close to an empathetic mood. He didn't seem ready to say anything.

"Wha," I said shakily. My throat was dry, and my words came out in a voice I didn't recognize. "Wait, why are you two here?" I said out loud, turning back into my case officer self and wondering why the Chief of Station and his right-hand woman were in my presence in a public place. I had a lot of questions, but that was all I could get out. And probably all I should have, under the circumstances.

"You had an accident just outside the Piccadilly Circus tube station. Fortunately, there's an emergency center there and you got help within minutes of your fall. The medics saw the blood and what looked like a wound on your arm, then called in the police. Word got quickly to the main station, and, luckily for you, up to Garvin. As 'friends of the family', we got notified right away."

"What's wrong with me? What's with the tubes?" I asked.

"I'll fill you in," Perlman interjected. "But first you need to follow up with the doctor and we need to get you well."

"I'm fine. I feel much better already," I lied, trying to pull myself up, barely mindful of the tube attached to me. The doctor walked in and ordered me to lie back down.

"Where's my purse?"

"You're not fine, Ms. Raines, but you will be. All your belongings are secured here, in the hospital."

"You're very lucky," the Pear said quietly. "As for the purse, I have it. It was partially under you when the ambulance came. You fell very professionally," he whispered, a slight smile on his face. "We'll leave the room, give you and the doctor a little privacy."

"No," I shot back. As I continued to take in the scene, consider what I'd just heard, and began to remember, I felt the tension rise in me and, strange as it seemed, didn't want the Pear to leave. "Please stay."

"Relax. We'll get you taken care of. I'm Dr. Wilders," the doctor said, shooing Perlman and Gladys out, then reaching for my pulse and checking my vitals. He tapped on my bandaged arm. "You're doing well," he said perfunctorily.

When the doctor was finished, Perlman came back in and asked to talk to me privately. Dr. Wilders nodded but said he would be nearby. He directed the Pear not to pressure me, to stop if I had any trouble getting out words or seemed at all faint.

By now I was concluding that something serious had happened to me and assumed the Pear needed to get anything he could from me as quickly as possible. It suddenly flashed on me that it took Litvinenko days to die. I was beginning to recall my last moments of consciousness. And remembered the blood on my arm. Then I knew.

"Was I poisoned?" I blurted out.

"Decky, let's take it slowly. I'll tell you what I know and then have the doctor advise you, but first, tell me what you remember."

He sure was interested in getting my info as quickly as possible. Not encouraging. Struggling to talk around the tube, which was more annoying than painful, I gave him a slightly breathy account of my long surveillance detection route after I left the White Dolphin, ending up at Piccadilly Circus thinking I had avoided surveillance.

"Was I poisoned?" I repeated.

"I'd prefer the doctor explain everything to you, but—"

"Then please get the doctor in here," I interrupted, as Dr. Wilders, hearing my plea, walked through the door.

"Ms. Raines, you were unconscious when you arrived here, and we sedated you additionally to ensure a full recovery."

"Please, just tell me what happened. How long have I been here?"

"When we examined you, we saw the blood on your arm, and scoped it for analysis. There was a smattering of tiny white particles amidst the blood."

I gasped.

"Whoever attacked you left a nasty little dose of a toxin in rare use these days. Curare mixed with another substance we're still analyzing."

Yes, I know. No need to explain any further, I thought. *I'm sure you'll find the other toxin is Star of Bethlehem.* Perlman didn't interrupt. He was too smart to hint that he knew anything, just a family friend checking on me.

"We haven't seen anything like this for years, certainly never in my experience. Curare rarely surfaces in any kind of attempt on someone's life in this country, much less in London. But the good news for you is that the amount was so small that you will be back to yourself in short order."

Short order? What did that mean?

Perlman asked again if he might have a moment alone with me. He knew I'd be totally aware of what this poison was and who likely delivered it. He didn't want me dribbling out words or commentary in my condition. He looked over at me and paused, as if to find the right words.

"Decky, you've been under sedation for over forty-eight hours. I told Dr. Wilders I'd break this news to you. They, we, had to find out exactly what had happened to your body before you awoke and started moving. You had to stay completely still until we knew, and, I admit, I told the doctor it would be hard to keep you down once you woke up."

My mouth fell open and I swallowed to ease the soreness around the tube.

"They tried to kill you, Decky. When we learned of the cut and the white specks, we asked for an urgent hospital analysis, and thanks to Garvin, were able to get a small sample to his people as well. The curare was quickly confirmed, but of course, we knew what we were looking for."

"This can't be," I whispered, knowing of course that it *could be*. The truth had now sunk fully into my brain. I was stunned, but at the same time, I completely understood.

"You're all right, Decky. You're going to be fine. Grace will stay here with you tonight, and they think you can be released tomorrow."

"What happened after we aborted?" I felt tears sting my eyes, which I certainly didn't want Perlman to see, but I needed to know.

"We met the following morning, as planned, a full postmortem. It wasn't an easy discussion. Obviously, Ivanchukov's people know we're onto them. The good news is that our targeting was correct, and we confirmed that the two individuals who came into the pub are with the Russian Embassy. Neither we nor the Brits have anything more on them, but we now have pictures of the twosome and a suspected intel affiliation. The pictures you took earlier on your walk through John's Place with your concealed camera showed the female that was at the White Dolphin. We were able to match yours and the ones we got at the White Dolphin with the blurry photos we had on file and confirm the identities."

"They're the twosome who followed me into Harrods and Harvey Nicks. I didn't see my other surveillant at the White Dolphin, but I'm sure the two are the very same."

Perlman's eyes widened. Of course, he couldn't have known that. I was the only one who could recognize them. I felt the tube pulling at me as I tried to go on, croaking out questions.

"How did they find out about us? What was the result of the postmortem?"

"Stop. I'll tell you what we have, but just rest and listen. No one knows what alerted them. We've considered every option, based on all the intel we have, and as you well know, we have no inside source who can fill in the blanks. I'm sorry to say, the conclusion we reached was that the only loose thread is you. We think they spotted you, disguise notwithstanding, signaled their colleagues when the rumble began."

I was so clogged up, I couldn't even respond to that announcement, and my throat wasn't about to let me carry on much longer.

"Sergei?"

"Don't worry about him right now. We've been trying to get in touch with him but don't want to do anything that would draw attention to him or his family."

I wanted to know how Sergei was, but I understood that my colleagues were being cautious in following up with him since his only point of contact, me, was definitely not available. I could tell that was the end of our discussion, and I was going dry, literally. I felt the tears leak down each side of my face and closed my eyes.

"And the bad news?" I whispered.

"We have to wait for them to attempt a recontact."

CHAPTER 47

I was considered healthy enough to leave the hospital three days later. By then the drugs had worn off and I was no longer drifting in and out of sleep, my mind wandering aimlessly. The only reminder of my attack was a stitched wound on my upper arm, no nausea, nothing else.

Gladys had gotten me a new room at the Langsford, in the front and a more active part of the hotel. I was told that my tail had moved as well but was nearby. All done with little curiosity on the part of anyone at the Langsford. I should have been deeply relieved, but I wasn't.

No one had answered my questions about Sergei.

But Perlman was about to. As soon as I was settled in at the club, he came to see me. I hadn't even considered what he was about to say, but "I don't want you to get upset" didn't bode well for good news.

And then he delivered the update. After the incident at the White Dolphin, our group, which now included Garvin, had lost sight of Sergei. He was missing, gone, and so was his family. What the hell had happened?

I was absolutely furious when Perlman told me. There'd been no plan for increased surveillance on Sergei after the meeting at the pub. How could we possibly have failed there? It was Intel 101. I couldn't let the fury overtake me. I had to get well and back in control. My type-A personality was just beginning to resurface.

In the hospital, Perlman had fended me off by leading me to believe he'd tried to contact Sergei using the cell in my concealment device, my CD pocketbook. I didn't have the energy to pursue the topic further that day and presumed that even if Sergei was upset about the aborted op, he would ride it out until we had a new plan and until I could get to him.

Perlman had saved the bad news until I was out of the hospital. Sergei had disappeared.

After Perlman left, I curled under the blanket, ready to be alone. *Where is Sergei?* Like a broken record, until I drifted off that question played over and over in my mind. The phone woke me sometime later.

"Decktora, are you up for a short visit?"

"Jason? Sure, just give me a few minutes to wake up, then come on up. Would you be so kind as to bring me a cup of coffee?"

His slight chuckle was my answer. I hung up and headed to the bathroom to freshen up and make myself as presentable as possible.

I opened the door to his knock and all but grabbed the coffee out of his hands, then settled into the armchair in the corner of the room. Drake smoothed out the bedcovers and sat on the edge.

He looked down at his hands for what seemed like a long time. When he turned to me, I almost winced. The fear and fatigue in his eyes were startling. "So, you're okay?" he asked.

I took a sip of the hot brew and tried to savor it. Was I okay? Guess it depended on how you defined okay.

"Aside from being pretty tired, I'm good. Thanks for the coffee. Do you know where Sergei is?" I said.

"Everyone's upset about this, and I'm not going to lie to you. We have no idea where he is, whether his wife and child are with him, or whether he has been taken by the Russians or taken off on his own. We're using every kind of technology and groundwork at our disposal to find him, but so far, nothing."

I groaned. Nothing comforting in those words. I wanted to yell, "How could we/all of us/you have been so stupid!" but I held my tongue. Little to be gained in going off the rails now. The mistake we "professionals" had made was in losing site of Sergei. It shouldn't have happened, and my confidence in our cadre was diminishing.

"Decky, I do have one piece of good news for you. Bredon Aberforth didn't want to bother you in the hospital—"

"But what, what, what…," I interrupted, no longer needing the caffeine hit.

"Between us and Langley, we have the location where Alex and the others have been held. Technical oversight worked brilliantly, once Bredon got the info from his SAS colleague. Everyone is alive, and we're in contact with the Kremlin, who will handle the Syrians involved. The Russians aren't eager at the moment to add another layer of conflict between us in that region. They're saving their chits for a chemical weapons disaster levied by Assad, which they know we will blame them for and which we all know is coming."

"Are you telling me what I think you're telling me?"

"I'm telling you that we expect Alex and the others to be released and sent back to the West within the next few weeks."

"Oh my God, I can't believe this." I jumped to my feet, ready to kiss Drake, then sat down again, realizing my joy—and a good deal of dizziness—was overtaking me.

He grinned at me, then the smile faded.

"That's all we have, Decky, but you have every reason to be optimistic. It's going to be all right. In the meantime, we want to keep this separate from the Ivanchukov matter. So far, so good. The situations fall into their own columns."

I flashed a big grin, my spirits lifted. "Bet Garvin's glad I didn't die, huh?"

Drake's sudden laugh was more of bark. "Of course, he's glad you didn't die. As is Perlman, and Gladys, and *all* of us."

We sat in comfortable silence for a minute or two. He knew I'd barrage him with questions, but it was the post-op disappearance of Sergei that I couldn't let go of. Drake was upset too. He explained that Sergei was a trained professional and had slipped away with the rest of us as originally planned.

Drake saw that I was sinking, finished his coffee, and got up to leave. He smiled, opened the door, and slipped out into the hall.

"Lock the door, Decky," he said softly from the other side.

The following day, I sat down again with Drake and Perlman in Drake's office over at Vauxhall, and got the full update.

Sergei was gone, and so was his family. Discussions with his neighbors had revealed nothing. Everyone contacted assumed the family was on vacation, with school out for the summer. Drive-bys of his house continued but the place was dark, car still in the garage. Garvin even used the British police's modern national network, the Holmes System, to find out if anyone matching Sergei, his wife, or son was seen anywhere else in Britain. All checks nationwide had come up empty, including in Cornwall, where we knew Johanna had family.

Not only had Sergei vanished, so too had Ivanchukov and Olga. MI5 picked up their trail at Heathrow the day after the White Dolphin disaster. They had been on the afternoon flight to Moscow. We wanted them back in London. Now. Dangers aside, we were all driven to finish the operation and nail the Russians. The assassinations had to stop.

"If that bastard stays in Moscow, we'll be sitting on the edge of an international incident," the usually cool Drake argued. "The assassins who killed Litvinenko got out of London in the blink of an eye, and as far as I'm concerned, we did nothing. Relations too sensitive at the time, the Foreign Office declared. This cannot happen again," Drake said, his face reddening and his fists clenched.

"But how do we get them back here? What evidence do you—do *we* have against Ivanchukov? Everything's circumstantial," I replied, feeling no less vengeful than Drake.

"We can, among us, build a case, just as we did leading up to the White Dolphin. And even if our killers don't resurface in London, we will find them anywhere else they go—outside of Russia. If they've really disappeared, we begin a media blitz on this entire matter, link it back to Litvinenko, all the rest of the murders." Drake was firm, confident this time that his government would be on the same page. He went on to say that MI6 in Moscow had been brought in and was trying to find out what they could about Ivanchukov and Olga.

But Sergei, was he alive? The only tidbit that gave me an ounce of hope, and the bar was set very low, was that Johanna and Georgie were gone as well. Maybe Sergei had taken them somewhere and was still alive, I dared to think. Right then, I made the decision to stay in London until this whole thing was resolved.

Garvin could keep my passport, for all I cared now. Thankfully, Perlman bought into my plan, as did Drake. Coverage on me was increased, but I didn't stray far. I was still weak and back to the old waiting game, though I couldn't remember—at least not since those early days when I'd "lost" Elena—ever having felt such a high degree of anxiety.

I was soon reminded that patience really is a virtue.

CHAPTER 48

LONDON, JUNE 21-25

It was eight days after the White Dolphin op went bad. Perlman had given me back my cell, though not the purse, because he considered it compromised. I kept the phone charged continuously and the ring volume at its highest level to make sure I missed nothing, and in the blind hope that I might hear from Sergei.

It was just before midnight when the phone jolted me awake. "Hello, Decky. Hope I didn't awaken you."

"No problem. I'm awake," I said, immediately recognizing Sergei's voice and overcoming my immediate urge to say, "Oh my god, where are you?"

"We were out of town on a little summer trip. All is well and I would love to catch up for lunch, if you have time."

Of course, I have time, I felt like screaming. He was obviously being careful what he said over the line, even though it should have been secure, but at this point, I was ready to double-talk, too. It was hard to trust anything since our aborted mission.

"That would be delightful. Just tell me where and when." What I didn't say was "You're alive. I can't believe it!" I could barely hold my emotions in check during our short chat, but, of course, I did.

"Our old hangout at one o'clock for lunch?"

"Dandy. Glad you're back and look forward to hearing about the trip," I said, matching his calm and maintaining the superficial level of the conversation.

I hung up, knowing I was to meet Sergei at noon tomorrow at Chequers. We could move elsewhere as we had done before if we had to.

I called Perlman, waking him up. "My dear friend is back in town and I'm looking forward to a catch-up lunch tomorrow." I felt a slight in-drawing of breath on the other end of the cell and would like to have seen his face.

I knew he would pass the info on to Drake. I didn't plan to see or talk to anyone else involved in the op. I would lie low in the morning but hoped Perlman or Drake would have me under full surveillance. I couldn't believe the Couple would be on me, but neither could I believe that the Russians would have no surveillance covering me.

Sergei was already seated at a table in the rear of the pub. I barely saw him at first, and when I did, I felt a mix of fury and elation.

He stood up and we embraced, like the longtime friends we actually were. The place was already busy, but I recognized no one. I did notice he was wearing the watch I'd given him.

"I don't think I need to tell you how I feel," I said through gritted teeth.

"You don't."

"I thought I had lost you—"

"I'm sorry," he interrupted. "I had no choice. After the collapse of our plan, I went home. I didn't know then if they would try to kill me that night, or what they intended. I have to admit that after the abort I had no faith that I could count on anyone, even you, my dear Decktora."

"I understand," I said, and I did, angry as I was that he would take such an extreme action.

"I called Johanna, told her to meet me at a friend's house a few kilometers from ours and to bring an overnight outfit. She knew that meant pack for three and come prepared not to return home right away. She's learned enough during our years together that she can read between the lines when I do something that seems out of character. She and Georgie met me, and I told her the barest bones of what had happened that afternoon. I knew she was alarmed, but she understood. I borrowed my friend's car, and we headed to Bruges, where she had a cousin, and we could seem to be on a legitimate vacation."

"Are you all back home now?"

"No, they are still away. Don't ask me, Decky. I have them in a place that I believe is safe."

There's no such place, I wanted to say, but I realized I had no right to. Not now.

"And I'm going back to work."

I didn't argue that either. What was the point? I told him Ivanchukov and Olga had fled to Moscow, said we were looking for them, while continuing to assess what had happened at the White Dolphin. I didn't mention that while he was disappearing, I had my own brief encounter with death.

We made no plans for next contact, but I told him I was staying in London until we got some resolution on this dreadful situation. He didn't particularly want to tell me where he was staying, but I insisted he keep the cell phone with him at all times. Something could happen, and when it did, it would likely be fast.

Later in the afternoon, I went to Grosvenor Square and briefed Drake and Perlman on Sergei's story. There was a joint sigh of relief, but, like me, they were both angered by what he'd done, the concern he'd given us, and the risk he took in disappearing. When I added that Sergei had lost some confidence in us after the incident, they got it. None of us was proud of our work at the White Dolphin. Drake promised me that Sergei's office, Russian Antiquaria, would be watched.

* * *

Two days after my meeting with Sergei, Ivanchukov and Olga returned to London from what looked like "rest and recreation," or as we call it, R and R, in Moscow. We had no details on their activity there, except that they flew Aeroflot to and from Sheremetyevo International Airport.

Both were back at work in their embassy, but even the signals intel pros over at General Communications Headquarters (GCHQ) in Cheltenham were unable to get anything on them from telephonic or other communications. However, the daring duo interpreted the results of the aborted meeting at the White Dolphin, their act was now foolproof. They were giving us nothing, now cautious to the extreme.

Drake, Perlman, and I had a long session over at Thames House to try to figure out what their return meant. As far as we could tell, they were the only ones who fled to Moscow after the failed meeting. The couple who'd surveilled me at Harrods and had been seated at the pub hadn't been spotted anywhere near an airport, which we assumed meant Moscow had no plan to get them out of London. This gave us the slightest hope that Moscow thought we hadn't identified them.

We asked each other why they were back. Were they in trouble with Moscow? Had they returned to finish this operation and to give the appearance of business as usual? And, most worrying, would they resume their targeting of Sergei?

Having thoroughly reviewed the files and data on all of the Caesars, we believed Sergei was the only remaining live operative among the Soviet and Russian defectors who had worked at Kamera. MI6 had had communications with stations across the globe who might also have relocated Russian or Soviet defectors who had been affiliated with the poisons lab, whether briefly or long-term, but none remained.

Once again, we were in a waiting game—hoping that Ivanchukov or anyone in his group would make a move.

Sergei received a late morning call several days later on his office phone.

"Mr. Devlin?"

"Yes," he said, immediately recognizing the voice.

"I am so very, very sorry about our meeting. My mother was taken ill, quite seriously, and I had to go to her. I was already at the airport when we were supposed to meet, and I was so upset that I did not think to call you. I am very sorry."

She needn't keep repeating that, Sergei thought, noticing the tearful-sounding voice she'd adopted. No surprise that she would be a good actress.

"I do hope you didn't wait long for me. Were you there?"

Sergei was tempted to say that he had not gone either, just to see how she'd respond, since he knew her colleagues had been there.

What will be her next play?

He assured her that there was absolutely no problem and that he had not stayed long at the pub. "It gave me a chance to get out of the office, away from the noxious paint, for a little while," he said.

"Well, perhaps I can make it up to you? I propose a lovely high tea at a place where we can find a private table. I owe you that. Yes, I do."

"I didn't know if you were still interested in your project," he responded, intentionally excluding the reference to "her friend."

"Oh, most certainly, very much so. And you remember I want you to meet my friend. He will have very big business for you. Perhaps I can make up for my impolite behavior." She'd gone from remorseful to voluble.

"There's absolutely no need for that," Sergei said, intentionally underplaying his interest. She had, after all, contacted him. "But perhaps we can work something out. I had planned to take a vacation."

"Oh, yes, we must get together, soon, I hope," she interrupted.

"Is it pressing?" Sergei pushed.

"My friend is in town this week, and it would be so very nice if we could all meet. I can make it easy for you. The place I referred to is not too far from your office."

"My schedule is a little busy this week, but let me—"

"What about Wednesday at four at Café l'Orange in Kensington Gardens? It's a lovely, elegant place with the best tea service in London." She wasn't giving up.

"That should be fine for me. I'll meet you there, hopefully in the sun."

"Excellent. We are most happy."

"We?" Sergei mused. And the restaurant, so close to the Russian Embassy and full of light and windows. So easy to observe from afar.

Sergei hung up his office phone and extracted his doctored mobile from his briefcase, then dialed.

"Hello, my friend, won't you join us for tea this Wednesday at four in the afternoon at the Café l'Orange in Kensington Gardens?"

Sergei trusted this phone. He had to.

CHAPTER 49

I couldn't reach Grace or Perlman when I tried immediately after Sergei's call. To my surprise, neither answered. They seemed to have dropped the "immediate" response they'd promised regarding my special cell.

I did get through to Drake, who sounded as if he'd been waiting for my call. In the fewest words possible, I let him know we needed to meet right away and that he should try to track down Perlman, to coordinate. Drake agreed, and I headed over to MI5. Perlman and Grace arrived shortly after me, along with the MI5 surveillance officer who had been, and still was, my floormate at the Langsford.

"Sergei contacted me about an hour ago, telling me Yulia—ah, Olga—has called and requested a meeting with him at the Café l'Orange in Kensington Gardens, four o'clock, Wednesday afternoon. In short, it's a go," I said, getting quick acknowledgment without any argument from Drake or Perlman. Grace and the man I now knew as William listened. "I think we have to assume that they got word that Sergei has resurfaced and were sent back to London to carry on as before."

After my announcement, we all sat quietly, as if each in a private trance, mulling over the new situation and what problems we might face. The questions spun in my head. I wanted a perfect plan before the l'Orange rendezvous.

"Do you think our friends are in hot water with their bosses in Moscow, that they were told to get back over here the minute Sergei was spotted?"

"Very plausible, Decky. My read is that they will act fast and lethally. Olga's quick invitation supports my first thought, the second, an assumption. We need to accept that they have likely identified each of us," Drake said.

"Not comforting, but believable."

"As with the White Dolphin, we'll have some of the same people on site, but I plan to bring in a few extras. They'll be unknown to the rezidentura and will enhance our security and response capability. I'll get to Garvin, but I'm confident we can move quickly. He's as driven now as we are. This time Sergei will not be sitting in a dark corner. Unfortunately, there's no way to fix that with this restaurant. I know it well. It's very open and, for their own reasons, they chose a place close to their embassy. We have to consider why that choice. I'll arrange for the concierge to take Sergei to a specific table. If the Russians have their own contacts at l'Orange, we'll soon find out."

Perlman then jumped in with his own imaginative update. "We're going to change your disguise, Decktora, and I want Grace to go with you, to have you show up as a twosome at one of the tables."

I smiled. I should have seen that coming.

"Attractive a female as you are, we want to put you in a masculine disguise."

I laughed out loud. My first time as a male, but he must have had the equipment on hand, and there was no time to spare. I was fine with the twosome idea. The main thing for me was that I would be there. Period.

"We'll give you a modest shock of silver-gray hair, nothing showy, and put you in a fat coat. You could use some extra weight anyway. And we might do something about your teeth, a jutting upper tooth to give you that British look."

My eyes rolled, but I didn't disagree, especially not after the last time.

"Grace will have a wig and a rimmed cloche hat that will cover most of her upper face, specifically her eyes. You'll look like a couple. You can read the newspaper and look up occasionally. Grace can watch the scene and interact with you."

"And our secure contacts in case we have to abort again?"

"As before, each of us will have an earpiece. But I want to make a change with Sergei and the watch. Can't be too careful. Who knows what they saw at the White Dolphin. A pen, with mic capability, will be sitting on his table. He should pick it up and keep it in his hand at all times, as if he's doodling or about to take notes. If anything arouses his concern, he should tap the pen two times. Can you communicate that to him? Will he buy it?" Perlman asked, in earnest. He glanced at Drake, who would have to place the pen.

"Yes, and yes," I said, grateful that we still had our minimally used secure phones. I would tell Sergei, probably in something as brief as a street encounter, almost a brush pass. We didn't have a lot of time.

Sergei wanted this to end as much as anyone. He needed his revenge, and now, I thought he deserved it.

CHAPTER 50

LONDON, JUNE 27

Grace and I took the table Drake had chosen for us, in the garden salon of the Café l'Orange at exactly three-thirty.

Sergei appeared at three fifty-five and headed back to a table four removed from us. I could see him well enough, but Grace and I weren't the only participants, so I satisfied myself with my earpiece and Grace's reassuring presence.

As the man, I comfortably dove into today's newspaper, with a table full of elegant tea, watercress sandwiches, and cookies, ordered by my faux wife. I took a sip of my tea, flipped the page of my newspaper, and then briefly looked up.

Then I saw her, in person, for the first time. Elena Radzimova.

It isn't possible. She was alive and, worse than that, she had to be Yulia. Or rather, Olga. *Gads, what tangled webs we weave....*

Grace looked up, not knowing what had caused me to make a slight sound. Sergei's descriptions had been perfect. Trim, compact, the fake yellow hair a poor match for her sallow complexion. And the eyes, yes, those eyes. I could see it even from where I was sitting—why she was called Snake Eyes. Why hadn't that grabbed me those many years ago, as it had Sergei? Her glasses, or perhaps special contact lens? She'd played me in Estonia and done it well, but this game wasn't over.

Olga nodded at the bartender, gesturing that she was heading to Sergei's table in the back. As she moved through the café, I sensed the slightest movement of my MI5 compadres in the corner. I glanced up at Grace, smiled at her and returned to my paper, careful to turn the page.

No matter how many times I'd done something like this, I always felt as if I were in a movie, watching a scene unfold. It wasn't really me, but this other person in disguise, playing out a scene, hoping it would proceed as rehearsed. Today unnerved me in a way I hadn't experienced in years, learning firsthand of the Elena–Olga connection. I had to turn my brain on to remote or else I could blow the op, and that wasn't going to happen.

Sergei rose from his chair to acknowledge Yulia, Olga's character for this play. He was as smooth as I expected him to be, showing not a hint of tension. She sat down, facing my general direction, which gave me a better look at her. I felt comfortable in my extreme makeover with the support of my temporary wife.

I sensed the harshness in her. In spite of the smile, coldness emanated from Olga. Her outfit was as colorless as mine, a simple dark blue suit and a white blouse with no trim. But one thing caught my eye. On her left wrist was a large piece of jewelry, a bracelet. It appeared to be decorated in oddly colorful bird feathers or some sort of unusual fur that formed a design I couldn't make out. It didn't fit with the overall look of her.

My earpiece picked up the initial conversation between Sergei and Olga. Social chitchat, drinks ordered, and then Sergei moved into the heart of the issue, asking when the potential client would arrive.

"He just texted me that he's in a cab and running a few minutes late. You know London traffic."

"I do indeed. Tell me, how are you? Your family?" Sergei asked, trying both to draw her out and to keep the discussion relevant to the stated purpose of their meeting.

"Everyone's good, but I'm thinking of moving back to Russia. Things have changed so much," she said, offering nothing more.

I strained a bit to discern every word through her accent. Thankfully, they were speaking English, per our prearrangement with Sergei.

"That's quite a decision."

"I guess I'm more Russian than I thought. With all the changes and progress, so much good happening in Moscow now. We have such a brilliant president. It makes me want to go home again. And I have even some excellent business possibilities back there."

I bet you do, I thought to myself.

"I can always visit my uncle's place in the south of France if I need a change." She offered a strained smile. "What about you? Don't you desire to go back?"

"My wife is British. She would never leave. I get enough from my work, speaking the language, hearing about the old days, to satisfy my Russian needs. No houses in southern France, just a small apartment here. You seem to have had a successful life, an uncle in southern France, good connections in Russia. How very fortunate."

"I've been lucky. My uncle became a big success in the new Russia, and he treats me well. And I have my contacts at the embassy. That has made my time here so rewarding. Still—"

"The embassy?" Sergei interrupted.

Be careful, I thought.

"Yes, the embassy. I said I would bring you some new business. A friend from the embassy is going to join us."

Though my stomach tightened as I heard what she'd just said, I had to believe that each of us heard those words and were ready.

"There he is now." Olga raised halfway out of her chair and pointed toward the front door of the café.

Without moving, I could see Sergei's nemesis walking toward him, the stolid, imposing form of Vladimir Ivanchukov. When he reached the table, he did not take a chair.

"Sergei, I thought I had lost you. But here you are, alive and well," Ivanchukov said in heavily accented English.

"Ivanchukov," Sergei stated coolly. He did not offer his hand.

"Ah, my friend, you don't look happy to see me." Ivanchukov paused. "But let's speak in our native tongue."

"I live in Britain. I no longer speak Russian," Sergei responded firmly.

"So, Mr. Devlin, or should I say Dumanovskiy? That will be easier for me." Ivanchukov inclined his head, then pulled out a chair and sat down across from Sergei.

"It has taken me a long time, but I am a patient man, as you must recall. There I was back in Moscow on the fast track, and suddenly one of my officers went bad, right under my eyes. You know, you all but ruined my career. Of course, your treachery began in Washington, but your downfall came under my authority. And then I saved your life, sent you to America, and what did you do? Tell my people that I was a spy too. So, as you can see, I have been waiting for this day. Waiting and planning...." He paused as if to catch a breath. "If I had had my way, you would not have...," Ivanchukov stopped himself, his tone bitter and sarcastic.

I was surprised he launched right into that conversation, his voice rising and his anger increasing as he spoke. Then he lowered it, as if knowing he was going too far too fast. I could sense the anger smoldering inside Sergei. But he was an expert at control and showed virtually no emotion, even though he was now in the direct sights of the man who wanted to kill him. The same man who had destroyed his family, his sanity.

"So, Vladimir, you want to learn about your ancestors, do you?" said Sergei.

"That's not really what's on my mind. But I did want to see you. In fact, I've wanted to see you for many years."

"We're in London. You're a senior diplomat. I am but a small businessman with little to offer anyone. What could you possibly want with me now?"

"To be honest, it's been hard for me to get you out of my mind. In fact, I have never really succeeded in forgetting you, hard as I've tried. But never mind about me, I bring news of Katya."

"News of Katya?" Sergei repeated evenly.

What dirty plan did Ivanchukov have in mind? The very name of his beloved wife Katya had to have Sergei nearly ready to jump across the table and beat the man to death. The man who'd told her she'd died all those years ago. But Sergei had never learned the details of exactly what had happened to the woman who'd been the center of his life for so long. The mother of his two beautiful daughters, stolen from him by Ivanchukov. Nothing showed on Sergei's face but patience. I applauded him in my heart and mind.

"Sergei, I'm sorry about Katya. I used to visit her from time to time. You know we had to arrest her. We just couldn't be certain what she knew. I'm sure you understand. Of course, you would have known that before you left us, wouldn't you?"

Keep calm, my friend, I thought—perhaps prayed.

Sergei shook his head slightly. "Why would you bother with Katya? A chemistry professor from a musician's family?"

"I could not have left her alone. I *would* not have left her alone. But I'm going to make it up to you a little. Let bygones be bygones. I'm a diplomat now and have more important concerns than you and your treasonous past."

"I believe our distaste for each other is mutual, Ivanchukov."

"Well, then let's move on to something more pleasant. I've brought you something, a gift, you might say. It will not surprise you to know that Katya had tried to write you. I promised her that I would make sure her letters got to you one day. Of course, she didn't believe me. But I am keeping that promise. Olga, show him what we have."

I felt a chill go down my spine as Olga reached into a bag, the feathers on her arm moving slightly as she did so. I was confident all eyes were on her in case she pulled out her weapon—whatever it was. I heard a slight movement of chairs where the two MI5 officers were sitting, as she took out a small packet of envelopes, wrapped in a pale pink ribbon, and handed them to Ivanchukov.

"It's not all of them, Sergei, only a few. In spite of my contempt for you, I am making retribution to beautiful Katya by delivering them to you now. Take them. They're yours. Consider the score evened. I want nothing more to do with you or Katya."

Sergei paused. He looked at the packet but made no move to open it. Olga's hand now covered the brooch on her arm. I watched her and listened to Sergei.

"Aren't you going to open them, Sergei? I thought you'd be happy to get these letters," Ivanchukov said in an acidic but controlled voice.

"I can read them later." He wasn't about to give in to Ivanchukov's challenge, and I suspect we all now feared what was inside. Still, Sergei had to play it out. Nothing could happen without perfect evidence. He understood that.

The table grew quiet, and then Sergei picked up the top envelope and pulled out a pocketknife.

"You're so cautious, my friend. Don't you trust me? Just open them."

Olga didn't flinch, but I could see that her eyes were glued to the packet and her hand remained on her left wrist, fingers toying with the feathers.

I watched her as discreetly as I could, then moved my gaze back to the table. Sergei inserted his knife neatly into the slight opening at the edge of the envelope, and careful to hold it only at one end, he started to slice the envelope open with his knife.

Then he tapped his pen. Twice. I got it, and I signaled Drake instantaneously, as he then did the others.

"What's wrong, comrade? You'll enjoy the letters," Ivanchukov taunted.

I could hear the conversation but did not know what Sergei had seen. When it looked as if Sergei was about to take out the contents of the envelope, Ivanchukov started to rise, Olga as well, though she was now grasping that bracelet.

"Goodbye, Sergei, may we not meet again," said Ivanchukov.

I couldn't take my eyes off Sergei but sensed activity to my left.

When the Russian turned as if to leave, he faced the two MI5 officers. No one moved, including Olga and Ivanchukov. One of the MI5 officers reached down to pick up the envelope, protective gloves on his hands.

"Mr. Ivanchukov and Miss Semenyova, please come with us," said the other, showing them his badge.

"I beg your pardon? Who are you?" spat Ivanchukov. He glanced at Sergei, who remained in his seat. "I'm an official diplomat, and I don't go off with anyone under orders, unless my own."

The MI5 officer remained polite but firm. "Please make this easy. Come quietly. If there is no need for concern, we will issue a statement of apology to your embassy."

Ivanchukov's face began to redden. "This is highly unprofessional and insults our diplomatic relationship. You're going to lose your job," Ivanchukov barked, but now had no choice except to go with them, along with Olga.

As they left, Olga dropped her arms to her side, the feathered bracelet falling to the ground.

"Don't touch me," she screamed as one of the officers reached for her arm. Startled, he stepped slightly aside but stayed close to her and quickly leaned over to pick up the feathered bracelet with his gloved hand.

The rest of us, including Sergei, remained in place until the foursome had moved by. Then Drake gave a hand signal, which told us we could leave. As arranged, everyone went off in different directions, secure now that MI5 had Ivanchukov and Olga in custody, but careful to reveal no connections to each other.

I hated to see Sergei walk off alone, especially after the last time. But I was now most pleased that the Pear had forced this awful disguise on me. I looked nothing like Decktora Raines or Carolyn Shaw today. My concealed identity had prevented the whole op from blowing apart.

CHAPTER 51

LONDON, JUNE 27-28

Events moved at breakneck speed. Drake knew he had no more than two hours, typical close of embassy business hours for the day, to avoid a diplomatic incident with the Russians. If the evidence didn't come in as expected, Ivanchukov would be sent back to Kensington Palace Gardens. An official apology would be forwarded to the Russian ambassador and a huge flap would ensue, probably causing the end of Drake's career.

Because they already had samplings from the previous clawings and knew their components, the techs were able to determine almost instantaneously that the envelope did indeed contain Star of Bethlehem, a deadly quantity of it, mixed with calebas curare.

There was the evidence. It was all that would be needed.

The three blue envelopes inside the larger envelope were addressed in a script that looked feminine and personal. The Russians had surely forged Katya's handwriting. As for the contents, Forensics advised that once the envelopes were opened and the toxic particles exposed and touched, the effect would be lethal. But the particles had been contained, even with the slight cut into one of the envelopes that Sergei made, a cut that meant he was close to death, which is surely what motivated him to activate the pen. The medics later reported that Sergei had made no contact with the toxins.

The envelope on top contained a chilling message, also in Katya's forged hand. *Your time has come, Sergei. I will see you soon. Katya.*

If Ivanchukov was the puppet master, Olga was the puppet. All we needed was enough evidence to send them home PNG—persona non grata. With pressure from the British government and the accompanying evidence, Drake was confident they would be expelled from England. It wasn't the death sentence we thought they deserved, but they were perhaps in for something worse once they returned to Moscow in disgrace.

Drake and Perlman agreed to let me take the lead on the initial debrief of Olga. I had earned that. Now we would face each other after all those years, both with different names and clandestine histories.

I walked in and looked directly at her, all emotions held in check.

"I know who you are," she said, glaring at me, a hateful and ferocious look in her big eyes.

"And I know who you are, too. I have a question for you," I said as coldly and directly as possible. "How is Elena Radzimova doing?" I didn't expect an answer, and I didn't get one.

She just stared back.

"Okay, well then, tell me about that fancy jewelry you were wearing."

She sneered, looking at me as if I were a fool. "I don't know what you're talking about."

"I'm talking about this," I said, holding up the tightly sealed plastic bag containing the bracelet.

"Oh, that. A family heirloom. I wear it all the time. Surely you can't begrudge me such a small indulgence? It's just a frivolous thing. It fell off my arm when your thugs pawed me."

"Perhaps we should take a look at it together."

"Give it to me," Olga hissed, grabbing for the bag.

Now in plastic gloves myself, I gently removed the feathers from the bag and handed the bracelet to her, praying she would make the move I was hoping for.

She took the bracelet and made no attempt to put it back on her arm. Instead, she pulled at the feathers.

A claw popped out. Olga tried to stand up, frantically reaching out, first for me, and then the others. She swung the claw almost maniacally, but we all moved back quickly, each managing to completely avoid her.

Garvin's people, dressed for the occasion, grabbed Olga's arms and pulled them tightly behind her back, lifting away the feathery bracelet. As they did so, they pointed to the tiny specks of white on the claw and to the detritus on the table. There wasn't much of it, but we all understood not to get near to any of it.

Drake immediately called a forensics officer who appeared in mask, suit, and gloves to remove the white substance and to thoroughly clean the room, the table, the chairs. We remained frozen in place, none of us moving until the officer checked us for any specks.

There it was. All of it. The claw—the weapon. And the lethal powder.

Drake was about to begin his interrogation of Ivanchukov when he saw me appear outside the slightly darkened window of the small interrogation room where the Russian sat, tethered to an iron chair with very solid metal cuffs. He beckoned to me, and I slipped into the back of the room. Drake knew what I wanted to ask, we had preplanned it, but he was the lead on this one and would, appropriately, go first.

"You've made me a happy man, Ivanchukov," said Drake, looking across the debriefing table at the imposing, irreverent Russian who stared icily back at his captor. Separated from Olga when they were brought in, Ivanchukov did not yet know the murder weapon had been identified.

"How's that?" Ivanchukov's hid his anger well, but his eyes focused tightly on his enemy. He didn't even acknowledge my presence.

"You know perfectly well," said Drake, leaning back in his chair to further irritate the Rezident. "I do have some questions for you. Your degree of cooperation will help determine what happens to you and your protégée."

"No questions. You will get your full reward. You know you can't hold me," Ivanchukov sneered. "We have diplomatic immunity, and I'm certain your people don't want any problems with the Kremlin."

"Your diplomatic immunity isn't as secure as you seem to imagine, not in this case anyway."

I knew that what Drake was saying wasn't exactly true, but he had to dig everything out of the Russian in the very short time he had before the incident turned diplomatic and the top dogs on both sides took over.

"Spying is one thing, Vladimir. But murder is something else again, and you're not going anywhere until we get to the bottom of at least five claw murders and a sixth by garroting. Several of those were British citizens who have never come under your authority. That is murder, not a political cleansing."

A flicker of something—anxiety perhaps—appeared in Ivanchukov's eyes.

"I don't believe you."

"It doesn't matter who or what you believe. You're here, and I'm the one asking the questions, but I'll give you a small break and turn the discussion over to my colleague," Drake said, nodding to me to move to my part of the interrogation, but not introducing me.

"Decktora Raines. Should I say, nice to meet you?" Ivanchukov asked with a raised brow.

"No need," I said, not surprised that he knew my name, but somewhat so that he would use it. In this, he revealed his awareness of me. Drake offered his chair, but I chose to remain standing. I wanted Ivanchukov to see me looking down at him.

"Let's talk about poisons. Russian poisons. Let's talk about political assassinations using poison. Tell me about that." I watched his reaction. Eyes tightened, a sneer emerging onto his lips.

"What are you talking about?"

"You know what I'm talking about."

"Kamera?" he snarled back in Russian. "You Americans, so stupid."

"Kamera, you said. Did you mean to say that?" I responded in Russian. His eyebrows raised. He didn't know I spoke Russian. In fact, he had no idea just how much I did know. I almost felt that the word Kamera fell out of his mouth, assuming none of us would have a clue what he was referring to. "You mean that special chamber Lenin developed way back in the day, to find ways to deal with his enemies."

"Whatever you're talking about, it's a thing of the past, if it even existed. I think you've spent too much time reading fiction and perhaps ancient history."

"Well then, let me put it another way. What about Institute Number 2, Scientific Research Institute Number 2, Department 12? Any of those names familiar to you?"

He glared at me in stony silence. If he could have killed me in that moment, he would have. I saw it in his eyes, and I knew I was headed in the right direction.

"You people are insane," he said.

"It's my assessment that each of your Russian victims worked at Department 12. In fact, I believe you were there when some of them did," I said with complete confidence. "But I thought you worked with more advanced toxins these days, radioactive ones, nothing so simple as Star of Bethlehem and curare."

Ivanchukov surged forward, suddenly trying to rise from his chair, and I sensed Drake tighten as the cuffs clanked against the iron framework.

He sat back down, drew in a breath, calming himself.

"Well, my dear, I have a piece of news for you. You remember, oh, way back when your family was in Moscow?"

Oh my God, where was he going with this?

"I'm so very sorry about what happened to your mother, but it was necessary."

I stood stone still, facing him icily, but I would not let a tear form.

"Am I upsetting you?"

"Please go on," I said.

"We knew your father was CIA. Did you know that?" He sneered. "And he was getting involved with some people who were very important to us. Not smart. Apparently, he didn't realize that we were onto him, so we had to send a message. It was time for your father to go home."

Drake, clearly sensing the horror in what Ivanchukov had just said, stepped in.

"Stop this right now," he ordered, blocking me from Ivanchukov.

"I have nothing further to say, and I demand to see my ambassador," hissed Ivanchukov.

"I'll make it easy for you, not that I want to," Drake said, taking over the conversation. "I have only two requirements. If you meet those, you will be able to return to Moscow. I will even escort you to your Aeroflot flight and make sure you're on it.

"First, you and Olga Fortenskaya will be removed officially under PNG status. And your leaders must agree not to reciprocate by sending any British diplomats home. In other words, no tit for tat in this case. Once you are both safely on your flight to Moscow, we will release the story to the British media, all the details of the murders. The end of the serial killer scare; now a story of SVR revenge and murder."

Ivanchukov sneered. "This will never happen. My people won't accept this, nor will your government. Our relations are too important."

Drake and I both knew that Ivanchukov's confidence was based on the Litvinenko case, but the mood in his government had changed since 2006, and relations with the British were more fractured than they had been then.

"They'll do whatever they can to get you home. Discussions are going on right now, and you will go only on the proviso, to repeat, that there is no reciprocation and we release the story without interference of any kind from you or your people."

Ivanchukov was silent. Drake could only conclude that the Russian knew he had no choices—not now. Ivanchukov would go home, no matter what consequences he would face in Moscow.

"As I said, there is a second matter," Drake added. "You will tell us the whereabouts and status of the two daughters of Sergei Dumanovskiy."

"Hah," Ivanchukov spat the word.

"You find that amusing?" Drake said.

I prayed that Ivanchukov had the information. It had been my idea to ask about the daughters. It was a stab in the dark, but a calculated one. We hoped to give Sergei a gift in return for all he had done. The answer fell out of his mouth.

"You and your American friends, you think you're so smart. But they were right in front of your eyes, and you weren't clever enough to find them, to figure it out. We wondered how you could be so dumb," Ivanchukov hissed.

"Go ahead." Drake pressed for every detail.

"They're in Paris. We sent them out years ago. Together, in fact. We didn't have much use for the daughters of a traitor. One of them teaches Russian outside of Paris. The other one is some sort of musician. We debated how long it would take you to find them, if you ever would."

"You, your government, will provide the details of where they are, and we will confirm that before you depart this country," Drake said sternly.

Drake didn't ask about Ivanchukov's surveillance team, specifically the couple. Time was running out for our part of this game. It had been a long day and night. We'd timed it so that the diplomatic escape door was now closed. We had what we needed.

CHAPTER 52

LONDON, JUNE 29–30

My stay in London was coming to a close. I was ready to go home, but still heady from the finale. And I was elated that Alex could once again join me back in Georgetown.

I had one more meeting with Sergei to wrap things up. The tabloids were full of the story, front-page headlines in every one of them. Even the Sinclair-Jones killing was being replayed. The top journalists saw it all fitting together. It was the Russians. All the Russians. Though the evidence was still unclear about the garroting, the media believed he'd met his fate at their hands. And though there was some caution, there was also euphoria throughout the city over the news that there was no serial killer on the loose in London or its environs. A senior Russian embassy official was being sent packing, along with a mysterious, unnamed female colleague. Details kept emerging, and the tabloids couldn't get them quickly enough.

It was *The London Hour* that carried the main headline: "Serial Killer Turns Out to Be Russian Diplomat." It was written by a select staff at the newspaper and dedicated to "Alastair Sinclair-Jones for his heroic efforts in covering this story."

Hello, London. You will be happy to know that Jack the Ripper has not been reincarnated. Not at all. But the story we are going to tell you is every bit as good and much less scary to us locals. So, unlock your door and take a relaxing stroll. The streets are safe again.

The latest Jack the Ripper has been captured, and he is not an Englishman. In fact, he is Russian. A Russian diplomat named Vladimir Ivanchukov, the senior intelligence officer in his embassy, a former KGB official who is now high up in its successor service, the SVR. As we write this story, Mr. Ivanchukov is being escorted to Heathrow, where he will unceremoniously be delivered onto the next Aeroflot flight to Moscow. Once home, the Russians will make sure he is off the media screens. They will deny the story, of course, and close the door, just as they did with Alexander Litvinenko. Chief Inspector Cransford Garvin of MPS has given us the following wrap-up of the case and said he would make only one statement, and this is it:

"The top intelligence officer at the Russian Embassy to the Court of St. James's, the Rezident, has been arrested for the murder of five individuals, including three former Russian citizens, and the attempted murder of a former Soviet intelligence officer, a defector now living in protective custody in the United Kingdom. The Rezident is on his way back to Moscow. He was apprehended with his subordinate, a female who carried out the murders. Her murder weapon—a claw dipped in a combination of lethal poisons. She admitted the weapon and poisons had been chosen to make the murders look as if they were carried out by a serial killer. With the resolution of this case, I am happy to announce my retirement.

I will head with my wife to the English countryside, where I intend to take up gardening and enjoy my dotage. We honor all of those intelligence and Metropolitan Police officers who helped solve this set of crimes."

For now, Londoners, you can stop worrying about a serial killer. As they say, "Case solved."

CHAPTER 53

After a round of self-congratulatory drinks and toasts and, at last, a good night's sleep, I headed out to Heathrow. Now I had time to sit quietly for the long flight home and review everything that had happened. Langley would want a full after-action report from me, of that I was sure.

I leaned back into the comfortable, roomy aisle seat I'd been assigned for the long flight home to Washington, a glass of white wine already in my hand. I was grateful Sergei had treated me to business class, but felt I'd earned it. What he had started in his initial FedEx to me led ultimately to a remarkable intelligence coup.

Together a small group of us had closed the circle on one of the darkest unresolved cases in Russian intelligence history. The case didn't bode well for relations between the Russians and their old Western enemies, Britain and us. All of what came from the Ivanchukov–Olga business would now fall into the hands of diplomats to resolve.

MI5 would no doubt increase their surveillance of the Russian Embassy, with special focus on anyone in the old Ivanchukov network, which left those who Ivanchukov referred to as "the Couple," and I don't know who else. Drake would figure that out. And Perlman, who had obviously learned a good many things about proper treatment of people over the years, was now quite pleased with me and with the kudos that he was receiving from headquarters. The crotchety DCI Garvin had become so fond of me that he said I should remain in London, that he would not be returning my passport. His wife invited me to stay with them anytime I was in England. We ended up being a team after all.

"Mission accomplished," I kept repeating the phrase in my mind. The message had been sent back to the Russians, to the top of the Kremlin, and to the good old boys of the SVR: "Don't ever do this again, not to the Brits or the Americans."

I wouldn't exactly call it vengeance, but it was close to that, especially for Sergei. And although we hadn't discussed finances, he let me know that he was doing well. By the time I said goodbye to him and his Johanna, I knew that his second life was a happy one, the desperate and seemingly endless suffering he had gone through now a thing of the past. Sergei would even find his daughters. He was excited to introduce them to their young brother, too.

Would the Russians try to get back at Sergei and his family? I didn't think so, nor did Drake or Perlman. They would have to lick their wounds for a while, and we would be watching them, just like in the old days, because as I had said to my seniors back when I joined the Agency, eventually the Russians would return to their old tricks.

As for me, it was now clear that I'd be better off inside the Agency than outside. So much for my leave of absence. It didn't suit me anyway. Time to go home to Mother CIA, where the Russian target had been reincarnated, once again a high priority, and where I was one of the few who had the requisite expertise and language skills, the old Russia hands mostly gone in the nineties. What I'd learned about my own mother was shocking and enlightening. At least now I had the answers.

The mystery surrounding Alex was the extra pull. I understood that I'd been probing into a rigidly compartmented black operation and that I'd stepped outside the box in tracking down Bredon Aberforth, but that act of independence on my part had recharged Langley, even though MI6 was the lead on the op. I might get some grief on that when I got back, but I was confident they'd keep me in the loop now.

When he got home, and I knew now that he would, it was time to get married. My struggles these past months had shown me that.

The plane touched down smoothly. My car was sitting alone where I'd left it, looking a little the worse for wear from being outside for so long. The inky sky held a sliver of pink, signaling the end of the day. I wound my way onto the George Washington Parkway and headed toward Georgetown. As always this late in the day, the parkway was dark and uncongested. I was going home to an empty house. The lonely highway darkened my mood until I got near Key Bridge and saw the glowing lights of Georgetown.

As I drove up Thirty-Second Street, I could see my single timed light on in the living room, the one I set whether I am in town or away. Tonight especially, it felt welcoming. I parked in my usual tight spot, pulled out my suitcase, and dragged it across the cobblestones to the house. As I unlocked the double-latched door and walked in, I almost tripped over the heap of mail and magazines dumped inside during my absence. The pile looked daunting, but I swept it up, knowing I would at least have to glance through it for anything personal before unpacking.

I kicked off my shoes, plopped down on the sofa and dropped the stack beside me. I tore through the junk mail and catalogs, putting the magazines in a separate pile. Just a few real letters. One from my niece, thanking me for the birthday gift, two from friends stationed abroad. I was dog tired and even debated making it to the second floor to my bedroom. I looked around the living room, happy to be in my own surroundings. Life was good again. Full color, no more grays. I got to my feet and walked toward the stairs.

Then I noticed the bottle of Cabernet sitting on the kitchen counter beside a half-drunk glass of red wine. I didn't drink red, ever.

"Alex!"